THE GRADUAL GATHERING OF LUST

Also by Toni Davidson

Scar Culture (1999)

THE GRADUAL GATHERING OF LUST

TONI DAVIDSON

CANONGATE
Edinburgh · New York · Melbourne

First published in Great Britain in 2007
by Canongate Books Ltd,
14 High Street, Edinburgh EH1 1TE

1

Copyright © Toni Davidson, 2007
The moral right of the author has been asserted.

The publisher gratefully acknowledges subsidy
from the Scottish Arts Council
towards the publication of this volume.

Scottish Arts Council

British Library Cataloguing-in-Publication Data
A catalogue record for this book is available on
request from the British Library.

978 1 84195 898 9 (13-digit ISBN)
1 84195 898 0 (10-digit ISBN)

Typeset by Palimpsest Book Production Ltd,
Grangemouth, Stirlingshire

Printed and bound in Great Britain by
Creative Print and Design, Ebbw Vale, Wales.

www.canongate.net

For my father

To Kate Orson

Something we were withholding made us weak,
Until we found it was ourselves.
>> Robert Frost, 'The Gift Outright'

Contents

Affections of the Ejaculation Centre • 1

The Gradual Gathering of Lust • 47

The Inert Penis of the Man Who Had Just Been Shot • 89

Like a Pendulum in Glue • 117

Some People are Born to be a Burden on the Rest • 135

For Solace Fled to Parts Unknown • 179

Raul and Petra, Uri and Renzo • 219

Miss Globe X • 269

Affections of the Ejaculation Centre

HIS MOTHER WAS strapped to the bed. The men were not in white coats. They wore blue, short-sleeved shirts and blue, baggy trousers. A moment before, a nurse had come into the private room fussing and fluffing the pillows, positioning them at the usual angle while making sure that the sheets were tucked in as tight as they could be. Using both hands palms upwards she worked her way around the bed.

'All safe and sound.'

'Yes.' He answered on his mother's behalf.

'Is there anything you need, Mrs J?'

The nurse pinched the sheet line and pulled it closer to his mother's chin. She cocked her head to one side perhaps trying to gauge if the line was straight enough or flat enough or tight enough. Rean wasn't sure.

'I was told she wouldn't be able to answer.'

'That doesn't mean you shouldn't ask, does it?'

There was a reproachful tone in her voice and, as though acknowledging her abruptness, she warmed it up by adding, 'You have to keep trying. We all do. It's the only thing we can do, isn't it?'

The men in blue came in, each with a brown leather strap in their hands, the buckles striking the bed with a cold, metallic clang. A dull yet resonant tone. He had sat often enough in the room to be able to keenly pick out and identify the sounds of the hospital. Sometimes he thought he heard distant wailings or the high-pitched rush of breath, quickly inhaled, painfully withheld. More often he heard the nurses and doctors go about their business, or the squeak of trolley wheels, a regular motion, that teased him with horror then comforted him with reassurance. They were being carried leaden to the morgue. They were being charioted from a successful and triumphant operation. It could be both. It could be either.

His mother was going nowhere.

The blue attendants fastened the straps across his mother's chest and legs. The nurses tch'd and gathered up her bottles and plastic tubings.

'She's not going anywhere.'

'Standard procedure for patients . . .'

One of the blue attendants looked at Rean suddenly

aware that his language would have to be adjusted, sensitised.

'... for patients liable to move a lot.'

The nurse tch'd again and left the room. Rean followed her.

Rean reached out and touched her arm. When she turned he saw the smile that had caught his attention when he first saw her. It was attractive, warm. She was pretty he thought. This wasn't a sudden realisation. He had known it all along.

'It looks bad, I know. Extreme, yes, but it's for her own protection and ours. You would be amazed how strong elderly people can be when they are ...'

Rean lean forward so he could smell something of her, something different from hospital air. He was meant to be listening.

'... when they are here.'

Rean nodded, smiled and watched the way her uniform rubbed against her body as she walked away.

'I'm too old for this, for Christ's sake!'

Rean was arranging chairs for his guests. A 69-year-old widower in fawn slacks and white shirt fretting over the arrangement of furniture. It had come to this? It *had* come to this. He hadn't entertained a lot since his wife had died two years ago and this was an effort. This was him making an effort.

'You should make an effort.'

'You should get out more while you still have your health.'

'You should exercise every day. A healthy body means a healthy mind.'

He did all the things she used to do. He spent hours in the kitchen chopping, frying, studying the grease-stained cookbook which he had broken the spine of. It wouldn't stay open. He noticed a fingerprint next to the photo of the expected result. It wasn't his. He had removed all sight and sense of his wife in the torrid weeks after her death but it had not been an efficient operation. He missed details: a comb with her hair still attached that had fallen behind a chair; a book he had not read, her dedication in pristine condition, 'To my husband, wise before his time'. It was a little joke, a running parody of themselves, a fragile jab at their mortality. Weeks after everything had been cleared and rearranged, he had been cold called by a company selling security and reassurance for the over seventies. The caller had only just begun her pitch when Rean interrupted her, 'You're too late.'

'Oh, it's never too late.'

Rean hung up.

For a moment his wife had regained consciousness. It was only a moment, a fluttering of eyelids, a brief stare at something invisible to Rean, and a soft, barely audible sigh. There wasn't time to whisper last words or to reach out for one last grip. It had all happened so quickly. She had been laughing, playfully ridiculing some eccentricity Rean had recently acquired and then the laughing had lurched into coughing, great heaves of air being spat out of her small body, the rattling of her ribs cracking the silence of their nurtured, suburban life. Rean noticed the spots of blood flecking the thick-pile carpet. One moment she was falling to the ground and the next she was being lifted into an ambulance, a small crowd shifting their gaze from the stretcher to Rean, who stood frozen, rigid.

'You should come with us.' The paramedics whispered into his ear.

'Please stay with us.' The other paramedic shouted into his wife's ear.

'You must come out with us.' His friends said to him as they devoured his food.

'This is good.' They said as they toasted each other, congratulating each other on their surviving friendship.

'I remember.' They rushed to dampen that tinder sentence, making sure they stuck to the unwritten plan that no-one alluded, no-one inadvertently compared. It hadn't been long enough.

'It's been ages since you came out with us.'

They went on outings or sojourns as they liked to call them. They visited historic sites and nestled poor china in their hands. They speculated on the age of things and nudged each other about another coach party arriving at the tearoom.

'We will never do that. En masse? Not for us.'

They were entertained night after night by soothing violins and the sonorous tones of war reporters touring their tales of near misses: the music and words from somebody else's life. After years of family and domestic hiss, there was finally something else to know, to experience. They had all lost someone. They all had something that needed to be replaced.

'It's good to get out in the real world.'

The sites they saw were of battles fought long ago; the words they heard described only pageants of foreign experience and the music; the trilled words of an incomprehensible libretto were but safe confusion, a turbid clarity darkly lit.

'Wasn't the lighting good?'

Rean spent much of his time with his eyes closed. Being but not being there.

Rean turned the light on in the middle of the night and saw the nurse standing at the foot of his bed.

The lighting was good. She was in spotlight, her figure hugging the shadow of the room. She didn't have to move much, she didn't have to do much. Being there. It was enough.

'What are you thinking about?'

His wife had asked him this many times. Before, after, during.

He had never been unfaithful.

He had spent forty years happily married.

He had loved his wife.

'You must have been thinking about something.'

'You.'

'Or someone?'

'You.'

'Ahh.' His wife sighed and shifted closer to him on the sofa.

He told himself, 'There was never anybody else.'

His voice sounded, weak, sleep-blocked and pitiful. He didn't like the way it came out. He didn't like the way thoughts were being shaped in his head. It wasn't better out than in.

He was told, 'You're doing well. And at some point you will want to move on. There is only so much bereavement a person can endure.'

That made sense of course and he was expected to creakily get in the car and be whisked off on regular theatre trips to watch drama unfold. He watched in silence and refused the detritus of entertainment as mints were prised out of tins, ice-cream tubs passed round. With laughter, in tears, whatever it was they were watching he had seen it already. Rean felt enraged by the drama's rigid display, the enforced cohesion such comfort to those around him. For him, it was a white-knuckle ride on red velvet seats.

'There was never anybody else.'

It sounded stronger. He heard it in his voice, felt it in his arms. The nurse moved on to the bed, the spotlight following her. He raised himself up to the usual angle, pushing the pillows against the headboard. By the time his hands were free from the bedding her lips closed on his. He kept his eyes open and watched his hands slowly descend on to her back, the tight line and crease of her uniform, quickly and easily disrupted.

The home help, Shan, came every morning from nine until twelve.

'What can I do for you today?'

She cooked him meals he could have made himself. She cleaned surfaces he had wiped the night before. She brushed spotless rugs and polished invisible dust from neutral ornaments. Everything his wife had bought had been sold or donated. There were no photographs for him to linger over, for dust to gather on.

'Is this all the washing you have?'

He took clean shirts and trousers from the wardrobe and crumpled them in his hands, dipping cuffs in plant soil, dribbling unnecessarily into underwear, spattering jumpers with food stains that could only have come from a loose and aged mouth.

'Is there nothing else you need done? Don't be proud. I'm here to help.'

'I feel tired.'

'Then sleep. Dear God, if you aren't allowed to nap when you get to your age I don't know what.'

He settled himself on the sofa and three quarters closed his eyes.

He left enough to squint. Shan moved a duster over the television he never watched.

'I think I pulled the cable out by mistake.'

Shan shook her head. 'I'll never understand why they put these sockets so low down.'

She bent down and fumbled with the cable that had become tied in knots.

Rean opened his eyes so wide the light hurt them.

'She had a bad night, I'm afraid.'

The nurse opened the door to her room.

Rean looked at her breasts with a quick roll of his head.

His mother was straining against the leather straps.

The nurse rushed forward to hold on to his mother's

hands which were reaching out, taut and skeletal, trying to grip something. The air, her life, her past. It could be any of these things.

'There will be moments of lucidity, like the sun coming out from behind a cloud on a dull day. It is best to treasure these moments because it will become overcast again. This disease, like the weather, is not predictable.'

One of the buckles on his mother's bed had loosened. Her thin and tiny arms were pushing against the restraints and it was with some difficulty the nurse managed to clasp her hands and fold her arms back to a restful position.

'This won't last long.' The nurse reassured him. 'The strength they can find is soon lost.' His mother was opening and shutting her mouth as though she was struggling for air. She was out of her depth. Simply existing beside such a struggle seemed shallow to Rean.

'It's good that you come so often to visit your mum especially since I know you have lost your wife recently. Many people don't bother to visit patients with dementia. They say it's because it's too upsetting but I think it is because they hope that it doesn't matter. What is there to remember?'

She turned round from the bed and noticed Rean looking at her.

'Sorry. Sometimes I say too much but it takes quite an effort to be tactile.'

'Tactile?'

Rean moved closer to the nurse.

'No, I said tactful. It's the air conditioning. It's difficult to make yourself understood.'

Tactile.

Rean rushed towards the nurse and pushed her on to his mother's bed, pinning her arms wide either side of her.

Rean walked authoritatively over to the nurse picking her up in one swoop and walking out of the room. The blue attendants dropped their belts in surprise.

Rean stood there wondering. Wandering.

'Are you okay?'

The nurse was looking at him, her head tilted to one side.

'I'm fine.'

'It's difficult, isn't it, seeing your flesh and blood in such a state?'

'Yes.'

At home he could hear his wife in the kitchen downstairs. In their bedroom, in the long wardrobe mirror he saw what he had been told.

'You've always had an athletic build.'

'Most other men have gone to seed by your age.'

'Women like a more mature body.'

In the mirror he didn't just see himself. He was not alone in reflection.

Shan was in the living-room, hoovering the packet of digestives he had crumbled close to the bedroom door.

'It's quite a mess. What have you been doing?'

Rean flexed his biceps then puffed out his chest. With both hands he smoothed back his silver hair and slowly allowed his gaze to drop to his genitalia.

'This is why I have stayed with you all these years.' His wife laughed into the pillow while she pushed his balls lightly with her fingers.

'I've never seen so many crumbs in one place.' Shan shouted over the noise of the hoover. 'Did you jump on the packet when it fell?'

Rean used his left hand to stroke his penis and his right to tweak one nipple then the other.

'I like the way men's nipples are just there. They don't have to do anything.'

His wife swirled her fingertips across his chest in an ever widening spiral.

*

'It's like there's a trail of breadcrumbs into your room. Did you have a midnight feast or something?'

The hoover crossed the threshold into the room.

Rean's penis twitched as it grew, gulping into its slightly crooked erect state.

'It's a good hoover though . . . oh my!'

Shan pushed the hoover to the last of the digestive crumbs that had been scattered on the pale cream carpet.

'Oh God, I'm sorry, I didn't know, I didn't think you were . . .'

Rean turned away from the mirror, folding his arms across his chest.

'It's okay. I was just looking at myself in the mirror.'

***

The PIR bus shuddered to a halt and forty bodies creaked forward.

'It's a good idea. Without Possibilities in Retirement we just wouldn't get to see these places.'

Rean whispered under his breath, 'Oh, God.'

'I know, the old bones do suffer a bit on these journeys. Fish oil. That's what I take and it's made the world of difference. I just slide off the seats these days.'

His wife's friend laughed and bustled down the aisle

rousing some of the slower moving passengers with her now familiar rallying call.

'History won't wait.'

Rean watched her as she gathered people together at the visitor centre.

With practised ease she went over the itinerary for the day's event. As organiser of such trips it was her responsibility to make sure that everything went smoothly and that everyone knew when to gather in the tearoom or understood when the giftshop closed for lunch. Rean remembered her a decade ago. They had jumped out of the car driven by her now dead husband. They did what they always did on a Sunday. A walk in the country, a flask and a slice of cake at their destination, some windy hilltop with a few stones still standing. They sat as they talked, husband with husband and wife with wife.

He remembered her husband droning on about work, his business that once was, its ups and downs.

He remembered the wives talking about decorations for a Christmas a long way off.

He remembered looking at both women, the wind flattening the beige material of their windcheaters. While the husband ruined the view with his myopic conversation, Rean manoeuvred himself, sandwich-filling, between the two late middle-aged women, their legs wrapped around him, their hot breath making clouds above their heads. It felt like the right thing to do.

He remembered telling the husband about the User Guide.

'The pictures are quite erotic but tasteful.'

Rean mail-ordered top-shelf magazines which arrived in A4 manila. As a novice at such purchases he had been made sleepless by their imminent arrival: he had feared that clear plastic might reveal his intentions and undermine his secrecy. This was his after all. In all the glory of matrimony and shared lives, this was and had to be his.

'We all need a valve to help us let off steam.' The husband had said, keeping his voice low in case the wind carried his words to the wives sitting perched and engrossed on ancient rock.

He cut out the brunettes and ignored the blondes.

'Do you like my hair?'

His wife had asked him this for decades and he always said yes and only cared that he was lying when it wasn't dark. Reassurance was not a lie.

He cut then pasted the women into a ring-bound A5 folder that he had had made up at the local printers.

'You're quite right,' he was told, 'DIY photo albums are more personal.'

Rean was sure he was meant to have holiday snaps and architectural curiosities in the album but he deflected such enquiry. He wasn't to be bound by anything.

On the left-hand page he stuck the image of the topless young woman in the centre of the white sheet being careful to avoid greasy fingerprints on the white cartridge paper. On the right-hand page he cut out the brief description supplied, the tamed words of sex, the lettering dropping off the page.

> Cassandra has taken all her clothes off and is waiting for YOU.
> Melissa loves to be watched, to be undressed by the eyes of men.
> Anastasia has been in prison, now she wants a different kind of correction.

There had been many times his wife had shouted up the stairs.

'Dinner's ready. Don't let it get cold.'

Rean wiped the sweat from his forehead,

'What do you do in that study of yours?'

The husband hadn't wanted to hear too much. When Rean's hands enthusiastically conjured up the User Guide in the thin cold air, the husband had huddled away from the wind, wrapping his arms around himself, shrinking his neck into his windcheater.

'Be careful with all that.'

Rean was. He had been faithful in body but not in

mind. That was enough as far as he was concerned and more than was usually expected. In body he had walked around the ancient monument, nodding when the tour guide pronounced, laughing when history revealed itself in some simplistic, prophetic way. In mind he quickened his pace so that he came up close behind his wife's friend.

'Imagine how our ancestors must have felt,' the guide gushed as he opened his arms to reveal a view of valleys and hills. They all for a moment were resident at Finlagen, the ribaldry of the clan replaced by the chatter of wishful thinking.

Rean imagined how it would feel when he pressed himself against his wife's friend, his arms closing around her.

In the hospital, he felt young again.

'You're a good boy, a good boy.'

His mother patted him on the arm, her long, emaciated fingers tapping a languid rhythm on his sleeve.

'She's having a good day.'

The nurse carried a small tray into the room and set it down on the bedside table.

'And so chatty. I don't think I've heard her say so much in one day.'

Rean looked the nurse up and down, taking in all the

details he had been dreaming about. These images gleaned in the sterile, brightly lit room were the new User Guide. He would copy and paste; recall and enact.

'People say some dementia patients become talkative close to death.'

The nurse dropped the small glass bottle she was holding. The shattering glass skated over the linoleum, spreading out under the bed, a few pieces even reaching Rean's feet. He looked at the tiny fragments glinting under the glare of fluorescence.

'If I was you I'd be careful who you listen to and certainly who you believe.'

Rean looked up as the nurse bent down to pick up the glass. He saw what he needed to see. It wasn't the uniform, it was the way the nurse fitted into it.

'You're a good boy, a good boy.'

His mother reached out to pat his arm again but Rean was already crouching down beside the nurse. He could smell her. Again. But it was stronger, closer. He heard her uniform rustle against her tights, her skin, and all he could do was close his eyes.

His mother's fingers reached out, drumming the stale air of the room.

'Be careful you don't cut yourself.'

When he stretched his arms forward, it could have been for glass fragments; it was possible he had seen something the nurse hadn't. She wasn't sure until she felt his hands on her breasts, his thick fingers clawing at her hidden flesh.

'What are you doing?'

She pulled away from him but her balance was upset and she tumbled on to her back, her legs hoisted into the air, the glass fragments loosened from her grip. Without hesitating, Rean threw himself on top of her, his arms pinning hers against the floor.

'Get off me, for God's sake!'

In his night dreams and many waking moments, Rean had already been here. His tongue was dancing with hers, his hands exploring every inch of flesh and bone. He had stripped her and himself so many times already. But he had not thought about the shouts which now bellowed out of her as he thrust himself against her. He put his hand to her mouth but her shouts escaped through his fingers, her saliva wetting his skin, her teeth biting through to the bone.

Rean heard his mother's voice amid the shouts.

'You're a good boy, a good boy.'

She always used to say that even after she'd had to scold him for some childish act. Her raised voice was always tempered by a reassuring whisper, the whiplash of the back of her hand countered by a comforting hug.

He always believed her.

'I can't believe you did that.'

The nurse managed to slither out from Rean's body

and without reassembling her uniform ran out of the room.

'I need help here.'

'I need you here.'

Rean had wanted to go up to the study, to add to the User Guide and check its function, its ability to work, to work on him. The thicker the album became the longer he stayed in the room, at his desk, its surface strewn with unread magazines opened and ready, notebooks with only half-written lines scrawled on to the paper.

On Sunday we attended the service and then had lunch. It was a beautiful, sunny day.

'What are you writing in that journal, anyway? I hope it's not all about me.'

There were things to do, household chores that could not easily be ignored.

'You have to do it at some point.' His wife reminded him.

He carried the paperwork upstairs with him.

'It won't take long.' He shouted as he jogged upstairs.

'That's what you always say.'

He shut the door and wedged it shut with the paperwork.

*

Melissa smiled at him then whispered into his ear, 'I want you to watch me undress.'

'It's so tidy in here.'
   Shan was in the kitchen when he reached home.
   'How was your mother?'
   Rean went straight to the bathroom. He had run from the hospital and he was not a fit man. Once, yes, he had run for miles, training for a college bout but that had been years ago and there had been a toll taken after years desk-bound and chair-ridden. He was kept in some kind of shape by a fluke of nature, by 'lucky genes' his wife always said. Still, the hospital was more than two miles away and his face had reddened, his pulse quickened. In more ways than one he felt feverish.
   When he stood without clothes, sweat trickling down from his face, dripping on to his shoulders before being dammed by the hair on his chest. He saw the nurse on her knees, her mouth around his erection. He noticed how the sweat dropped occasionally from his forehead on to her upper lip as it moved up and down his penis, the pale lipstick leaving a trail smeared pink for his eyes to follow.
   'Illness is a terrible thing. It robs people of their dignity.'
   Rean closed his eyes and still saw the mirror reflecting

him, the nurse, his wife as she tapped at the door to the study.

At home his wife is at the door.
'I said the dinner is ready. What are you doing in there?'
She tried to push the door but the papers blocked its way.
'Just a minute.'
Rean shoved the User Guide between other manuals and pulled himself together.
It was a sham.
It wasn't a sham.
Making love to someone in your head isn't the same thing.
'It's okay, I'm just finishing off. I'll be there in a minute.'

'Do you want some dinner?'
Shan shouted from the kitchen. After last time she avoided walking through the house without directly signalling where she was going. People were allowed their privacy after all. Just because they were there to help, paid to assist, didn't mean that they could act like one of the family. On the many orientation in-services she had been on, it was stressed over and over again.

Widows but especially widowers have an individual and unpredictable response to personal space. One minute they want no-one near them and the next all they want is to be reassured. The skill you need to acquire is knowing which they need at any given moment.

'Rean?'

He pulled the nurse into his study for closer inspection. A like for like comparison; a page-turning decider. The angel versus the home help.

'Are you alright, Rean?'

Shan was taller than the nurse, longer legs and prettier face.

In the User Guide he flicked the pages impatiently to get to the face, the body he knew he wanted to see. Yes, he knew them by their names but it was their bodies he remembered. Flesh tones, curves and smoothness of skin; the way their nipples would pierce the page, the angle their legs wrapped around the photographer's lens. All of it. He felt he had been released into a secret world.

Shan's voice was incredible. Rean had never heard it so sultry. It was smoke and mirrors; alcohol and soft, soft furnishings like the chaise longue Cassandra relaxed on, her thighs nestling the centrefold across the watermarked paper of his photo album.

'I'll be there in a minute.'

Rean needed a moment to prepare himself. He wanted Shan to see him at his best. She had commented on how handsome he looked when he made an effort just as the nurse at the hospital had speculated that he must have been quite a ladies' man when he was in his prime.

His wife has always wanted him to dress for dinner. Being from humble origins made good he always found it a little bizarre to suit up for dinner for two. Sometimes his wife would be running around the kitchen, balancing plates and pans, stressed by the need for everything to be just right. She would curse the sauce, the soufflé and her hands, wrinkled by water. Then there would be a lull, a near silence broken only by the soft simmer of water, the snap of fat in the oven. He would wait, stiff and uncomfortable in his suit and tie, trying to watch the television but distracted by the thump of yet another pair of shoes being thrown back into the wardrobe.

Dinner with their friends followed the same pattern except everything was amplified. The courses were longer, the sauces richer and the dresses more exclusive. But it wasn't just his wife and her friends who politely competed, the husbands too upped stakes in their conversation turning casual references to business and success to extravagant pipe dreams, clouding the dining-room with thick, unctuous smoke. By the end of such dinner parties he was intoxicated by riches and more than a little ashamed by the unspoken acceptance of them.

Rean walked out of the bedroom. Unsuited. Unclothed.
    He could hear Shan clattering plates in the kitchen.
    'I hope you've dressed for dinner.'
    She laughed as the kettle boiled and clicked off.
    Rean sat down at the dining-table, drawing the chair tight against the table. Years ago he would have waited for his wife to sit down and then poured her a glass of St Emilion, recommending it without gusto. It was expensive. It was usually fine. The conversation was of the day, a ship to board and sail through steady waters avoiding storms or outcrops of rock. After his wife had given him the details of what they were to eat and rushed from the table after barely touching her starter, he was left becalmed.
    'I must rescue the roast.'

'At last.'
    Shan rushed in with a plate she held in both hands, lightly juggling its weight in her hands.
    'Be careful, it's hot.'
    She put the plate in front of him and then hurriedly looked away.
    'Not wearing a shirt? It is cold outside you know. You don't want to be catching a chill at your age.'

At his age, Rean thought, he was lucky to be alive. The Group of Who Was Left, splashing out with pensioned money on sites of antiquity, was dominated by women. The few men still around seemed to be nuzzling the tombstones they visited.

'I'm sorry the food isn't great. It's all very processed nowadays. It used to be that it was made by cooks who served the whole city. Now it's just made ready to heat up.'

It would have been sent back in years gone by but Rean wasn't interested in the food.

He kept his hands under the table.

Shan wouldn't eat with him. On the in-service she had been told

Guard against over-familiarisation. It might seem friendly but it can be viewed as intrusive.

She busied herself with unnecessary tasks. The pile of mail he hadn't looked at was fanned out on the table, the most recent on top.

'You really should look at your mail. You might get a nice surprise.'

Rean kept both hands on his penis, holding it tightly until it reached the underside of the table. He pushed it against the rosewood, rubbing it against the fine grains.

'You may have won something. You never know. A

friend of mine filled in a form the other week and someone phoned her to say that she'd won a holiday!'

She let the last letter drop askew from the neat pattern she had made.

'What's that sound?'

Rean was watching the nurse squirming on the floor, her eyes screwed shut, her lips pursed and puckered as though his was the first kiss she had received.

His wife turned over in bed and kissed him lightly on the cheek.

'We still love each other, don't we?'

Shan walked around the room, her head tilted backwards trying to find the source of the knocking.

Rean varied the rhythm depending what came into his head. He stroked his penis gently, pushing it in a slow tap against the wood then when he saw something else, felt something else, he increased the tempo, and slammed it as hard as he could against table. In anticipation of orgasm he leant back in the chair and aimed for the long-life bulb which stained the room with dull, yellow light.

It was then that Shan screamed. Not a horror film scream, a tonal pitch and volume that could make your head stand on end. This was a rush of breath inward that whistled into her body. The tepid dinner of stewed vegetables and tough meat slid from the plate, keeping its shape and form as it fell to the floor taking with it the glass of cloudy tap water, the untouched cutlery and triangulated paper napkin.

Rean stood up and spread his arms out wide.

'This is more appetising, is it not?'

He shouted the words and Shan's hands concertina'd between her eyes and ears, shutters and mufflers being brought into hurried and indecisive use. She didn't want to look or hear. She didn't want to be there. The in-service training hadn't taken her this far.

The elderly out of all the age groups the care services are involved with is the most sexually benign. On the rare occasion it isn't, the client is usually both easily placated and distracted.

Rean cleared the table with his feet and climbed on to it, closing his eyes for a moment, initially to steady himself as the rush of blood and adrenaline threatened to unbalance him but then to concentrate on what he wanted to see.

'You'll be a heartbreaker one of these days.' His mother had said.

'You're breaking my heart.' His wife had said when he wouldn't bring himself to talk about anything.

'You'll break something for God's sake!' Shan shouted at him.

He knew what she meant but the best glassware was covered in dust anyway.

Rean started to gyrate, bending his knees as far as they would go while his hips thrust violently forward.

'I'm leaving. Now!'

Shan slid her way around the dining-room walls while Rean pivoted on the spot so that his rhythm was uninterrupted.

'Please, don't do that.'

Rean took a deep breath and jumped off the table. He saw himself leap into the air, his body hanging for a brief moment before he slammed to the floor, his tongue flicking at her cheeks and lips as he came to rest. He was close enough to smell the scent of his own home on her skin. This was familiar. She was familiar.

Shan ran quickly from the house into the street pausing only to make a wild but accurate grab for her handbag. Her car was parked close to the house and even before she reached it her fingers had already snared the keys, her head jerking round to see what he was doing. She wished she was back on the paediatric shift.

Rean knew exactly what he was doing. He followed her out into the street, not opening or shutting the wooden gate but jumping it.

*

'You could have been an athlete.' His mother had said.

'We should have been athletes.' His wife had whispered as they both reached the summit of the hill before their huffing and puffing friends.

Before he even made it another step however he could already feel other eyes on him. Not Shan's but his neighbours, their carers, their dogs and cats all peering around doors or slitting eyes through blinds. In a silent neighbourhood a refuse lorry can cause commotion and so Rean knew that there were many living, breathing things between him and Shan.

Shan fumbled for the right key to the lock. There were only three keys on the ring and yet each one slipped from her grip as she shook with fright.

Rean turned towards his secreted audience and exaggerated the pull on his penis, flicking his wrist so that he pulled the circumcised head first left then right then straight on.

He could see himself in the mirror while his wife lay on the bed.

'Time has been kind to you.'

Shan locked the door when she slumped into her seat, her feet getting stuck under the accelerator pedal, her bag straps getting caught up on the gear stick. Without taking her eyes from Rean she fumbled in the bag to find her phone. Only once before, years ago, had she made such a call; the in-service had recommended it and she knew of nothing else she could do.

It is good practice to follow procedure in extreme moments. Reacting is not enough and can often cause more problems. Considered, procedural action is the only way out of a difficult situation.

Rean was now in the middle of the road. Two cars from opposite directions had pulled up at a safe distance. The drivers were used to speed bumps that prevented anti-social acceleration in a built-up area and Rean, remembering when years ago he had raced out into the road and shaken his fist after a speeding motorist, now shook his erection at both cars.

Before Shan could finish the call, Rean was already on the bonnet of her car, spread-eagled on the metallic paint, his tongue reaching the wipers, licking the rubber, his eyes rolling back into his head. She rushed to switch on the wipers as though their sweeping motion would brush away the horror. Shan could see the veins on his head, the silver flick of hair, matted with sweat, pressed into his forehead. She was closer to a client than she had ever expected. He was such a charming man and now his saliva was dripping on to her windscreen, his teeth sliding off the Perspex, his fingers leaving slug trails as they clawed and dug in.

***

'This is it. You will have read about it. Abnormally easy ejaculation from the absence of cerebral inhibition, resulting from excessive psychic excitement. All it can need is the simple conception of a lascivious situation which is sufficient to set the ejaculation centre in action.'

One of the students peered through the opening in the door.

'At least he doesn't have to worry about his Viagra prescription.'

The other four students laugh and Dr Sitruc allows a smile to hover briefly over his pale, institutionally toned skin.

'The case is unusual because it challenges popular conceptions that arousal follows stimulus, a stimulus that comes from a body represented in the flesh, on film or in the pages of a magazine. For this patient, the stimulus is solely located in the mind.'

The other four students push to look through the small slit in the door. A woman, short enough to have to stand on her toes asks, 'Is there a medical condition to be diagnosed here or is he simply being held because he represents a threat?'

Dr Sitruc nods and begins to walk away from the door, gently urging the students to follow him into the middle of the long corridor.

'That's a useful question. What shoot from the hip, textbook diagnosis would any of you give at this moment?'

There was a long pause which Sitruc expected. Students on their psychological rotation rarely expected the cut and thrust of instant diagnosis that was the bread and butter of other clinical modules. He liked to remind students that his department, small and underfunded as it was, would be just as likely to challenge their skills as any other.

This was an ideal case to challenge the imaginations as well as the knowledge of the students, especially compared to the pitiful sights they had already seen on the morning rounds. It wasn't so much bedlam but boredom he reminded them. They were not likely to see people in violent self-abusing frenzies. The main activity for most of the two dozen or so patients was staring into space. Any space for any length of time.

'You have obviously heard of nymphomania?'

The male students nodded uncertainly.

'This is the male equivalent.'

'Satyriasis,' the woman said firmly.

Sitruc smiled.

'Exactly. The textbook definition in case you need reminded, gentlemen, is a morbid, overpowering sexual desire in men. Forget about textbook cases. They offer general descriptions to assist general diagnosis but as in any other area you will be studying and visiting and maybe even working in the patient's individual response to their condition will dictate both diagnosis and treatment. The textbook is a guidebook, nothing more, nothing less. The man inside that room was once a healthy member of the community. Whether he is again is possibly up to us.'

Rean could see the nurse coming towards him.

At last.

His wife used to complain that sometimes he would avoid coming to bed.

'What do you do in that study, anyway?'

The nurse stood in front of him.

'What do you want me to do?'

'As if I didn't know.'

Rean wasn't sure he had heard his wife right. This was a rare exchange, a brief flirtation with argument. When the intercom had been installed between the kitchen and garage, to allow for quick yet unintrusive communication, there had been a quick tension and a steady gaze from his wife that unsettled Rean.

'Why do you ask?'

The nurse unclasped her hair as she held his gaze.

'You know you can share things with me. Because, in

spite of all our years, I'm still the one who knows you better than anyone.'

Rean smiled at his wife's sultry voice, the confidence of intimacy, the entrapment of familiarity.

'You don't know me, you just think you do.'

Now that the moment had passed, Rean wasn't sure who had spoken. The words recalled a sense of threat, of knowing and a reminder of how brittle things had become.

The nurse bent over him. He was in the twin-bedded hospital room. When he glanced to the left his mother lay sleeping on her back beside him, her mouth slightly open, her breathing faint but rasping. Her skin looked pallid, a shade of grey Rean had come to associate with hospitals, where skin tone was dulled by illness and then artificially brightened by the strip lights. Here we are: packages of meat in a supermarket fridge glossed and revitalised by tight cellophane.

It was okay. His mother was asleep. It was just him and the nurse. There was no-one to see. He pulled the sheets away from him and reached out. The nurse hesitated.

'Don't you find me attractive?'

The nurse smiled.

'How shall we begin today?'

Rean smiled and grabbed his penis.

'Try this.'

*

The nurse smiled.

'This won't hurt a bit.'

She daubed Rean's forearm with cotton wool and carefully inserted the point of the syringe.

Rean watched as the nurse straddled him. They didn't break eye contact. He raised his knees up so that he supported her weight, so that he could pull her closer to him. His hands slipped under the uniform, his fingertips pressing into her skin.

'I hope my hands aren't cold.' His voice was husky as though he hadn't spoken for some time. His throat felt dry but otherwise in every way that mattered he felt in good condition.

'This will feel cold for a moment but don't worry, that's normal.'

The nurse discarded the syringe and pale latex gloves. She rubbed his arm vigorously.

'This will help.'

Rean wrestled with the nurse. First she was on top then he was then she was again. They rolled in the hospital room. He grunted, she squealed and his mother snorted rolling over in her bed, turning her back to them.

They waited, both of them, for a moment but the

only sound was of the clinical hiss and whirr of the hospital building around them.

'Oh yes.' Rean shouted not caring whether his mother rolled again, this time to wake up, to intervene.

At home the User Guide fell from his lap on to the floor.

'Oh for goodness sake,' his wife had shouted when he still had not come to bed.

'How long are you going to be?'

'Oh no you don't.'

The nurse changed from rubbing his arm to holding it down, pressed on to the bed. A man he hadn't noticed before grabbed his other arm, keeping it pinned down. Rean flexed his fingers, curling them in then out. Many times. It felt like it was the only movement he could make. Nearly. He discovered he could move the lower half of his body up then down.

'Oh yes.'

The nurse glanced anxiously over towards Rean's mother but she was still asleep and, with a spare hand, Rean brought her face back close to his. He pushed up and inside, closing his eyes so that nothing would prevent him from seeing.

*

In the bedroom, Rean turned on just one small lamp.

'Why do you always want it to be so dark?' His wife asked as she climbed out of the dip in the mattress, entwining her legs around his.

'Grab him, for God's sake.'

The two nurses rearranged their hands so that each of them could hold down a leg and an arm.

'We need some restraint here.' The male nurse muttered.

'You're holding back from me.' His wife whispered into his ear.

'Don't stop, don't stop.'

Rean liked the way that sounded. Liked that he was being told something that he wanted to do.

'Oh yes.' The nurse purred like Cassandra. Or was it Melinda?

Sitruc stood with the young female student, a bright, breezy woman called Alecs, outside Rean's room. The three male students had taken advantage of his offer of a coffee break while he did his rounds. Alecs asked quietly if she could accompany him. Sitruc was more than happy to accommodate this subtle enthusiasm. It seemed, as ever, psychology was a near last choice for most specialising doctors and he felt honour bound to encourage interest whenever he came across it.

'He's showing all the signs.' Sitruc whispered into her ear as Rean lay convulsing on the bed, the leather straps digging into his arms and legs. 'Progressive loss of intelligence and increasing perversion of his moral sense.'

'It's very sad.' The student said wistfully, writing down Sitruc's statement word for word in her notepad. 'But I must admit I am surprised too. I didn't expect it to be so . . .' She underlined and capitalised MORAL. '. . . so . . . obvious.'

Sitruc nodded wryly, 'The most private of men can become the most expressive at times like this.'

Their mutual friends dropped off one by one, on the mountain and in his house. The last walk up the striding edge had seen him out of breath and alone looking down at his wife's friends as they struggled and slipped over the loose slate, their dubbined walking boots kicking into the air.

'Whoops. I don't remember it being this slippery.'

'Ah, it's that slippery slope.'

Rean listened to their laughter, his hands digging deep into his waterproof trousers.

He broke a plate filling up the dishwasher as everybody rushed to clear up after his dinner party. When he joined the group of widows and widowers, when he entertained them in his home, it was taken for granted that there was both a fanfare for what they had achieved and a last post for what they had lost. There was no question that anybody would be left alone with themselves, their thoughts.

'Keeping busy.' Someone said as they fought over the last few spaces in the rack. 'That's the key.'

'Whoops, those plates are slippery.'

The plates had been a present. Of course, Rean thought, this was the moment when anything of any importance would and should come unstuck, unhinged, fragile and brittle as the china once so proudly displayed.

'It's heritage.' His wife had told him. 'That's always more than just simply flesh and blood. '

The cheerleader for them all, the tour organiser for PIR, the very image of a brave face, kissed him on the cheek as she left with the rest of them, in silence. In his ear she whispered, 'You did very well.'

He should be proud of himself.

Alecs walked down corridor G2 in fitful steps. Every time she heard a sound, a low groan, a rising scream, whispered words, she would stop and try to work out where it was coming from.

'Behind each door is a human being. Sometimes you need to remind yourself of that.'

Sitruc happily unlocked the ward door. He wanted to

encourage the curiosity that Alecs was showing. Most of the students regarded their clinical time in the corridor as the medical equivalent of the graveyard shift.

The male nurse tried not to look at Rean's lolling tongue. It wasn't just hanging out of his mouth but was thrusting into the air, darting at the fug of the room, licking invisible skin. It wasn't just his tongue. His body was arching as though being shocked, his penis hammering into the sheet, quick bruises appearing then disappearing.

Rean could see the shape of the body in front of him. The curves beneath the sheer angles of the starched uniform were clearly visible. With one movement of his hand he knew it could be easily achieved. The white material would disappear to reveal sheer silk barely hiding white skin. Then he would be where he wanted to be. His tongue, his fingers, his nose would revel in the emotion of flesh.

The male nurse struggled to find a vein. He was aware that the thrashing and the visible throbbing were part of the condition but they still unnerved him. He was used to being sworn at, attacked with anything from walking frames to overcooked hospital food but the patients in G2 always unnerved him. Their uncontrolled explosive behaviour was both difficult to predict and awkward to cope with. It was not violent as such but the provocation was nonetheless acute. He was never sure the injection would be enough.

Alecs peered through the spyhole. She had wanted to be in the room with Rean but Sitruc had shaken his head at the suggestion.

'I understand that you want to be closer to the patient. It is the instinct of the doctor, the healer who believes in the hands-on approach. But, in cases such as this the hands-off approach is the only possible strategy. Putting you in there would be like lighting the fuse with one hand while holding the explosive in the other.'

Alecs's notepad remained limp in her hand. She couldn't tear herself away from the spyhole to record clinical notes. Now was not the time. It was enough to see a patient, a man, writhing as though caught on barbed wire.

Rean feels like he is about to explode. Melissa, Cassandra, Shan, the nurse are wrestling around him, fighting for space, fighting over him. Their lips clash, gums merging as they push against his skin. He can feel teeth both sharp and blunt, he can smell breath both fresh and rank. Tongues, many tongues push and tug at his penis. There is nothing he can say. 'One at a time' wouldn't have worked. It was all so urgent. It had to be now. The timer hadn't been set. The appointments hadn't been made. The bus would have to leave without him.

The male nurse rubs the skin where the syringe delivered its drug. He hoped it would work. Other patients in G2 had been quelled into a coma-like state with this drug. It was not without its potentially traumatic side-effects but it was being trialled as an antidote, as a much needed intervention. To combat the physical impact of satyriasis and its associated symptoms. He could see the symptoms writhe and flex before him and they weren't good. The penis looked like a boil that needed to be lanced. Fortunately it wasn't his job to wait to assess the effects. When he closed the door to the room and turned the key in the lock he said to the young student hovering around the door, 'Take some notes. Anything could happen.'

Alecs wanted to know what was going on. Her fellow students had laughed as they rushed off to the canteen. Alecs knew the humour, it was the usual medical coping strategy in an early stage but she also knew that she didn't want anything second-hand. If it was that bad she needed to see it for herself.

There were so many women gathered around him now that he could no longer see where he was. He could be anywhere. The room was filled with the heat and smell of sex. When he looked up at the ceiling juices dripped like condensation until it too disappeared from view as body after body clambered on top of him. Rean felt an immense pressure on his chest and while every part of his body was being caressed or kissed or licked, a panic rose inside him. He was being caged by limbs, torn by nails drawn across his skin.

'It could happen to you.'

His mother in a moment of clarity gripped his arm as he sat beside her bed.

'Look at me, son.'

For the first time in months he held his mother's gaze. It was too difficult to look her in the eye and see the child, the need, the pain in her.

'Sometimes I think I am losing my mind.'

Rean slid his hand into hers.

'I know.'

She was closer to the truth than anyone expected her to be.

The doctor told him. 'We like to comfort ourselves with the notion that people like your mother are unaware of what is happening to them, that they are oblivious, blissful. But what if they aren't? Can we cope with the possibility that they are being slowly dragged into some kind of personal hell?'

The nurse sighed and shook her head when the doctor left the room.

'Don't mind him. His bedside manner has always been a little too grave for my liking.'

The nurse rearranged his mother's pillow and turned and smiled at Rean.

The nurse fought her way through the throng of bodies, twisting limbs like pipe-cleaners to clear her way. Her face pressed into Rean's as her naked body manoeuvred itself on top of him.

'I'm here for you.'

Rean closed his eyes and no longer felt any pressure on his chest. He entered her body and the rush and chaos of the room subsided into their breathless, mutual sigh.

The male nurse walked slowly even though Alecs was screaming at him to hurry up.

'Something's happened, for God's sake. I think, I think he's died.

She wouldn't, couldn't move. This was her first death. For all the hours she had spent in A&E and the critical wards she had never witnessed dying. Even when the nurse attempted to move her gently away from the door she struggled with him and in the end they shared the same view through the spyhole in the door. Rean lay still, serene, yet every part of his body was still taut. In his last frenzied movements, the sheets had fallen from the bed and they both saw the strings of semen dripping slowly from his penis on to the mattress.

The nurse pulled away and led the shaken Alecs down the corridor.

'An enviable death.'

'A heart attack?!' Alecs looked at him as what little colour she had drained from her face.

The nurse just smiled.

The Gradual Gathering of Lust

Monday, above the South Pacific Ocean.

It feels good to have the family together again even in a rattly old plane that has seen better days. It's too noisy to talk, so I write, just like I've always done. Since I married, since the kids were young, it's always been my way of treating the world, to season and add flavour to an existence where so much is verbalised, painstakingly rationalised for consumption and methodically ordered for reaction. It takes the whine and whirr of these creaking old engines to take us into a silence that I like to think is contemplative, that I like to think is more about spiritual engagement than emotional estrangement.

The turbulence is getting worse. I have to stop now.

It was the same. His head was on its side, half in, half out the shallow warm water. His eyes opened then closed. The glare of the setting or rising sun made it hard to see. He didn't know which it was. It could be dawn or dusk. He didn't know enough. He was the dreamer of the family after all. He had no facts, no hard and fast ideas, just revolving feelings that spat out meanings in lyrical moments. This was a beachhead. It was a test, to recreate the time and place of his awakening on a deserted shore with only the sounds of waves, wind and scuttling crabs for his senses to pinpoint. His senses had alerted him *then* but did not inform him. It could have been dawn or dusk. A sun rising or setting on a bruised and bloodied body, pierced by jagged rock, wrapped in layers of seaweed.

He knew now. He had watched enough, felt and seen enough to know the progress and process of the day. This was the time as exact enough as it needed to be. This was when he had woken. Like a broken doll thrown up by the sea and chance; spat out by fate to be churned with the weed and the limpets, broiling in some foreign . . .

'What are you doing?'

Karine was fighting with the debris shelter; its structure had been made unsafe by high winds and torrential rain. The vines and saplings she had spent a day twisting into shape over the sturdy boughs from the crashed-down trees had sprung loose and were weaving and writhing around her in the stiff breeze that threatened to do yet more damage. It was a difficult task since her hands were still swollen and bandaged but it was an essential one. They needed shelter. Her father had told her tales of bivouacking on mountaintops and creating swamp beds in jungles, and shelter, as he never grew tired of telling her, all of them in fact, was primal. It was practical. They did not know what they were facing and to lie exposed night after night on the beach as they had done was not acceptable. She could hear his voice, 'In a survival situation shelter is a high priority.' Of course it was. The dampness from the rains was rotting the improvised bandage she had made from jacket fabric and she couldn't bare to think of another night with nothing between her and this unknown land and sea. She could hear his voice, the same words now whispered into her ear, a warm comfort turning to a cold rage. Minus. It was his fault. He wanted to roam and yet would hurry under the shelter when he had had enough of the elements scorching his soul. He should be here, with her, tying down tangled vine. Minus.

On the island, the atoll, as her father would have wanted it described, they had to eat, they had to sleep safely, they had to keep the fire going. These were simple facts to be agreed and acted on, maybe even rostered so that each survivor would take his or her turn in such essentials. If they followed some elementary rules, some rudimentary guidelines they would be able to survive long enough to be rescued.

Minus.

'I said, what are you doing? There's no time for . . . this . . . or whatever you call it.'

Minus lifted his head out of the water and looked down at his body, still wrapped in the torn shreds of his winter clothing. The air inside the plane had been cold and they had all kept their layers on. After the crash his sister had ripped his clothes into strips and applied them to the many gashes that had covered his body. He giggled putting his face back into the water, watching the bubbles froth briefly into foam. Karine winced as her fingers touched his flesh. The skin she remembered as smooth and white had been torn open.

'Nothing's properly healed yet. If you get an infection . . .'

His sister shook her head and kicked the last few waves dissipating on the sand, her ugly, angry swipes spraying the water back into her face. He giggled again, this time letting the water spurt out of his mouth. Like a fountain cherub, Minus thought, a bedraggled and fucked-up sprite bleeding on some unknown atoll, spewing forth with crimson innards. The fountain of youth. He had discovered it and should now grow old with his discovery. So be it.

Minus picked himself up out of the water and lurched to the dry sand. He watched his sister now kicking the fine sand of the upper part of beach as she made her way back to the shelter at the start of the tree-line. Just like it ever was. Not her way? Then off in a huff she goes. His body would heal he told himself, inspecting his gashes and grazes as he stood on the beach balancing himself on a piece of driftwood. The skin was a resilient layer, it could stretch and transform to accommodate wounds, to gradually heal the torn, the ruptured. He watched Karine now at the shelter and felt goose pimples rash over him in the tropical heat. His injuries made him feel alive.

When the pilot had screamed – and he did scream – BRACE FOR IMPACT, Karine had expected her life to flash before her, a ready-made biopic that everybody apparently has in waiting. She wondered what it would have contained. A potted history of dreams limping into reality weighed down by the high expectations of her parents. A catalogue of limited exhibition, of ambition yet to be fulfilled. She doubted the flashbacks would have been long enough. It didn't happen. Anyway. The last words she heard on the plane were the pilot's frightened repetitions, the trained exhortations reaching through the rush of noise and clamour. The last sound she heard had no lexical cohesion but its meaning was clear enough. They were in brief harmony, all four of them, strapped in and huckled down, their heads rammed between their knees. They were in unison of action, of impending doom and of sound: the chest-tightening, air-suctioned AAAAAH they chorused before being engulfed by the sea.

Karine watched the shelter being dismantled by wind, she noticed her T-shirt being blown along the beach and she saw her brother's baseball cap lofted into the palms that stood swaying, brooding with intent. These were signs, visual signifiers both familiar and disturbing to her. She had lived and breathed photographs, seeking out meaning in other people's lives. This time she was more involved and their clothing being whipped up by the sea breeze was symbolic of their pathetic attempt to achieve some kind of normality, some kind of civilised survival exercise.

They had fallen out of the sky and into the sea with nothing but what they had been wearing and of course their pockets had hardly been bulging with Bowie knives, survival rations or emergency flares. Minus's smoking habit gave them a still-working lighter but all she had were sodden tissues and a packet of gum which she had aimed to be chewing as they descended into Honiari. As it turned out she had barely had time to swallow before the sea greeted them.

She had regained consciousness in the water just like her brother except he was worse hurt than her. She had fallen thousands of feet and emerged from the sea with barely a scratch and her thoughts had turned to driftwood she could bind together with vines, to green saplings she could tear from the ground. But this was not all she could think about. This was not all she saw. Her mother had reached across and touched her father's arm. He had leaned over and pushed his ear close to her mouth. They had both smiled after the exchange of . . . of what . . . a joke, an endearment, an important anthropological thought about their forthcoming trip to the Solomons? She didn't know and, as she reached one last time high into the air and caught the sleeve of the shirt, it flashed into Karine's mind that she would never know. Such was the snare of the still image, of a memory, of a life made into portrait, seeing something didn't necessarily make sense. Suddenly, as she exalted in her timing, she felt ashamed that she had believed so much in the encapsulation of a moment. What had mattered didn't matter. Her still lives were still there. As she began to tear strips from the shirt to use as fresh dressing for Minus's wounds, her gaze drifted to her brother rolling around on the sand. What would such a snapshot mean for her, for him? Karine shuddered. It had already been over-exposed and such a memory of him, of them both, should be torn up before it could be allowed to develop. It's not the photograph that matters. It's what happens after it that counts.

This will be good for all of us. We both agreed on that. Eventually Torr had to be dragged to the conclusion that if we didn't take the kids with us on this trip it would mean another half-arsed Christmas, another opportunity allowed to slip by. 'The kids have their own lives, let them lead them.' This. I mean this was his clarion call, his off the cuff strategy that's supposed to pass for family. We've never agreed on this. It's an old, creaking argument. We play the roles that we have recorded for nearly three decades. I fret, he forays; I smother while he is the distant lover, caring but not showing. We have processed our findings, written out conclusions and know everything about our subjects but nothing about ourselves. Yes, a kind of kinship.

But that's not true, I let my words ramble on and sometimes their meaning leaps too far forward for me to justify, rely on. We know we have two incredible kids, caught up in an adventure that could lead anywhere, to any particular ending. Torr teases me when I tell him this — and I do tell him a lot of what's in here, not everything but enough — 'Sure we do,' he says 'they know that we are going to land on the Solomons and have a great time.' He knows what I mean but it's not to be talked about. He nods and rubs his hands with that kind of show-some-strength attitude that has probably been passed down his pioneering family. 'We're all going to get on fine.' He smiles to himself and you can feel the rue being churned over and over in his head. 'They are great kids.' Nobody had said anything different and yet why do we let a silence grow?

Minus thought of Richter as he staggered up from THE PLACE WHERE HE HAD BEEN FOUND. Richter had sampled the sea, taken a DAT to the shore and, encasing it in some plastic, had submerged the machine beneath the waves. When he returned to the studio he took the basic, natural sound and layered it against loops of sand being ground beneath bare feet, of drips of seawater languorously falling into rock pools and of driftwood or human debris bumping against the rocks with each surge of the sea. It was mesmerising stuff and through headphones it was just like it had been. Just like he remembered. Putting two shells up to your ears and shutting your eyes. You were already there and yet suddenly you were there even more. That's what Richter was about, that's what most people missed about him, dismissed about him as a niche new ager providing a backdrop for a tinitis generation who could no longer bear the thud of dance but needed the wash of nature. He called the music 'Somewhere There Is A Space For Us'. Exactly. You can't rely on memory, your own or other people's. You have to find something new in what you think you know. What most of his contemporaries didn't realise is that it wasn't about wallpaper: a safe and securing backdrop that would harmonise simply with a childhood moment. And it wasn't just about the sea, its sounds. Minus liked the music because what he heard and felt, what he saw and could taste, was him then, now and maybe even as he would be. He could hear himself in sound.

'Christ!'

Minus could see his sister trying to keep the fire going but he wasn't ready yet. This was some kind of anniversary. His sister didn't understand. Everything was about survival to her. The shelter, food, fire, water. These were elemental concerns to her and yet she would wake him each and every night by leaping out of her bed of leaves and shouting for their parents, screaming for them as though she was ten and nightmarish. It could have been sleeptalk, the somnambulant walk of the ill at ease, but she seemed wide awake and aware and nothing would comfort her, not a hug, a kiss, a reassuring word. She had to be wrestled back to the makeshift bed and held down until her limbs were at peace. Still longer for her mind to be calmed and Minus would stroke her forehead, pushing the sweat-matted blonde hair out of her screwed-up eyes until, finally, screams would slide down into whimpers then slur into strange gurgles. The leak would somehow stop just as his lips hovered above hers, her warm breath mingling with his. His body trembled as this air from deep inside her filled his lungs. THIS WAS THE PLACE WHERE THEY HAD BOTH BEEN.

In the morning she would wake with the dawn and rush about duties that she had assigned to herself, that had been given to her by necessity; the mother of reinvention. Nothing was said about the night; the terrors that she had succumbed to. It was just like it always was. A significant event should always be down-played.

Minus wasn't sure how long it took but something had drawn him back to the water, to THE PLACE WHERE HE HAD BEEN FOUND. When his sister was crying into the sand, splurting words up into his bare chest, he remembered Richter's music and found something new again, in the gaps he allowed, the artificial stretch of silence he created between flood and ebb flows. He wasn't minimal but infinitesimal. Minus had space to breathe when he recalled this music. With a simple scratch of rock he could breathe huge sighs of relief and not care whether there was fire or food. And he needed to breathe before his sister smothered him with the insistence of everything they didn't need.

At THE PLACE WHERE HE HAD BEEN FOUND he recalled not just how he had got there but why. Karine said she couldn't remember, that the last moments were held and caught in memory in the plane itself, a horror site of regurgitated images that no doubt fed the night terrors. But Minus could remember. It was a list, a sequence. A smile leaked in his direction from his mother as his father whispered or maybe shouted above the plane's

57

noise into her ear; a nod from his father as he withdrew back to his own seat; a quizzical, worried glance from his sister to their parents then to him, a gaze that lingered for a moment and then was gone. A look that fell from her face.

They were all there, a rare gathering under one rattling roof. They should all have stood up and cheered at that moment, Minus realised, but they were all strapped in. They were all strapped in and then the pilot lost control. 'She's going down,' someone shouted and they braced, braced, braced. Water woke him up from the jolt that had sent him dark; more water rushed around him as lights flickered off then on around him. Where there had been air, there was only water, coloured water at that: streaks and currents of red and black, of his own blood mixing with chemical ooze from the plane as it bumped its hulk in slow descent against the rocks that lay close to the island. There was no pain he could recall but there was evidence of the injuries that had challenged and threatened his life on the first few days on the beach.

The anniversary celebrated this. Not just survival on the beach bleeding, but the memory of body parts now lost. He was an amputee who could still feel his leg twitch; he was an impotent lover who could still feel his cock pulse. There was the sensation of something still being there. When the plane impacted all fittings either screwed in or loose had flown in his direction; objects sharp and blunt had thudded and torn into his body. The lacerations were multiple and by chance his sharp awakening into the disorientation of a shaken-up world gave him sight of both of his nipples swaying in front of his eyes, like deep-ocean creatures, strands of fleshy tentacles moving languorously in the cloudy water. His chest had been scraped by some cabin furniture and a vicious tick across his chest had scooped up not one but both nipples. It was a fairground jackpot and he was as ready for the world of freaks as he ever was.

Perhaps he would have stayed there if his sister hadn't tugged at his buckle and then pushed him through an emergency door. She was stewarding him to safety but he remembered not the drill of life jacket and emergency air but the feeling of what he was leaving behind. Feverish he might have been but Minus always knew what he felt, heard, saw. And understood. First there were his nipples brushing against his chest as he was being pulled to safety, the ripcords of shredded skin tantalisingly close to impromptu reattachment, then, there was the sight of his mother and father slumped in their chairs, their legs raised improbably by some unseen force, their heads lolling gently from side to side.

They had fallen from grace.

That's what the anniversary was about. With his head half in, half out the water he had a perfect view of both worlds. The surface and the submerged. He didn't know what he was talking about. He had no way of knowing what he was seeing. Everyone else did. His sister snapped at every chance, every moment that would catch and keep, that would display and pursue; his parents on some tropical scape, some sub-Saharan terrain, would watch and observe, creeping close to understanding, and then would draw back, taking notes and comparing, like for like, matching culture for culture and rushing to conclusions. They – his sister, his parents – noted the world they saw and this sustained them, this nourished them.

Minus was no longer at the THE PLACE WHERE HE HAD BEEN FOUND. He was dead centre in the place where it had all been lost. Not a place exactly, but an existence. The rushed moments of home life tagged on to the beginning or end of a journey; they always had an important reason to leave, to be taken away from the here and now. Anthropologise this! He was crying at home then vomiting at school, retching and wretched with nerves. He was for ever waving goodbye and sulkily welcoming home. They were both packed off to distant schools to be reclaimed for the holidays. When his parents did come home their skin glowed like tanned leather and their suitcases were bursting with artefacts, their words full of remorse for distance that was still there as the heat from their other life made the air humid.

They were never there. The nanny assigned to look

after them took cover when it came to the holidays while his parents were still away, as they increasingly were, on some foreign soil. When the crunch came, when the buck had to find some place to stop, the nanny slammed the door and left them to their own devices, their innate vices. It was true but his sister didn't want to photograph that particular truth. Her lens cap was on and of course it was his fault. The anthropological data could be fed into the home computer and it was the man, the boy, who had done the damage. In the place they never reached, she was given a grant to record not only their parents at work as they studied the effect on the natives of the Solomon Islands of the rapidly expanding trade in eco-tourism, but also to document the natives themselves for her own project. She was encouraged to swap the gritty reality of urban estates for the sandy illusions of a paradise well and truly found.

Minus was there because he was their son. Anthropologise this. The parental obligation never leaves. Just the parents. This is what he tried to say, this is what he tried to shout into their jet-lagged ears time and time again as they returned from longer and longer expeditions. He was the poet of the family. On the rare occasions they entertained, it was invariably other anthropologists attached to various universities and the parties would only be wild in terms of tales, as each leatheretted and slacked academic would flex their storytelling muscles and whip out stories which stretched the earth to breaking. They had been everywhere, seen everything and as a result knew everything. There was no room for Minus and his like. There was no space for that. He served drink, allowed himself to be patted on the head well into his teens and then had to endure the sympathetic smiles when he was introduced by his father as 'our struggling artist son'. He might as well have said cripple.

It wasn't so much what was said but what was left out.

They had fallen from grace. They had spent a life in pursuit of the truth, watching it, capturing it and regurgitating it for eager minds. Their ambition had been clear. When THE NEWS broke, they were simultaneously shocked and shamed. It was a hands-free telephone conversation that quickly growled into recrimination. Not for absence but for lack of restraint. 'She's your bloody sister, for Christ's sake.' Minus could hear his father kick some African dirt. 'Oh Minus, how could you.' His mother sounded profoundly weary as though he had broken something fragile.

As a child, Karine had never wanted to play at houses. Her girly friends tupperwared an existence, cutely enterprising all manner of household objects into miniature replicas of domestic arrangement. But here she was, setting out palm leaves as plates while she dug out the last slithers of flesh from crab shells readying them for the skewers she had fashioned from the bamboo splinters. She was taking on a role that had been forced upon her. Her parents would tell her tales when they came back from their many journeys where women the world over would be subjugated into servant roles, reared to rear and manage the daily routines. Her mother, lubed up by spirits, swerved off script from the antiseptically neutral anthropological tone and railed against a litany of injustices visited on women in the name of religion and biological expectation. Her father would chuckle and say nothing. He would sit at the table and wait for the dinner to be cooked and served on fragile white porcelain. It was their game, their professional duel. Refusing to be calmed, her mother would leave the food to burn on the stove as she grabbed a drink and went to sit in the garden even if their return home had coincided with a sharp winter. There, on the patio, she would gulp down her vodka and look out at the frost-covered garden shaking her head in disbelief. 'It's the same. It's always the same,' she would say. Karine didn't know what to say or do. Her mother would be animated if you asked her where she was going next but would forlornly look down if she was asked how long she was going to be home. 'Home?' she would scoff. 'The world is our home and each return feels like I am setting fire to it.' She could be volcanic when she wanted to be and the jet-lagged, fuelled-up woman was a tortuous sight. Karine wanted to be held and instead she could feel herself kept at arm's length. At eight, ten, twelve and fourteen. Touching was taboo. It was, her mother was right, always the same. The rituals were as established as the ones they detailed for their journals and books.

Karine shouted for Minus. It seemed that was all she had done since they had fallen from the sky. That and dress his wounds. She had been relieved a few days before when the bleeding had finally slowed. Her younger brother had always been thin and pale, a ghostly pallor made even starker by his jet black hair. As a kid, his hair was always long and he treasured this mop, vainly brushing and combing it until it was as straight as he could get it.

She wondered when things got bad, really bad, on their first few days and nights on the island whether he would survive. The score across his chest was deep enough to reveal white bone and when he got feverish in the tropical heat she knew it was serious. His pale skin was leaking blood, not just from his chest, but from his arms and his legs. When she took off the shredded clothes and tried to calm his fever, her eyes were flooded by his frail, fragile body. It was the same blurring, the same seeing but not seeing. THIS WAS THE PLACE THAT COULDN'T BE.

Karine shouted for Minus again and this time he stirred from the ebb and flow of the waves. The food was ready, there was fresh water to drink that had been collected from the night's downpour and the fire had been stoked. 'It could be worse,' she whispered to herself. 'It's always been worse,' she bellowed with full force towards the sea.

'I'm coming, I'm coming. You don't need to shout. You're not my mother, for Christ's sake.'

***

Torr says it's okay. He always says its okay. When we were being lashed by a typhoon in Palawan, he kicked out his legs and made like pipe and slippers; when we were ducking from uncivil crossfire in Guatemala, he pushed his head on to my chest. The same words, their repetition aimed to provide reassurance. As if that was enough. As if that shouldn't be enough. I don't know. I know rituals. I've lived and breathed rituals. They become showcased and enlivened by participants who rush on into the harshest, most extreme of situations. But they are a mechanism, a regurgitated reflex where the process can so easily overtake meaning.

It's okay?

I know, I've taken all the symbolism I can get. That totem is no longer taboo. I admit it, full on and fully fledged. In a difficult situation you take the hands of anyone, friend or enemy, lover or stranger. I succour this. I need this. But not this. He won't talk about it. Is that our ritual too? The man keeps stumm while the woman vibrates with worry? We have seen it all. Where men have led, woman have followed; where girls haggle over some possible future, boys lurch into innate stoicism. Whatever the source, the result is eminently predictable. As if I didn't know this, as if he doesn't either. We act it out so that we can hide behind the shield of our own drama.

'It'll do us all some good, I guess.' I guess. The throwaway care, the flexible understanding that allows for both sides. But both sides of what?

Either he thinks it was a terrible thing or it wasn't. He wants to dampen flames, so that there will be no fire, just straight to embers so that they can be turned and considered once the heat has gone.

So, I say to him before the year is planned, before we know exactly what we are doing. Christmas with the kids. 'Both of them?' I can hear and feel the panic in his voice. Things have been dealt with separately, independently allowed to grow and prosper according to individual needs. This was the tactic, this was the way it was planned and panned out. We were not parents but social workers; referees in a fight where not a punch was thrown. It's okay? Of course it's not okay but I can't stand the divide, the ever-widening gulf. Jesus, it's so fucking hard. I can't find the words. I want to let these tears drip and emboss this paper, let them rain and stain so that they can be felt like braille. We have been witness to history's horrors, we must find the strength to view our own.

When he moved to the interior of the island, Minus felt he had seen the foliage before. Not the leaves as such, nor the vines or clinging plants that seemed to move and writhe around his legs as he hacked his way through the growth. Not so much seen but felt. The dark green, the rotting brown, the stench of life and death wrapping itself around him, coating his skin like sweat brushed on. He was being crowded out by growth, smothered by vitality which thrived in spite of his crashing blows, his whipping arms. He had already been here.

Everybody had moved on and was now still, safely trapped in snares of their own making. He hadn't. He had spiralled downward while they aspired upward. The smokers, the pill-takers, the powder-snorters had now all found reasons to find a sense of calm. New reassurance for closing minds. They had all to a man and woman become variations of their parents, rushing to replicate a sense of posterity, of profound, life-changing progeny. There were less visits to his stinking hole of a flat. Nobody wanted to breathe in his air. That was history, that was the weak that was. Now, there was strength to be found in securing a future. Not Minus. He was the poet of the family. He was the struggling artist amongst professional friends who had been given enough rope by everyone and everything. Welfare, parents and friends had all lent a helping hand with money and advice in equal measure.

Still, the poet of the family had not changed. The words he spat out as a teenager in verbose, visceral verse read much the same now that Minus had turned thirty. He was caught up in the flow. He was the preacher of a generation; the mouth voicing what everybody knew had to be said. He was angry. He was wild and crazed with the need to spew forth the dissent that nobody else could make coherent. They were all addled and made idle; they coaxed out a simple hedonistic belief and then watched it wane. Still, his words made sense to the dwindling crowd who couldn't take it anymore. The pub and club crowds he wrote for could no longer hear because they were no longer there. The few that were didn't know they were. Such was his audience. In THE PLACE WHERE HE WAS LOST, no-one could hear you read and everybody had underestimated the stealth of expectation. One moment they were partying for three days, coaxed on then egged down by the recreational hugs that exponentially failed to live up to their expectation, and then the drugs, the words, the music no longer worked. It wasn't so much the verve that had gone but the nerve.

As Minus coated himself with the warm, wet palm leaves that could be tugged off branches, he brought out one of the charcoaled sticks he had rescued from the fire and then fashioned into a rudimentary writing implement. He recorded this upside down on his chest, being careful to draw round where his nipples should have been. <u>You</u> <u>think</u> <u>you</u> <u>know</u> <u>me?</u> He underlined each word, pressing the stick into his skin. He knew he should run out of the jungle and back on to the beach, rushing full frontal to where Karine no doubt was doing something, repairing something. 'REPAIR US' he wanted to shout. She probably wouldn't. Just like everybody else, she had ceased to listen or desire to learn. They all knew what they wanted. It had taken them a while to learn it but then it clicked. If you become like everybody else then there is always safety in numbers.

It made Minus laugh to think of those first few days of delirium, of liberating nonsense. It was a comedy of manners as he ran the length of the sandy beach, ducking and diving into the edge of the trees as his sister ran after him desperately trying to get him to stop so she could apply the dressing to his wounds. He didn't want to stop bleeding. He wasn't losing lifeblood but gaining it. It was the adrenaline kick that everyone had left behind, going Judas on vitality. With each drop he ran on glorious empty. Giggling then laughing then erupting into disabling guffaws that sent him tumbling, his chest heaving, stretching the tick on his chest. He used his fingers to gouge his words, pour the content of his head on to the sand. It didn't matter. It didn't matter that the tide would wash and carry away the slur and smudge of his mind. It didn't have to last for it to matter. It didn't have to be nurtured to mean something.

It made Minus laugh but it also ate away at him like the infection that had started in his lower back where a deep gouge had been allowed to fester. Somehow he had managed to keep this away from Karine's careful nursing; somehow this had been allowed to develop all by itself. An independent pain.

His mother had said, 'So you would like to be a writer, that's good. Maybe you will be published one day.' His father had said, 'You'll have to work hard, make sure that you write things people want to know about.' His sister said suspiciously, 'What are you going to write about?' Everyone had an expectation of what it would or should be; he was told endlessly of the pitfalls, the shortcuts, the outlets for his writing. But not once was he asked about the truth. He was endlessly advised to join the human race, to prepare his own safety net for falling from grace.

It could have happened. If he had stayed in his stinking home for much longer, had to free himself of daily entrails any more he could have caved into pressure and let himself slide into the pit of other people's expectations. He was told he had skills that could be moulded and honed; he was told not to get niche nor abstract; not to voice a generation nor get too radical. He was being pushed and pulled back in the OLD WORLD. It's okay to do this but it isn't to do that. It's okay to be angry but not to show it. It's okay to have desire but channel it. It's okay to leave but it's never okay to come back.

He had craved a new world.

If Karine could read the words he was writing in the jungle soil, slurping the mud to fit his letters then watching them as the gloop reclaimed its structure. If she could read the words he had left at the water's edge rather than run over them playing some chase game, rushing to save him from himself, then it would be perfect. This. When she cried at night, she relived the crash, moments before, moments after. The terror dripped from her skin and her voice was strangled with pain, memory's frightful grip wrapping itself around her. She held her arms out to the dark night sea, her hands skyward, the fingers curling back into her palms over and over again. She was reaching out, he said. 'Nonsense.' She was reaching out to their dead parents. 'Ridiculous.' She was reaching out to their dead parents, decaying in the plane, and wanting them back so they could understand.

'Understand what?' The daytime Karine hurled this at him day after day as she ripped her hands on splintering wood she used to keep the signal fire going.

'Understand what, exactly, Minus? We were near-children badly supervised. It's all a long time ago.' The night-time Karine threw herself into the air and came crashing down on to the sand. She swore at him using words they hadn't exchanged for years. Sexual words, guttural, visceral words that had been thrown about in the empty house when they had become unstuck. Sometimes, at the height of her sleep-life, she tried to throw herself in the fire and Minus had to keep a watchful eye on her movements which could be sly and covert.

'It's okay, it's okay.' She whispered into his ear, reaching to stroke his hair, his sun-burnt skin with a tenderness she would forget the next day. Then, she would make for the fire, the calm suddenly burnt away. 'You want to feel something, feel this.' He brushed the embers from her skin and doused her singed hair. In the morning, she tutted at her state. 'I wish I had some sunblock.'

Karine watched him through the thick cover of the trees, his strange unpredictable movement made compelling but repulsive viewing. She had hardly ventured as far as this into the island. Minus had been all over, exploring, bringing back strange stones with fossilised creatures perfectly preserved and fruit which neither of them recognised but were both compelled to eat when there was nothing else. She worried about him when he disappeared for hours on end, anything could happen to him but she couldn't bring herself to say it. She was too angry with him. She would not be left alone on this island, she would not be abandoned. They could barely have a reasonable conversation without it flaring into accusation and emotional insurgency. She was a stone-hearted bitch who could only think in one dimension; he was a pathetic dreamer who took fragile dreams as some kind of solid reality. He lived in the past, emotionally; she lived in the present, coldly. They ate silently the food she had taken hours to gather and prepare and then with a quick thanks he ran off down the beach saying he had things to do. Karine felt like a housewife left to deal with the washing up.

Minus looked so happy. Writhing in the mud, writing single words and quick phrases before they were swallowed up, sucked back into the ground. She had seen that expression before. When she found him squatting behind the oak tree, in a childish game of hide and seek, he looked up at her and said, 'So, I'm caught. Do you know the penalty for that?'

Their nanny knew the penalty. Damnation, she said, you will both be damned and unforgiven. This is wrong. Minus had a good memory and had her accent perfectly. When he reproduced her words, when he levered the past into their present, he replicated not just the memory but the situation, the sensation of being caught, of being found. Karine didn't see the point. The past and the future were blots on the landscape. Now was all that mattered. In the now, that Minus conspicuously failed to deal with, was the bitter truth that their parents were dead and they were stranded on an island far removed from shipping lanes and search patterns. They had only heard the distant thrum of one plane in all the time they had been there and Karine knew enough to know that there was barely enough water or potential food of sufficient nutritional value to help them survive. Minus's wounds would not necessarily heal themselves and already he had lost body weight. Whatever twisted chemistry existed between them, their brother and sister bond meant nothing now. They were two people struggling for their lives. And Minus, this other person, was rolling in mud, scanning badly into warm slop words which held neither rhyme nor reason for her.

Maybe the nanny was right, this was their damnation, a decade later. Karine had to turn away from Minus as he stood upright. She had not noticed he was naked. She couldn't believe it. The mud would pour into still open wounds and soon she would hear his cries of pain that he tried to mutate into whoops of some primal scream. She knew more than he thought she did. He would run off down the beach to rediscover himself and then cry, literally, into the sea, the ocean dampening his howl. She couldn't bare to look. She hadn't seen him naked since that last time alone in the house. The knot she felt forming in her stomach made her gasp and clench every muscle in her body.

The nanny stood in the doorway and just froze at the

sight of Minus kneeling on the bed, naked, everything about him taut and ready. This is what Minus wanted her to remember. This is what he tried to bring up by the fire, as though the flames curling out from the burning wood would bring back their fiery embrace. The scream the nanny had let out when she unfroze, the fury of her reaction when she rushed downstairs to gather her things was all Karine could remember. The nanny had not looked at either of them again but shouted up her prophecies for their future souls as they lay cowering and shocked in the bed. They were just kids, they were just playing with live ammunition. It was hide and seek, nothing more, nothing less. It didn't matter any more. After all this time, after the flow of blame, disgust, confusion had nearly drowned them all, this was a chance for them to move on. Truly move on. Their parents were dead, swaying at the bottom of the ocean. What had happened happened to them too and now they were no longer here. Surely this was an opportunity more than any other attempt for them to consign their little, bitty game to its sordid place in history. They should understand that it was okay to forget.

The jungle was Minus's place. No doubt he enjoyed the claustrophobia of it, the pressing intensity, the living slime. That was him. It was not her. She hacked her way back to the beach to make sure the fire was still burning strong.

I have seen and done so much over the years but I still can't understand Torr. I can watch him work and sleep, I can feel him inside me and I can listen to his considered words but nothing I hear, feel or see leads me to understand him. The question I never ask and the question he would travel the world to avoid is left hanging there between us, whether it's on this plane or knee-deep in a far flung village. What are you afraid of?

The nanny made it up. Suddenly we were in a bad thriller where the audience can see all the clues but the hapless actors fumble their way into dead ends and melodramatic cul-de-sacs. Torr phoned the agency and formally sacked her from her position even though it was clear she was never coming back. He wanted to take it further and have the agency itself questioned, its regulated credentials brought up to be examined for flaws. The flaws were in ourselves.

This didn't go down well. The intrusive nanny, the abject agency were nothing when such a brief admission was mentioned in the heat of some transatlantic moment. While other passengers nested in their privileged cocoons on some long haul flight, Torr leaned over and spat words into my ear, the hushed menace decompressing the air of indulgence. 'You of all people should know that they must take responsibility for what they have done. To blame us is too easy and so fucking typical of their knee-jerk, self-reflective generation who completely and utterly deny the truth.' 'And what is the truth?' I foolishly asked him. I could feel his lips on my ear, his saliva on my cheek. 'They neglected self-control; they forgot about accepted behaviour and above all they ignored the natural order of things. Just because you have a sexual desire doesn't mean you should express it.'

I had to wait until we were off the plane for that one. This was an anthropological problem which after much investigation reveals that the problem was not only the act itself but the effect on the tribe, the group, the people involved. Gene pools are never something I like to wade into. It always seems that we, as anthropologists, are paddling in waters much deeper than analysis can truly display. We record the results, conjugate the possible reasons and leave our understanding open ended.

This was not an anthropological problem. Torr could extemporise all he wanted but academic cloud nine is still floating on thin air. He was a master at obfuscating, he could wrench status quo from the most volatile of situations and then, to cap it all, he could offer solid, scholarly reasons for his conclusions. There it was, parcelled nicely and ready to deliver. Except it wasn't. All that mattered diddley. All that mattered was that he had to pass the phone to me while we were in Tanzania and let me hear all about it. After two minutes he had gathered all he needed to hear, all he needed to understand and judge the situation. I listened for half an hour to the tears and shock of a young woman who had never seen the like. I had. It was there in black and white, in print on glowing screen in the testimonials of cultures across the world, each one of them citing marital, tribal and traditional reasons for their actions.

We have seen it the world over but hadn't expected to find it at home.

There was assumption, presumption and unbridled complacency. I drew up a list of mistakes and accepted them all while simultaneously trying to reassure Torr that there was still love to be found and given. 'After this trip, we'll spend more time at home, get to know our children all over again.' Torr grunted and suddenly the words felt more like a funding application than the words of a distraught mother.

So we had left them to it.

Torr was already gearing up for this, already moving on. I just thought of my children thousands of miles away being lost to something they should not have had to find. But then, I'm just being emotional. Let Torr gather that shit.

Oh, God. We left them to it.

When Minus emerges from the jungle, the jungle comes with him. He drags a long stick behind him, stopping occasionally to see what word he has dragged from himself to leave temporarily on the jungle floor. Maybe the word says Karine, maybe it doesn't but in the jungle mud, in the ooze of the soil running in rivulets around his trudging feet, there is no second glance, no editing. What was written was meant.

'Why did you do it?'

His father screamed at him down the phone.

'Tell me you didn't do it.'

His mother cried at him down the phone.

Their instinct and learning told them that the poet of the family had become too literal for his own good, and poor, poor Karine, who could build a storm shelter out of a rag had nothing to do with it. She was the innocent victim, the wreckage of a good life now ruined. But she had done okay. They had given her a helping hand in every way they could while he was cast out into the wilderness with ever diminishing means. This journey years later was to be the balancing act between them all. They were to be reunited on the move. It made Minus smile to think of that. It was always going to be a desperate journey and now they had fallen from grace. Some shamanic twister his parents had wronged in a foreign land had rattled some bones and they found themselves cocooned in a tin box falling from the sky. And all they could do was whisper their dissent, sigh with their heads between their knees that it was never going to work. Fate was their co-pilot and he couldn't give a fuck.

When the jungle gets too thick and he has lost his way, Minus pricks up his ears and leans into the air. He can hear the sea, Like Richter would have wanted, he can feel and taste the sea. He doesn't chop or hack at the vines creeping around him, he just pushes through.

He knows that strange thorns are tearing at his skin, bizarre purple fruits are being pressed into his wounds but it doesn't matter. He knows where he is going and there is no pain.

Karine leapt off the bed when the nanny slammed the door and rushed around the room gathering up her clothes, pressing socks against her breasts, a shoe between her thighs as she staggered out of the room. She stumbled from grace. She wouldn't talk to him for the week they had left before their parents were due to return from Africa. They fended for themselves, they survived somehow on canned provisions and the last bottles from the drinks cabinet. They both retreated to their own stimulus. When Minus knocked on her door, staggering a little from the port that his sister hadn't touched, she shouted from behind her locked door. 'Go away, you've ruined everything.'

Minus remembered, slouching down with his back to her door, that he had got young on her, pulled some childish voice out of him and shouted. 'You got naked first. What was I supposed to do?'

Something, a book or maybe a clock was thrown against the door and nothing more was said. The poet of the family was left to his own version while everyone else got lyrical with theirs. It was a kind of rhyme.

The sinking sun was settling the waves. Minus knew

little about timings for dusk or sunrise, for tides and weather fronts looming over the sea. Nothing was being scheduled. But Minus knew light when it began to fade, just as he could feel dawn creep out of dark.

'You think everything's simple, Minus, that's your problem. You wave at the world and expect it to wave back.' Karine packed some bags and threw out one-liners as she stomped from room to room.

'You can explain it to mum and dad, I'm not going to be here.'

When she left, Minus could hear the silence of the old house, all its murmurings and reverberations slowly being muted until all he could hear was his own breathing. In the bed they had shared, he pushed down into the mattress pulling the sheets over his head. Like the shell to an ear, so the sound of the sea could be heard, distant yet persistent.

Karine was silhouetted against the tropical sky, brochured, resplendent, a photo so unlike her own. The fire was full, stoked-up for possible rescue. Karine's mood could always be judged by the state of the flames. He didn't rush on to the beach as he has done many times. Like a child it made him laugh to give a fright, to take a fright deep into him so that he was shivering with generated fear.

When he was left alone in the house, he didn't move from the bed even when the phone rang and rang. It could have been anyone phoning, maybe even Karine, gushing to take back her hasty departure. It could be the agency, the nanny, their parents, the police. So much had been made wrong by so little as far as Minus could see, and when he torched himself under the bed sheets, illuminating his desire, his still slicked memories, he found himself blind to everything that didn't matter.

And now, after so long in the wilderness of other people, he had come back TO THE PLACE WHERE HE HAD BEEN FOUND. Then and now. Not just the breaking curl of the waves but a moment of bliss, reclaimed from submerged ground. He was here to stay. In every sense he could muster. There she was, building the fire and looking forlornly out to sea. The fault is not . . . all of it. Richter would have recorded a shifting yet prescient sound and Minus himself would have written it solidly on shifting mud. They already knew what they wanted . . .

***

Karine didn't want to know what Minus was thinking. She had already heard it dozens and dozens of times. After she left, there had been a few years of calls decreasing in frequency but increasing in their slurred desperation and then it was only through her parents she heard about him. There was little sight contact and when they did see each other it was almost comical. As she was being driven back to the station one Christmas by her mother, her father was ferrying Minus from the station. They were a family on shift work; allotted moments and time cards punched to a traditional rhythm. They were all battered and bruised by it but there was no quarter given. Karine ignored his calls and wished that he would realise that it was easier to be apart, for her mother and father, for them. At home, with her parents already discussing their next trip as they dished out the shop-wrapped presents, there were gaps where memories should have been just as there was a space where Minus would have been, gleefully opening his presents, disregarding the advice to be careful with the wrapping paper.

'It could be used again.'

But no-one wanted to recycle anything. There was no attempt at a fresh start. In the years after she had left the house her parents increased their time away so that the home barely ranked as anything more than a stopover on their itinerary. They encouraged her to join them, wangling grants for a photographer so that she could have some role, some independence. When she returned from each trip, she tried to balance the exotic with the alien; from dust bowl to grafted climbing frames, children like birds roosting on their urban bars. This had become her way of seeing. Other people. Herself. There was structure, balance. As soon as the photograph was taken and the children moved to continue their play everything changed and Karine was the one now still. She had been caught without motion. She felt nothing.

The tiny fish she trapped with a makeshift reed cage, the crabs that succumbed to her traps and the strange fruit which dropped from the palms that lined the beach would help them survive and the storm water collected in shells would keep them going. She wasn't sure for how long but as she looked out to sea she was certain that someone would come. There were such things as search patterns, there was such a thing as never giving up hope.

Nothing was spoken of in all the years since Karine and Minus had been at home. Her parents detailed the lives of so many, recording the voiced histories of disappearing people but had no words to describe what had happened. When she asked how he was doing, her father rolled his eyes and her mother rushed to tidy up. Only when Karine brought up the idea of a trip somewhere, sometime, together did her mother stop what she was doing and sigh.

'You need to watch where you step among all the ghosts and memories.'

Minus thought he could not be heard. He imagined that after a short time on the island he had already blended into the scenery becoming indistinguishable from the foliage, part of the undergrowth. And that was it, he had not developed. It was clear that, for all his attempts at finding himself through self-medication, nothing had been changed. He was still the onanistic boy who thought it was all a good idea. His stealth was not as effective as he thought it was and she continued to turn the skewers so that the crab flesh began to char. Soon, they would be rescued and she could start again. She had had enough of still lives. She would not be stuck in the current.

Karine repeated her mother's words as Minus approached the tree-line, the words repeating and growing in volume. It helped her to see him as he was. A young boy running after his toys or jumping up and down when their parents deposited their presents from their travels. He had been cute and he was as everyone must have been at some point, innocent. This picture was the only one she would allow. It helped her not to hate him.

***

Minus knew what he would do first. As he edged towards the tree-line being careful not to tread on brittle growth he decided that the fire would be doused. Karine wouldn't like it but he would nurture her way of seeing, persuade her that leaving was not an escape but an entrapment.

He would present not just his thoughts but this action: once the fire had been put out, he would reach across the smoke and kiss her.

He made sure he was ready. The mud felt warm on his skin and the palm leaves moulded easily to his body, their texture easily sticking around his limbs and torso. The pain made it hard, not from the tick or other gashes across his chest but from the deep cut that had now gone septic in the small of his back. Already on his journey from the interior of the island he had found himself flat down in the earth unable to remember how he got there. It didn't and wouldn't matter. The pain wasn't his, it had been attached.

***

Karine stopped the chanting when she could smell Minus. She knew, from her nursing, not just the smell of his skin but the scent of his wounds. Of course it brought back memories, their whole time on the island had reaped many but she found it easier, now, to look out towards the flat line of the horizon. She wasn't dead. She had survived. It had taken death to shake her up and now she felt unshakeable. Determined. It didn't matter if Minus wanted to play his games, *she* would walk away from this. Minus would have to be dragged kicking and screaming on to their rescue vehicle but later he would thank her, later he would realise that he too had been caught in still life unable to move.

***

Minus would kiss her then caress her and then they would relive what had died. There was no shadow of their parents anymore. They were no longer here and no-one would know. This was their chance, it had to be grasped, it had to be allowed the momentum that had been cut short, abruptly and needlessly. There was no harm in the touch. It was the lightness of feeling something which was real. They didn't have to make a whole new home, they just needed to remember where it was.

The Inert Penis of the Man Who Had Just Been Shot

THIS IS A frozen, bucolic scene. There is nothing moving. A road stretches straight ahead as far as the eye can see while either side of this certainly hazardous, icy strip of tarmac are fields where snow remains untouched and where one solitary tree in the middle distance is dying slowly, its bark made brittle by layers of night frost. Its leaves were shed long ago and the once sturdy trunk seems fragile now as though the slightest gust of wind would snap it, frozen. There is no wind. There is nothing moving save the sun which lingers for a moment at the horizon before spreading its pale yellow blush moving slowly at first then in a sudden rush and the pale yellow turns orange then a vibrant, raging red. The fields, the road, the tree, its branches like lightning caught in motion, shrug off the shroud of darkness as the sun lurks in the sky. There is nothing moving. It is the same scene but warmly lit. By day the road sparkles, the embedded jewels yet to yield to the sun and the icicles on the solitary tree silently drip on to the snow.

There is something moving. A figure walking in the middle of the road in the middle distance close to the tree. It's not easy to tell what this figure is. Man or Woman. Old or Young. The clothes eliminate the lines of the body, such is their material and weight, and the walking pace is neither sprightly nor stooped. The clothes lack the brilliance of the snow in the fields and the colour of the slowly rising sun. They are neither old nor new. They bulk around a body which could be thin or fat. There are shades but only of grey and brown. When the sun stalls at its winter setting barely above the horizon, the figure is the only movement to be seen.

We can look more closely. A gust of wind can suddenly stir in this place, like a belly-boosted laugh thrown out into the air; like a mournful wail let out after so long inside. It lifts the snow-dust from the last fall, whipping it, teasing and tormenting before allowing white once again to settle. It is easy to be carried with this wind. A voice can be transported further than sight; the cracking of twigs can be heard unseen. There is a sense of movement, of rush and fitful panic, and then we are there.

And yet it is still difficult to make out who we are seeing. Or feeling. There is sound and smell before there is recognition. There is footfall. A slow, ponderous crunch that grinds into compacted ice. There is every chance of a falling here. One ill-advised move and it would be easy to take a tumble. Many have fallen late at night and numb by the roadside, their warmth leaking out of them as they dream of someone or somewhere warm. There have been deaths: stupid fatalities of men (and a few women) who should have known better than to walk home, their senses drummed out of all awareness of where they are. But this man's steps are careful, neither drunken nor haphazard. His faculties though slowed seem to be all there. This is a man in leaden retreat.

There is smell too. There is peat everywhere, a perfume of the land that coats the skin, gets into cloth and hair and stays like a wet dog on a hearth rug. There is a sense of the stray about the man – for it must be a man by girth and height of him. There is a vagabond air to him; a pungency borne of time spent away from certain comforts, functional necessities. He is beyond peat and has gone to earth; soiled and rotten as though he is of the ditch, the country gutter where everything gathers and nothing leaves. And there are, leaves, which have stuck frozen to his coat.

But not a coat. An old cloak, a murky brown thing that covers him from head to foot. This is not a man but a spectre; an image to taunt children or remind fate-filled adults. His sensual demeanour, his carnal body, in step and stench is that of the dead walking. A ludicrous possibility but his funeral pace, his burdened walk creeps the flesh and antagonises the rational. This is a man for whom journey seems irrelevant. He has already arrived.

It appears to be a usual day in the village. Its bustling life while lively is the product of routine. You can almost hear a voice call out from each clapperboard dwelling, 'There is work to be done.' And early too. Despite the cold there is no time to linger in the warmth. As the adults make their way to store, to field, to stand on the frozen mud and talk in billowing clouds that spiral above the huddles, the couples, the children eschew the routine that has nothing to do with them. Despite the cold there is no weather to hinder their play as they cavort and scoop up the fresh snow-dust, rushing to aim and fire, darting, fur-wrapped and swift, through the legs of gossiping villagers.

A few take cover under the houses, hiding themselves only partially behind the stilts that lift the houses above the ground. The village, Agder, had been flooded in the past by the sea that lay some miles to the west but which in a perfect storm had pushed into the heart of this small community retreating with untethered stock and a stray, unminded child. It had been a tragedy and all had raised their houses, their efforts so that it would never happen again. The children hiding had never known of such things. Theirs was simply a childish precaution and the houses as they stood now suited their playful purpose.

The houses themselves were of a particular structure. All followed the same design and even after many years all retained still a characteristic uniformity. Their salt-scorched walls were bevelled and slowly rotting; the doorways remained curiously low — only just six feet — and inside, the dark wood of the forest around the village had been used in every conceivable way. Nothing had been wasted. This was a village which had learnt to rely on itself, to keep its citizens secure despite the onslaught of the winter, the ravaging tear of time. Yes, they had to rise at dawn but it was a way of life, a blueprint for survival.

But this being said, it wasn't, with closer view, quite the usual day. The tracts of routine had been altered; recent events had called for detours and on this day the frozen mud paths mostly all led towards the centre of the village which in warmer months was the site for the villagers to commune, to be together rather than huddled around embered wood stoves, closed in against the winter. Here there would be games and stalls; wild antics of young men and poor performances from the old. The summer months brought a sense of togetherness the winter never brought. When the brittle cold clasped the village, the children, their play curtailed, would retreat into singular worlds watching icicles drip from the eaves of their homes.

Today winter was confounded, the cold ignored, and the men, women and the scattering children eventually made their way to the centre of the village. And then nothing; there had been a rush of activity, a murmur of expectation and then nothing. It seemed they were here to wait even in such a cold, which no foot-stamping could eliminate, no fur-wrapped hand-hugging stop its creeping grip. Towards the sea, all glances were fixed and towards the sea they kept their ears keenly pricked. It was both sight and sound they were expecting.

The girl who had been kept behind since the incident, kept locked to an old stump of a tree outside her parents' home, did not look in the direction of the sea. Her gaze, her wide-eyed stare, was fixed on the hazy horizon of the Agder Road.

One moment the cloaked and bedraggled man is walking steadfastly along the road away from the village and the next a single shot is heard, a crack of sound, the lash of a whip brought violently down. And down he falls. No staged or dramatic exit but a crumpling of the human form so that the man is now steeped in a flurry of snow-dust. And on it goes beyond the seemingly endless echoes of gunfire as the surrounding emptiness finds nooks and crannies to ricochet the sound, to make a storm out of one single thing. Nothing is wasted here. Not even sound. A single note becomes a chord amplified, keyed

THE INERT PENIS OF THE MAN WHO HAD JUST BEEN SHOT

up and down till it dies like a wilting and irritating refrain. There is no-one to hear it just as there was no-one to see this bedraggled man, touched by young skin, stealing out of the village at first light, his wet clothes sticking to his bones as he walked into the white.

And now, soon after this covert departure, the snow-dust takes its time to settle on the scene. There is no movement from the man. His figure, barely upright before the shot, is now still. It is possible there is a steady stream of red pouring out from his wound, to make some crimson evidence, ready for the imagination, easy for the eyes to see if difficult for the stomach to endure. But there is nothing so significant, no hot trail of relevant evidence for his fate to be judged and lingered over. There he lies, a brown, untidy heap on a whitened landscape. If there is no telltale red, no ooze or trickle then still something has been stained, something has been blemished.

Another sound, a discordant note, leaps out of the white like feet scalded on hot coals, a shrill yelp that tails off mournfully, its wavering, feminine tone becoming a steady background moan.

The villagers heard the sound they had been expecting. A grinding, grumbling ache that stopped then started. Without sight it might have been difficult to know what it was and yet they did. Memory quickly surfaced for such things: the slip of soles on shale and mud; the steady song and grit of groans more akin to men on a battlefield; the breaking snap of frozen roots as the object as long as two of the tallest men took twigs then branches from the trees. In the air, as always with these moments, there was the lugubrious intent of the object's pulsing movement . . . push . . . push . . . on and on. To a man, woman and older child they knew exactly what it was. The expressions on the villagers' faces announced more than the distant noise. They too would push and push until perversions and reckless, destructive desire was expunged from their community. There was no elation nor celebration at such a time, just brooding intent.

At last the sound was made apparent. Such a huge stone had rarely been seen. It matched the crime, the scale of the incident. Two lines of men were coming from the direction of the sea in the west, from the track that led to the point, the headland where cliffs had descended into the sea to make piles of rock that stood higher than all the houses of the village combined. The men were near horizontal with effort; their groans filled the air like a chant, an incoherent, breathless and desperate huff that made small all that could hear it. They had been chosen because of their strength, of course; this was no easy task but the awe at their effort by the many was mixed with the shame of a few. It didn't matter. What was done, what was decided had already been taken care of. All that had been talked about was now being put into action. It would be fitting. It would be right. Made right.

Nothing has changed for the dead man. That might seem a statement of the obvious but even in such stillness country things can move quickly. After only a moment some snow animal could have come tearing out of the white, a sleek fur thing camouflaged against the desolation. With a few vicious rips, the man could have been further disfigured and what was once warm flesh and sinew could easily have become a scattering of entrails on the road. And maybe not worse, maybe just the same kind of degradation, a rare cart could, with horses galvanised by the cold, have come rushing along the road, its hooves barely registering the bump of the man, the wheels churning up the remains into a red cloud of snow-dust.

Some hours have passed since the shot rang out. Not that it is easy to tell but the weak sun has passed its noon zenith, a paltry height to be sure, and now a strange twilight has begun to colour the country. The snow has turned a shade of grey, a metallic tinge to the frozen curls on the hedgerows, an off-white hue to the field ice-sheets which stretch on and on down either side of the road. The solitary tree looks less natural, more mechanical as though it was large scrap, deposited by the road, impaled in the frozen ground awaiting uplift.

No-one was uplifting anything. The sniper had not come closer to inspect her kill. This strange hunter, a killer of a lone beast without need for meat or pathology to gloat, remained secreted by the whiteout. The wail had lessened and blended with the rush of the wind but its pained vibration could still be felt, like the twitch of a torn muscle. Her continued but hidden attendance was strange. A cautionary assassin would have long ago retreated to a lair of warmth and security. If questions were to be asked at some distant time, it would not be sensible to be close to the kill.

When men, and it was usually men, had fallen by the wayside, had given up grace and were no longer in favour because of their actions, their predilections, it would be rare they would get this far from the village. In the warmest month the strongest man was unlikely to get more than a few miles without being cut down by scythe or shot; by anger or fear. Truly, this was the walk of the condemned.

An unexpected silence has fallen on the villagers. Unexpected because little happens out of the normal in Agder. There is sudden crisis when someone having drunk too much Litsch lashes out and descends into mindless actions but this is usually quelled within the houses by other family members. There are brief eruptions of joy when one of the children has a birthday.

THE INERT PENIS OF THE MAN WHO HAD JUST BEEN SHOT

The whole village gathers together to eat good food and tell bad jokes but there is still a routine to both these examples and certainly nothing like this has happened before. Many of the silent villagers most likely hope that it never does again.

Even the children are quiet and the youngest of them peer through their parents' legs, holding on to knees, slightly frightened by the stillness of everyone. Except Liena who has begun to gnaw at the metal links around her legs; except for the men sweating despite the freeze to loosen their burden. The stone is twelve feet long and six wide, a dense limestone formed from the ocean's ooze over many centuries. It had taken two scouting missions to locate the right stone for the villagers' purpose. At low tide the first scouts made the treacherous journey to the shore, using the little time they had to locate the appropriate stone while the second group planned the route for the bearers and tuggers to take.

And now that it is in the village centre, the task, which they had agreed on at a tense and volatile meeting just two days before, is set. The incident had seen to that. This is what has to be done. One of the many things that had to be decided was who has the skill for the job. The villagers had many trades; all basic requirements for sustaining a community set aside on wasteland so isolated that no ships passed offshore and no-one passed through on the way to anywhere else. Artistry was not considered an essential tool for living; the art was in the living itself. Aesthetic designs and neurotic, creative temperaments were hardly practical and actively discouraged. Still, by association, several of the craftsmen and women could have set about the task but it had been agreed that one person, one Silem Eeshen, should be given the task.

And it was he who now stepped forward from the gathered throng. He was an odd man by all accounts. Strong as an ox, a builder of the clapperboard houses who could wield a hammer as though it were featherweight; a hard worker who could barely tear himself away from a job until it was done. The villagers all understood that this task would be completed by Silem. He would not give up. In the bitterness of winter it needed someone as strong as he. Yet there was a strangeness about him too. Perhaps it was his twitch, a birth defect, which caused his head to jerk nearly ninety degrees always to the left at intervals no-one could predict. Perhaps, however, people had got used to it just as they gave not a second glance to the lame or maladjusted. It was the whisper that made it hard. It had been cute as a child, forgivable as a young man but now that he was in his late thirties it was considered threatening and unnerving. It wasn't that it was aimed at anyone or anything in particular; it was just there, a soundtrack for images and thoughts only

THE INERT PENIS OF THE MAN WHO HAD JUST BEEN SHOT

he knew. Still, it was difficult for the villagers and while they did their best to include him in all and any village activity, it was just simply awkward. The conversation could be flowing about crops and childbirth and there would be Silem, whispering at the end of the table in words that weren't quite catchable uttered with a childlike bewilderment, a seeping of air from his mouth, the sound of wind in the trees.

He drops the bag of tools to the ground, bends his head in prayer and his whispers become incantations while still inaudible, become something that everybody understands. This is, they had all agreed, God's work.

Not quite all agreed however: the old woman who was shouting about something from dawn till dusk tried to intervene to make herself heard but was pushed aside; and then there was Liena's mute observation as she struggled against the chains that imprisoned her. She was in full view of Silem and their eyes would meet when the icy mist would allow. Liena seemed as interested as anyone in the shape and form Silem was creating and she mirrored his progress. With her thin, blue-with-cold fingers, she marked out the progress Silem made in the hard earth, her nails digging into the ground, shaping the dirt as he sculpted the stone. She cut into soil as he carved into rock. Every now and then she would glance in the direction of the Agder Road. She had a likeness in mind.

*

You can hear laughter as the day dies, the sun finally giving up its attempt to warm this forgotten country. The pale red disc bisects the horizon and floods the sky with ever paling orange. There is more than a little beauty to the scene and the sound of the children's giggles and yelps creates a warmth all of its own. There are four of them – two boys, two girls – sliding on the shale, jumping on each other's backs, picking up snow-dust to force down necks tightly wrapped in fur.

The village school caters for more than just the children of the village but while the village children can tumble out of warm beds and reach the clapperboard school – built by Silem – in minutes, these children of the outlying houses have an hour's walk to reach their home. The gloom of the morning trudge is forgotten as, on returning, they loosen the grip of the journey's ache with simple playfulness.

They are used to dead and rotting animals that litter the fields and road as the cold takes its toll in the depths of winter. They have seen birds drop from the sky, rigored already with death and, it must be said, the two older children have come across a body on the road. A drunk who never made it home; a neighbour who was always thought ill of. The scene we know about is the same for all they know. And this brutal knowledge saves them from any shock or fright.

When they catch sight of the man there is only a

slight pause and the laughter begins again. The drunks who had passed by before had left nothing, not even underwear – although neither of them claimed to really want it. The man who had been shot had been stripped to his skin; the cruelty of such a death had been joined by the indignity of being revealed to the frozen elements.

None of these grave concerns mattered to the children nor did they hear or pay attention to the melancholic howl emanating from somewhere in the white. This was not their concern. He was an unexpected plaything, a somewhat stiff and ugly looking object, but a plaything nevertheless. They take it in turns to dare to edge closer to him, to hurdle him first across his chest then lengthwise. One boy aims to jump on his head then splits his legs at the last moment. The other boy aims a kick to the dead man's torso but his skinny leg swings high into the cold air. The girls meanwhile are shoving each other closer . . . touch his feet . . . touch his hair . . . and soon they are all hovering over the man wondering who will go the furthest, who will prove something they are not very sure of. You do it . . . you do it . . . Then the embarrassment eventually creeps in; it has been warded off by bravado and japes but the boys at least knew it would happen. Touch it . . . touch it . . . suddenly one of the girls grabs the older boy's hand and pushes it towards the frozen penis of the dead man. It doesn't hang or protrude, rather it seems to have curled in on itself, like a snail half home. The older boy uses his strength to pull his hand away but the younger seizes his chance to prove something and flicks the penis with his forefinger. They all scream and pull away from the body. They didn't know what to expect – he could have been sleeping and they could have woken him, to be chased down the road. Or something could have exploded, a sudden burst of bright light and all his insides would pour out.

It didn't matter what they might have fleetingly thought, their dramatic cries filled the air as they ran down the road, the screams quickly returning to laughter.

He hardly stopped. Silem, despite the cold, slept for an hour at most each night, lying beside the stone covered in furs which the villagers piled on top of him when they saw that he could work no more. When dusk fell torches were placed in a circle around Silem and the stone, their flickering light animating his twitch, illuminating the unflinching stare of his concentration. When finer work was needed, he would pull one of the torches close to him, near enough to singe his hair as he hammered and chiselled into the stone. By day, they brought him food and water – freshly baked bread, cured meat and the luxury of dried fruit. Some men tried to offer him jars of Litsch but he shook his head or rather twitched left then right vigorously and would have none of it. His head had to be clear for such work.

He was never alone. Nearly ten days after the incident the throng gathered around him was still at least two deep by day and by night there would be hardy souls wrapped in furs, nuzzling the torches and watching him. There was no conversation to be had but still they came and children would beg their parents to be allowed to stay up late and see Silem work by torch and moonlight. It was a community event; a village undertaking. They were being given the chance to witness God's work through such a task.

The stone was taking its agreed shape and form. The leaders of the village had debated for many hours after the terrible incident had been discovered early in the morning when Liena had been found near catatonic, her naked body half submerged in the frozen lake close to the village. It was not a scream nor a shout that had alerted the villagers but the ricocheting sound of her head being slammed into frozen ice, a jarring rhythm made by the soft skull of a child. Whatever had happened had happened suddenly, her hands quickly enclosed by the reforming ice were trapped like delicate lilies just under the surface, her fingers snarled in reeds, her legs stuck fast in mud.

They hastily convened a meeting for all to attend and it was a tumultuous event, a verbal and physical pandemonium the like of which the village had never seen.

Over the course of the day, parents locked their children in the clapperboard houses which had never been fitted with locks but somehow, using boards of wood and broom handles, they managed to secure them inside and with torches lighting the way they had stood frozen with anger in the centre of the village. No-one had yet built a house or a hall big enough for them all to congregate in. Perhaps it was the need to keep warm that fuelled the brief flurries of violence as the meeting meandered from cold evening to freezing night but of course more likely it was the anger, the impotent rage after the fact, that drove one family against another while still another tried to separate them. Man on man, woman on woman and then a scattering of any kind of decorum or restraint and men dragged women by their hair while women fastened their hands on to men's balls refusing to let go until their arms were belted with wooden boards.

It took much time and a few calm voices for the incident, as it was called, to be properly addressed. After much time, the few calm voices made not only their voices heard, but their reason understood. Liena, a ten-year-old waif, one of the palest, most withdrawn children the village had ever seen, was ushered into the torchlight, flame shadows streaking across her face. Her parents, her teacher, her friends couldn't understand where such a fragile creature could have appeared from. The stock of the village was generally strong and thick of girth but Liena was a stripling, a reed that if not protected, supported, would break during the first winter snap of cold. She has the look of a poet, some said. It was not meant as a compliment.

With all her sinewy strength Liena struggled against the hands that held her. The torchlight glare hurt and the cold was cracking her skin. She fought against her parents' grip which was quickly deemed to be too weak and so she was passed to the older women of the village. They had held wilder things in their hands. They wanted her to hear what was to be decided, what should be done about the incident and who had committed such a terrible crime. She was told she had to understand the wrong that had been visited upon her. There was vengeance to be discussed and justice to be meted out. Five generations of villagers had procreated not just family but a sense of truly belonging to the land. Transgression would not be tolerated. As the elders huddled, Liena, still held tight by old women, licked her wounds, letting the saliva drip on to the scores and scratches across her arms.

It had happened before. One Eli Cashen had taken something into his head. The storytellers made up what that was according to their own grinding axe. For some it was the local Litsch, for others it was bad blood and for others still, although this was but a bitter few, religion, the bedrock of the village, was the reason. But whatever route the story took, the basic destination was the same. The fields leading to the point were useless for growing the staple crops of the village and were used as grazing for the many goats the villagers depended on. Eli in hectic state had herded a huge number of these poor animals into some kind of funeral march – how one man could do this with so many goats and no accomplices was the subject of much debate – but both the long and short version of the story saw him lead the beasts to the cliffs of the point and allow them to gamble ignorantly over the edge, one after the other, until there was a pile of writhing and broken goats on the rocks, the tide taking swathes of them out to sea after each surge.

Speculation about how this actually could have been achieved by just one man was not encouraged. He was a piper, pie-eyed; he entranced the simple animals with a soft song; he whipped them into so much fear that the release of a deathly fall was the only option for the wretched animals. It didn't matter how it was done in the end, just that it was and with evil intent. To ruin the village; to starve the villagers; to wreck what had been so far achieved. It was a despicable act and one that could not and would not be forgiven. And this was where the simple law of the village was applied, the law that had gained structure and absolution through the generations. If he or she does harm to the life of the village – threatens to undermine the good will, the righteous

THE INERT PENIS OF THE MAN WHO HAD JUST BEEN SHOT

intentions of those who live there – then they shall be excommunicated and a monument built to their wrong to remind all others what was right.

It didn't matter for Eli nor for the many others who had followed him through the generations what season of the year it was or what health the wrongdoer was in. The village stood by and turfed them out, silently watching the departure along the frozen road until they were forlorn, darkened blots on the whitescape.

Now, many days later, Liena, chained to the spot so there would be no more careless wandering, watched Silem carving the stone. Her scores and scratches had healed and the clumps of her hair that had been torn from her scalp had begun to grow back. In silence she looked quizzically at a familiar face, emerging from the delicate chiselling of the stone. The villagers, she considered, the adults and all the other children, thought the man had gone, absconding into the night as her breaths grew sharp and shallow in the remorseless grip of the frozen lake. They always thought what they wanted to hear. He was still *here*. Not in flesh but in memory, not in skin but now in stone

In torchlight the dead man looks fatter than he was in life, bloated by lack of exhalation, by the process of his decomposition. Something has moved him, perhaps a passing animal, perhaps the larking children, but his face which had been glued by the frost to the tarmac was turned upwards at a hideous angle. The flames from the torch didn't fully light up his face and the shadows played tricks with the eyes, the eyes of the old woman standing still beside the man. His eyes appeared deep in their sockets yet his lips were puffed out and protruding. At least we know now. We know now that the single shot had penetrated his skull through his forehead and that the blood-pour had frozen; the bloodlines stopped and streaked. It was the deathly camouflage of the battleground where the fallen shared the same appearance as well as the same fate. Twisted, grotesque, not so much at peace but caught in violence; a life stopped by searing lead.

The old woman, cloaked and wrapped in furs, kneels beside the naked body. But not quite naked, not quite bare. A layer of ice has formed over his body, a second skin, tight and frozen, smooth and curved, hugging the bumps and lumps of his swollen body. He has been preserved, and perhaps left somewhere, untouched by man or beast, he would be dug up, years later, fossilised for the heads to nod and learning to take place. He would be the Naked Ancestor whose wounds would lead to speculation, whose form would tend to education. There would be much to learn from this earlier form of ourselves.

But in the here and now the old woman cares little

for what is to come. What has been has loosened her tight lips which tremble now, unable to contain the sorrow, maintain the facade that it was all for the best, that the community suffers each time someone slips; that each time an error is made, a correction has to be laid down, like the law they all agreed; the memory of near-ruins; the fragile network of life that could be and had been threatened by individual hubris or dangerous lust. If they stood strong, weaknesses would be bred out of them all and the moments of disaster would stop; the monuments would cease to be built.

The old woman strokes forlornly at the ice-skin; remembering in flashbacks everything that had been and nothing that had been bad. This was not an evaluation. The bloated man had been a mischievous boy; a wild 'un who would cause riot and mirth wherever he went. He had brought laughter not tears. She had held him when he cried and washed him when the village dirt caked his skin. He had been flesh and blood from her own and not this grim mannequin, a poor and unlikely replica. The old woman's hands pressed into his skin as her recollection grew deeper, as trails of memory slicked her grief. Moments of tenderness remembered, whispered goodnights and the soft touch of the child once been.

As her hand clawed at his body, the veneer of ice began to crack, like a series of shots in the countryside, a sound piercing the evening scene, as frozen as it ever was. The splintering sound began at his neck and continued down the body, the ice shroud falling in chunks on to the tarmac. Her hands jerked in fright and without any considered thought, just grief's own momentum, her hands cupped the dead man's genitalia and as the ice fell away, so did the penis, the half-home snail falling limp yet stiff into her palm.

Here was another shriek from this anguished woman, like the cry she let out when the bullet left her gun, but sharper even, a pained sound that could have cut glass but which made do with the remaining icicles that barred his mouth like primitive incisors and these fell into the gaping rotten hole. She staggered back from the body, the penis still in her hand, nestled, cupped, horrific in its familiar detail, its manifest connection to her now grotesquely reunited. But she did not let go, this piece of him, this piece of her remained in her clasp as she ran down the road, back towards the village, the loose twigs from the burning torch scorching her face.

They took it in turns to speak. The torch was handed to them and they stepped forward into their very own spotlight. They encouraged each other to both denounce and announce. They praised the courage and steadfastness of their fellow villagers – but ignored the violent frenzy which had erupted after the incident had been discovered – and spoke out against the evil that had visited them. It was indeed an ill wind, one woman said, but that is all it was. It carried with it not air to breathe but evil to suffocate, to subjugate their spirit. But, like any wind, it rushed swiftly and moved on and the villagers, the village were still there. Their children were both safe and safer.

They proclaimed the rock made statuesque by Silem. This was a marvellous and provocative *oville*, they declared, a fine example of that ancient craft where humanity in all its cruelty could be hewn from stone. The villagers remarked on his work and on his skill; they admired the attention to detail and the likening to the horror. Here was a reminder to them all. In the dark, the mother and father of Liena, standing slightly apart from the rest of the gathered throng, were gently nudged into the torchlight, each of them holding on tightly to Liena, who had been released from her chains. They and all the rest of the villagers bowed their heads for a moment and then gazed at the face on the statue, once one of them and now banished for ever. With their heads bowed, there was an understanding and a certain amount of imagination about the fate of the man. No-one who had been banished had every attempted to return, and along the treacherous road away from the village the man would find no welcome at any house; their lights would be darkened and their doors bolted. There was no prison nor punishment in the village but all the villagers knew any transgressor was not set free by this long road to nowhere. They were being imprisoned in year-round snow which blinded, numbed and eventually lured them into an everlasting sleep.

When the old woman stopped running, out of fright and out of breath, she gathered together her many layers and crouched down on the icy tarmac. The sun had long since gone and the moon had risen quickly into the sky, its shadows casting eerie forms into the hedgerows and fields beyond. Perhaps it was animals foraging unseen in the undergrowth of twisted, dead branches or perhaps it was the shadows themselves creating umbrageous voices whispering at her from both sides of the road. It was the madness, no doubt, many in the village attributed to her, that caused her to shout when there should be peace; that made her speak her mind when lips should be sutured and then nurtured by faith and community. It was the madness of a mother that could not accept the banishment of her son despite the horrors he had visited on a young girl, despite the shame and chaos he had brought to the community.

It was understandable given the loyalty and connection between mother and son but barely allowable and her remaining years – it was whispered hopefully they would only be few – would be spent in frugal aspect of living; given food and shelter but little beyond this. She had failed in her duties just as the parents of Liena had. They had allowed their offspring to stray without due leash and Liena would carry this with her until she died.

No-one had thought to watch the old woman. Just after the incident came to light she was vilified, shouted at and then dismissed as a lame excuse for a woman, a mother and a villager.

No-one missed her. In the violent frenzy, a few tried to find her, to bring her into torchlight so that they could make an instant statue of her; a spontaneous still life of the ill-conceived and the poorly nurtured but such was the melee that the intentions were trodden on and forgotten.

No-one missed the rifle, usually carried only by the named hunters of the village.

The voices didn't scare her as she crouched down on the road, she just couldn't locate them. They were not in the fields nor in the hedgerows. They were closer to hand, to her body. Despite the cold she shed layers of fur and wool. At the third layer the wooden handle of a rifle hit the frosted tarmac, its cocking mechanism sticking like a spike into the ice. After the fifth layer she was close to flesh and yet the voices were still distinctly near to her, close to her skin as though the words were seeping in through her pores.

The answer was in her hands and as strange to her as it was, as peculiar and unnatural as it would have seemed, it brought a smile to her toothless mouth and her head nodded at first in understanding and then became still, a long moment, to listen and finally acknowledge. Perhaps she heard echoes of memories past brought up by the magical light which emanated from the moon. Maybe the villagers were causing such a roar that it could be heard even so far away. But the smile showed that she was not looking for explanations just some kind of simple reassurance that seldom came the way of someone her age. Reassurance was so often reserved for the young and such a need was expected to dwindle with age. But it was what she wanted most right that moment on the ice-covered road. With her hand cupping her ear, the inert penis still in her palm, she listened to the single voice from such a familiar source.

Like a Pendulum in Glue

I DON'T WANT to be here.

Louche screwed his eyes tight shut. He pressed his fingertips into his eyes and tried to chase the lingering orange blotches away from the darkness. For a few seconds he could still see the strip light until its glow slowly faded into nothing. He was lifted on to the kitchen units while the voice, his voice, kept repeating *I don't want to be here, I . . . don't . . . want . . . to . . . be . . . here.*

BRING IT ON BABY, LET THE GOOD TIMES ROLL.

Louche heard his father singing, an off-key rendition, a vibrating sore that pulsed and throbbed, burrowing deep into his head. The tape was blasting in the empty kitchen and, although he couldn't see him, Louche could hear his father's dance steps, tapping and scraping at the vinyl floor. His father was a good mover. Sometimes when Louche's eyes were half open, that frightening slit of light searing his world, halting for a moment his voice, he had seen the quick steps, the body swerves and hip sways. His father was in no doubt of his own abilities. In half vision Louche saw him linger in front of his image in the long mirror which hung on the wall. He swerved and veered in front of it, checking his step every so often to twirl then sweep a can from the floor, a swift drink that didn't break his tempo.

LET'S SHAKE, SHAKE, SHAKE.

Louche kept his eyes closed even when he heard his father tap his way closer to him, his hands keeping time with the rock-'n'-roll beat, drumming an insistent rhythm on the kitchen surface, a vibration that rippled his skin and made the hair on his arms stand up.

COME ON BABY WON'T YOU DANCE WITH ME

The words were both in the air and in Louche's face. His father took Louche's bony arms which hung limply over the edge of the kitchen unit and swung them from side to side, but still he kept his eyes shut, not letting one ray of light into his head. The voice inside was still there, he didn't have to check to make sure. It never seemed to go away.

I WANT TO BE SOMEWHERE ELSE.

He didn't offer himself far-flung places or warm, curled-up spaces. Not wanting to be somewhere didn't mean he knew where he wanted to be. He had a map given to him by his father who had pinned it to the bare wall and tried to get Louche to investigate it with him, to look at incredible islands, like dust on paper; to look at vast swathes of desert where hardly anything could live. 'This is your world, Louche. This is your world.' Louche felt his neck get sore and his eyes go blurred. It was too painful to look at it after a while. His father had pins ready to stick in, ready for Louche to choose where he could possibly go with a leap of faith, a huge step into the unknown. The pins remained gathered at the edge of the map when he sank back on to his bed. His father sighed and marooned the pins on an island so distant there was no name for where they were.

In the kitchen, the music stopped suddenly and he felt his father raise himself on to the kitchen table to be head height with his son. His words were whispered, a long breath taken in and slowly released.

'Son, you have to learn to enjoy yourself.'

***

'C'mon baby, come closer.'

Louche's eyes were wide open in the pitch black. And he could see nothing. She wasn't talking to him. Louche knew that. But for a strangely dark and sparkling moment he thought she was. Who she was talking to, who in fact *she* was, Louche had no way of telling in the blackened arch. He sensed her close to his body, not just her scent but that sense of movement that doesn't require vision – like his own voice which didn't need to be spoken. Of course, he could have reached out and touched but his heartbeat quickened and a voice in his head surged.

Take a step back, move away from this corner, get back into the open.

For a moment he hesitated, just enough to feel another presence close to him, brushing past his near-naked body. Scent, movement and, yes, expectation told him that it was a man. Louche pressed himself tightly against the wall he knew was behind him and the woman's insistent encouragement first faded then became muffled, her voice swallowed by a kiss, the sound of flesh against flesh, the sigh of release . . .

Inside, Louche could hear a voice again, its tone pulsing with threat, its persistent echo refusing to fade until he listened, obeyed and once again squeezed his eyes half shut and groped his way along the wall and into the next arch.

It was a little brighter, illuminated by the lash of candlelight. Here, the dozen or so figures moved as though exercising some kind of penitence. A slow walking monotony weighed down their steps, their bodies rigid and shackled by chains, but their heads and particularly their eyes were alert to their surroundings. Their clothing was elaborate but not particularly sophisticated. Stretches of rubber held by stretches of skin. Some men had rubber masks, some women thigh-length boots. It was uniform. In front of him an overweight, middle-aged man was led by an erstwhile dominatrix, chain in one hand, a whip dangling limply by her side. The entirely neutral look on the man's face terrified Louche, galvanised his own self-reproachment into a frenzy, dragged him over burning coals, each with a spike that drove deep into his flesh, making his skin pop and sigh. *If you tore your skin you might feel something; if you cut away there might be a chance of taking hold of something, even yourself; even yourself would do. You are not at home here. It would be different. This is but once a year. C'mon!*

Near one of the elaborate candlesticks that lit the poor brickwork of the arch a man leaned against the wall, his hands behind his head, his eyes tight shut, a grimace of something on his face. On her knees a woman dressed as in Victorian times was sucking his penis, her quickening, thrusting movements dislodging her emerald green hat, the veil temporarily shifted to one side. There was a strange routine not only to their action but to the others in the room, single men mostly who watched with tight lips where lips were visible, with concentrated stares where eyes could be seen. But for the distant thud of music there was silence in the room broken only by the metal links of the dominatrix's chain.

What is the point of this? I should be the point of this. Wallflowers die in the shade, Louche. You already know that. C'mon!

The other voice inside him, the one that rose above doubt's persistent echo flashed like a torch in darkness. It reminded him why he was here. For a moment, just for one teasingly succinct moment. Until he felt overwhelmed by hope's bright glare, until he felt as though he was suffocating and unbearably hot, despite his near-naked state. Clothed only in rubber shorts and leather boots he felt restricted and, at the same time, both under- and over-dressed. He shut his eyes completely, not wanting to be part of the silent stare, not feeling he had anything to share.

***

'Come on, let it fly, let it go . . .'

His father gave him the kite just as it gained some height. He was jogging backwards up the hill, struggling and fighting with the string, both laughing and cursing as it dipped then soared then dived towards the ground, its brightly coloured tail close to the grass. As it climbed again, Louche closed his eyes and hung on to its tail, feeling the lift and rise into the air, his own dangling legs becoming part of its tail. He was jogging half-heartedly alongside his father who was willing and wishing the kite into the air. For one moment his father unexpectedly lifted him up off the ground desperately trying to give the kite a chance to fly in the light wind. When he lifted him up, Louche opened his eyes just the tiniest of fractions and saw the ground rush away from him. For that moment he too was airborne, the grip on his skinny hips gone, its safety forgotten. But then the kite nose-dived and he too found himself back on the ground, his father huffing and puffing beside him, dragging the sadly grounded kite back up the slope. Some part of him was still soaring yet another part was buried deep in the ground, lungs struggling for air, his eyes filled with earth. Louche sat beside him and watched through half-open eyes the sorry winding in of the tangled string. His father whispered into his ear, the words laboured, tense.

'You could maybe try a little harder, son.'

***

There was a peep show in another arch. Here there were more people than Louche had seen all night. They were two or three deep in front of the cage, which had been draped in black cloth. Around ten or so slits had been torn in the fabric, and the viewers, some with their hands on someone else, watched the participants of the peepshow. There was both a sense of concentration and strange distraction as these bodies pressed against each other. Louche joined the viewers. Of course, inside his head a voice gushing with enthusiasm was veering from one suggestion to another – that he should be on the other side of the cage, that he should be running wild and feverish, that he could have been dipping and sucking and entwined, sublime amongst the assorted bodies splayed out in every stage of coitus. He worked his way to the front of the cage and shut his eyes letting the thin wire of the cage press into his face, gently then forcefully. Then, another voice rose inside him.

What are you doing here if you're just going to . . .

Louche sank to his knees, and immediately people behind craned over him to view the orgy inside the cage. He felt a leg at his back, an elbow on his shoulder but these were accidental not intimate touches. When he opened his eyes there was only black cloth and the relief that not being able to see brought to him. From open to shut there was no difference. That made sense to him, but again the hopeful voice in his head came back to him, forced open his eyes like rusty hinges and made his hands tear at the black material in front of him. A small gap opened and straight away his eyelashes brushed the hairs on a man's arms which were pressing against the cage. Contact. His wildest dreams had never been this abstracted. His wildest dreams had him on the other side of the cage, his rubber shorts just another skin in a pile of limbs. His wildest dreams had brought him to this club of freedom, to set him free, to silence the undiminished voice in his head.

What are you waiting for, this is your chance . . .

The arm moved away from the cage, to be replaced by the smooth skin of a woman's thigh that suddenly buffeted the side of the cage, a rhythm growing ever more insistent. He tore more of the fabric away and more was revealed. He was so close he could smell something so personal that he scarcely believe it, he could see more than he had ever seen before. Louche put his hands down to his rubber shorts but his body felt numb, his nerves and senses blunted by the stimulation all around him until finally the persistent voice in his head reminded him what he already felt, already knew.

You are cold, cold, cold . . .

His father tried music. It was a tried and tested route. It brought on tears and dance; it reached both mind and body. At its most potent it was a panacea for the incipient numb, for the fear of feeling so quickly diagnosed as dumb. His father tried. This would be a challenge to one so young. The conductor's eyes were closed. His head rocked forward then shook vigorously for a moment before jerking back, his wild hair falling around him. His shoulders were hunched but his arms raged around him, tentacles, seemingly out of control then suddenly taut, suddenly loose. Louche turned to look at his father sitting beside him. His eyes too were closed, one hand brushing his eyelids while the other rested on the seat in front, his fingertips intermittently tapping the red velour. Through his own half open eyes, Louche could see other people in the audience in a similar state to his father, all of them reacting to the music as it raged towards a crescendo, the drums thundering through his seat.

At a quiet moment, his father whispered into his ear. 'Marvellous isn't it?'

He took his hand away from his face momentarily to squeeze Louche's hand.

And it was marvellous; Louche believed what he was told. His first concert, his first experience of live music, it was an evening of firsts. He should be proud. He was the only child in an audience of adults. There was something special about his presence there and yet his eyes remained half open, using quick, nervous glances, his vision squeezed into a loose line of blurred colour and unfocused bodies. He wanted to rock his head like the conductor, he wanted to run his hands along the harp, back and forward, laughing as the notes slid upwards. He wanted to run on to the stage and leap on to the cymbals crashing his way through the music. But a voice in his head offered no encouragement, teasing him only with the possibility of public humiliation.

How terrible it would be to be suddenly on that stage and expected to play . . .

He drew his body closer in, hugging his arms and legs, gathering his limbs tight against his chest. He needed to go to the toilet, he needed to clench his fists and stretch his legs so taut they would break and then there would be relief, a wash of wonderful warmth spreading over him and he could shut his eyes without thinking they should be open, he could let his voice out without fear of it being heard. He would not have to try anymore.

***

The Street of Shame, a central corridor of the club, was littered with couples in various states of sex. The light from the candles placed at even intervals along the narrow arch was surprisingly still, with little flicker to move or animate the bodies stretched out on the cobbled, uneven floors. Louche walked through these bodies with stealth, there still remaining a sense of expectation, a desire for invitation. Ahead of him, he saw another man, similar age, similar synthetic look, stop at one couple engaged in the early stages of arousal and kneel by them, outstretching a hand to the man's head and reaching down with his head to the woman's bare chest. Their arms welcomed him and drew him into their embrace. Louche smiled. This was what the evening was about. Encounters with strangers, exchanges of brief passion without guilt or long-term attachment; a sense of revolution and sexual freedom. He'd been told it was an ideal way to explore yourself and lose inhibition about sex and intimacy. His optimistic voice, that hopeful half of him, reminded Louche to retain the smile, to shore it up, fix it and anchor it in the face of doubt but even in the shadowy light of candles it was clear to see there was little humour creasing his thin lips.

Don't you wish that was you? Why can't it be you?

The warring voices in his head were the only thing Louche could hear at that moment. Yes, there was music, the sound of boots on cobbles, the grunts and groans of sex all around him but he was both deafened and muted by his own rage, clamouring for him to join in. Or not. He found another dark corner and pressed his bare back and legs against the cold brick. Now he was invisible, a white stain on the wall. He tried to stop all sound within him, to tighten it, strangle the words which kept coming back, on and on until his own breath stopped. Silence, somehow.

***

All they could hear was rain. The tent had begun to be weighed down by the torrential pour which had lasted more than three hours, just after the sun had set hurriedly at the end of the field. Louche could understand why. The enjoyment of the day had gone with the sun, the light drops of rain coming on as dusk shrouded them. It seemed to Louche that, with the sun gone, the clouds had rolled down from the hills surrounding them, rushing to corral them in their tents, one for the children, one for the adults. His cousins were enjoying themselves. They shed their given skins and let their naked limbs loose, a burst of energy, a smell of earth and breathing skin. While in the adults' tent maybe ten metres away he could hear the clink of glasses, the flow of murmured conversation erupting into stifled laughs and his father's ever-present good-time boom, inside the children's tent there was a worm out of control, tunnelling its way in and out of the sleeping bags as the other cousin tried to kill it with one of the plastic picnic forks. Out of his squinting eyes, he could see the worm get closer to him but rather than watch the small figure burrowing towards him he watched the fork in the other boy's hand, raised and poised to strike.

I need to be somewhere else.

Soon the torchlight began to dim and he felt able to open his eyes. His cousins smothered the light under the material of the sleeping bag and the bright-red glow became eyes in the gloom of the tent, their still playful bodies the tentacles of a serpent, the rain outside was the hiss and spit of its hunger. Louche was so lost to the sensations around him he could barely talk, though when they spoke to him he replied, he told them his favourite games, his best sport, he reeled off the litany of likes and dislikes, but whether they knew it or not he was simply going through his paces. The inevitable rituals. With raucous pageantry they showed him theirs while he hid from his, the palms of his hands pressed together, glued between his thighs. 'C'mon,' they urged, 'it's just a bit of fun.' Trace it to this, trace it to anything you want. There was no harm done but not, at any point, was it fun.

He waited for the torches to die, their batteries to deaden, until they were unable to ignite the darkness with their penetrating beams. When at last they were plunged into darkness Louche began to emit low noises, part animal, part machine that came from the back of his throat, maybe from somewhere deeper. They hung in the air with menace. His cousins stopped talking and giggled at first and called him names, half surprised, half impressed. But when Louche continued to vocalise these sounds they asked him to stop, they wanted to sleep, they didn't know why he was making the sounds anymore.

After ten minutes Louche's father poked his head into

the tent and told them to be quiet. He addressed himself to the cousins and not to Louche and this case of mistaken identity quietened him more than his father's irritated chastisement. While his cousins went to sleep he lay on his back, unable to curl up as they did, unable to get foetal as they did, unable to soften his grip on consciousness as they did. He lay awake all night, the sounds in his throat thwarted and held.

***

Near the end of the night, Louche made it to the last arch, a narrow corridor hung with black drapes instead of candles; it was lanterns held on metal poles which splashed tight, yellow spots on to the ground. The sound of his footsteps, the throb of music faded until all he could hear was the snarl of a whip.

He had expected to find more people in the arch. Everywhere he had gone that night there had been a throng of people, their desire and urgency, their lust and lingering desperation, being the brightest of lights, a beam that penetrated his half closed eyes.

A sign read 'The Dungeon' and an attempt had been made to recreate some mediaeval sense of torture. Whips of differing lengths and widths were racked on to the wall as were restraints and other devices, their function uncertain to his inexperienced glance. The lash of the whip had not been a performance to a large crowd but the action of one solitary, hooded man. A strangely angular man who stood in front of one of the walls raising the whip and then bringing it down, sending the dust from the loose bricks flying in clouds around him.

Turn back, turn back, this isn't for you.

Now or never, Louche, now or never.

The voices in his head were of course dominating everything, their ceaseless tussle reverberating as much as the sound of the whip in the empty arch but he swallowed hard and tried to take the voices with it, tried to take the voices and bury them somewhere deep and inaccessible. He didn't want to listen to them anymore and left alone he would have inevitably heard their insistence; left with no other distraction he might have surrendered and walked back along the gravel trail. The hooded man stopped mid-strike and through the black cloth Louche could see him squinting in the light of the lanterns, his eyes meeting his. He quickly looked away but just as his gaze suddenly found a missing brick in the wall his hand was taken and led towards it. The same hand was raised into one of the shackles; attached to the wall; joined quickly by the other.

One, just one voice, like a deep and unwelcome sigh, surfaced quickly.

Is this what you want?

For once the question was left unanswered in the air,

swirling incoherently with the clouds of brick dust. Without a word the hooded man stepped back, and Louche heard the whip trail along the floor. He was close to the wall, close enough for him to lick the dust from between the bricks, close enough for him to smell the dampness. He opened his eyes, fully, taking in all the available light, taking in everything within the limited scope. It seemed the richest of views. He waited for the persistent voice to say something, to make him balk and doubt his actions, but he heard nothing. The silence brought forward a surge of emotion, of tears and anger and laughter, rolling and gathering pace with each passing second.

Some People are Born to be a Burden on the Rest

1

THE DUST WAS bad that day. There's dust and there's dust, I tell ya, and that dust, those little specks and stones of horror and hurt, was being whipped up like the cry of the damned on a night for all souls. Sure, it had people runnin for cover every which way but it had people stilled, statued and stoned to the ground, rooted to the spot, n hot with the fire of those damned little specks, those goddamned stones of horror and hurt. Who would've thought? A summer's day turned storm in just a moment. 'It's not the time,' yelled old mother Flurn. 'It's too early,' she shouted as she gathered pies and cakes in her arms throwin them into the folds of her skirt as she ran for the shelter of her truck. Guess it was though, guess it was that time. Too early, too late. It doesn't matter when. Just that it was. The weather was not in our control. Nothin was in our control, her control, my control that day. Like it was just freewheelin any which way it could. Yea, tis surely a possible fate that I relate. I didn't hear much cept the whisperin and shoutin that day that's for sure. Someone went mad, it's said, went into a blind drunken frenzy. Or some simple-minded fool just spoilt it for all decent folks. If people don't know they just make it up I guess. But even before the dust-storm kicked the earth into her face I could already hear the screams. Yea, I could already hear my momma. You won't believe I could but I did. Her throat and tongue meeting in some stranglin touch.

Before the fair started in the early mornin with just a few people about and yea, momma with her sweat and bustle, there was nuthin much to it. Just a plain ol barn with a few wires and cables from a big sign that men were pushin and pullin at tryin to get everythin to fit into place. There were words but they were too jumbled up to read em; a long sentence gettin ready for somethin and then a whole row of light bulbs underneath with more words still. Dark. No-one knew what it was going to be. Momma didn't know that's for sure. She shoulda run a mile, thrown the bakin high into the air when men winked at her, their smiles snarlin, 'It looks like it's going to be a spec-tac-u-lar display.'

This was the fun of the fair bringin something to share. Yea Momma had been before and people knew her, could and would speak to her over some fence or in some store, but those same people now gave her a witherin look and some of the kids, the boys, the older boys it should be said, spat and curled their fists but she just went on through, actin like the day was purfect and she spoke like she always did, to the hot dusty air.

***

Shinton Galt swilled his drink around the bottom of the glass watching the liquid lap close to the brim. To anyone who had cared enough to notice, Galt seemed like a man lost in thought; an out-of-towner a little out of his depth, counting the bottles behind the bar and killing time. The bar was Toleka through and through. Hard-drinking hired hands wrestling with each other while ornery ol' boys nursed drinks and slapped each other on the back, another working week ended. The singing in one corner, the pool table argument in another was just background for Galt, the local colour he had come to expect. Far from being lost in thought, Galt allowed himself a little smile as yet another drunk offered him a drink, their payday bills wafted in his face. He was completely sure where he was. A backwater town riddled with generations of fools.

***

'Aperille, if anyone as much as twitches their lip, you stand proud. Everyone seems to think they are better than everyone else these days. Can't say that I've noticed. Folks are just folks and they do what they do. Good and bad. And we ain't done nuthin, y'hear, we ain't done nuthin wrong. We keep our heads high and we shall have ourselves a whirl of a good time.'

The boys would take a step back and look at the hot, dusty air makin like a cloud round momma then run. It was a whole lot of nuthin to them. To them. This was momma, just her and no-one else. This was what she was known for. Bakin and talkin to air.

Momma liked to bake. And I mean bake. On fair days the whole town ate better cos of her. She didn't just make one thing neither. She burdened herself with many things and she cooked it all up in a hutch few would call a kitchen, carryin it all and yea, carryin it all in the bakin sun all the way from her house to the fair.

'Aperille, don't skip now, don't upset anythin. We want it all in one piece otherwise people won't buy.'

Some people stepped out of her way when they heard this, some jumped out their skin. Some people laughed. They saw no-one, just momma sweatin to burstin point. 'The show's startin early' some of them shouted. 'Who ya talkin to lady, your better half?' The jokes just kept on goin. Like momma, in the bakin heat.

'Aperille, I swear you are the best little helper in the whole world. No-one could ask for a better pair of hands.'

Everybody kept well back, like they were feared what she had was catchin, like what she had could be dripped from her sweat and carried on the hot air, sweet n sickly. 'You better duck there, boy, the imbecile is sweatin somethin awful . . .' She carried and sweat so much her back hurt and her brow flooded. Buttermilk biscuits, cinnamon rolls, blueberry pound cake and almond cookies that folks had been seen to fight over at the last fair. People would come a long ways just to eat momma's cookin. When they got some hunger they didn't care whether she could count or not. They didn't care who she spoke to neither.

'Aperille, I don't know what I would do without you.'

No-one hoped more than me that she would never find out.

At school the kids especially the girls would gather round and make like it was a party and everybody was invited to play and make riddles. But not jokin, not laughin. There weren't no smiles on their faces, just licks n kicks that sent anyone who disagreed howlin to teachers who shook their heads and led them inside. It was sad because some of the days were just so pretty, blue skies and all. It would have been sad to be locked up for your own good. Can't see no good in that at all. Who's good? Sometimes it happened to a neighbourhood boy, Little

Bo as he was called, even though he certainly wasn't that little. Too big for his age folk said. Sometimes he got fed up and tried to trip up the girls and upset their rhyme with his long legs. He didn't like to hear names being called. He had heard it all before.

Anyhow, 'The bakin lady is an im-bee-ceele', that's what some of the girls would shout and get some skippin fun out of using my mother's good and honest name to dance to. Later, long after the fair had gone, the girls picked up another rhyme, 'The bakin lady sure can scream.' It made Little Bo mad but momma didn't want no-one to make scenes or start fights on her behalf even though Bo was big enough for anyone and would've won n beaten the livin daylights out of those prissy little girls, dolled up like they were on a shelf waitin to be bought. Even though momma got angry he lashed out sometimes, after school when they teachers could do nothin about it. He would grab their pretty blonde hair in his hand and yank it out of their scalps. You could hear them screech through the kicked-up dust and he laughed as they ran on home. 'You've left somethin behin.' He let the hair drop to the ground and left it there in the dust.

***

The Toleka Fair was something else. You could hear old Mayor Lounach saying the same thing year in and year out. 'Pork and Politics, it's all there at the Toleka Fair.' He cut the same old ribbon too, year in and year out, the red satin taut then flappin against the gateposts that showed us all into the field. And it was all there, all here at the fair. Momma said that, when she first laid out her bakin for all to buy, back in the real early days, when there wasn't much to do.

'Honey, there were lines for everythin back then, even to ride on ol man Hulsh's mare who must have been near fifteen years old. She could barely stand and yet all the kids and a few dults too wanted to have a seat on her. People said they just felt great when they were sittin on top.'

It didn't matter where you were comin from, you left it all behind at the fair – that's what they said about it and for sure I wished it to be true for momma's sake. I wish I could take back that day, take it back and wring everythin bad out of it so that not one drop of her blood or sweat would touch the floor of that fusty old barn. I could only look on with an airy touch; an invisible breath of fire and rage like smoke risin up into dark sky. The things she had to endure! She spent a day and a night doin what she does best then draggin it all the way up the Hernish road, past the bitin dogs and drunken Oakies still high from the night before who would swear their lust at her, say things that shouldn't be said to no livin person. Thank the lord that I didn't have to feel the anger and hurt and fist-curlin that happened to momma each and every time she stepped out her door. I was spared that. I was muted before all that. Still but not born. I was dee-nied even the suggestion. I wasn't there, but for momma I was there for her.

There are some things it's better not to understand.

But not many. Momma said you have to think the best of people and prepare yourself for the worst of them. She saw the worst of them n felt the worst of them. Sight and feelin. Fists and fury greetin and meetin her round every corner, in every hot barn.' You shouldn't be here.' They screamed into her face. 'We don't want you here.' They toppled over her table and it would take her an age to get everything back where it should be, the cookies and cakes back to where they were. It wasn't everybody, it was just a few and a growin few but like I said when people got hungry . . . You just had to keep an eye out. Keep them wits you are told you don't have.

***

Sticks and stones, they say, sticks and stones and names, they all harm you. When the storm came back, rushin up the valley floor bringin with it all sorts of foul air, it was said you could always see something in the clouds being whipped up by that vicious wind. If I could have I would have stood firm in front of all that natural violence and, though I had no body to harm, I would have stopped everythin from hurtin that dear woman. You understan? If wishin made it so, if god fearin righteous souls made me believe in somethin then I could have been a force to reckon with.

**

Galt's first day in Toleka wouldn't have seemed much like work to anyone shadowin him after he stepped out of the hotel. His tall frame and black city clothes drew some attention but everyone was too busy starting their day to worry about a well-dressed stranger in their midst. There was a routine in his visits to these small towns. Part of the day was spent in the local records office. Here he was careful to ingratiate himself with the clerk who would be usually only too happy for someone to take an interest in the pedestrian details of births and deaths. For some hours he would painstakingly record both consistencies and inconsistencies; patterns and anomalies in the deceptively simple cycle of life. While the clerk prattled on about the significance of twin births and multiple deaths, Galt satisfied his own criteria, his own agenda. The diaspora of human folly. In Toleka and in a hundred towns just like it, generations of mistakes had gone uncorrected and truly there was much work to be done.

In the afternoon he propped himself up at a number of bars and sat back. Anyone could collate names and dates but it was a different thing to watch, observe and listen into conversations that nobody assumed were any of his concern. Sometimes, he would sit out on the veranda of the hotel and do the same, chatting away to the proprietor who would fill him in on the town gossip. Who had done that and who was still doing this. It didn't even stop there. These two, preliminary days when he had the town to himself, so to speak, were no easy-going preambles to the main event. His colleagues had no idea how he truly operated. He didn't just arrive in a town and get to know its people. He infiltrated the population and patiently waited for revelation and information. By the end of the night, when he was helping drunks out of the bar and back-slapping locals who had no idea who their new best friend was, he was at his most alert. In this important work there was no such thing as too much information.

***

'This is what you need.' The man stood on the platform that had been made from any old box that was lying around. He was dressed real smart but dusty, like the clothes weren't used too often because they were so smart. They were heavy too, too dark and thick for the heat that was already in the day even though that old mayor had barely cut the ribbon. People weren't there yet. The dressed-up man with the thick moustache and a voice that rolled words round his mouth before spittin them out didn't seem to care. He just kept on sayin, 'This is what you need. Now. Right now.' He put a chart on some stand and began to point to it with a long wooden stick. It was real strikin. There were big black arrows pointin to small brown bottles with red and green and blue labels. 'Yes. That's it. This is FOR YOU. Your illness can be attributed to an imbalance of humours. They are locked into your blood and bile. This medicine is the key.' The moustache man jumped down from the stage and whispered into the air, happenin to be my ear, 'let's hope this works . . .' and then threw his arms up into the air like a shot had torn him and a small bottle with a pink label fell from his sleeve into his hand. 'Here it is ladies and gentlemen. Pink potion for pale people. It will cure your ills.'

They are locked into your blood and bile. The man sure could talk.

The fair was like this. One moment you could be walkin along looking for some ride or show, some 'shoot em dead' duck game or pin-the-tail-on type thing, and some fool would come through shootin his mouth off and giving people, certain people certain looks. Yea. Another man, a lanky, city type with a sharp, black suit and slicked back hair was doing just that, shoutin from the other side of the track that led to the rides and shows. He rushed out words like they were late and needed to be somewhere.

'There's too much dirt, too many unnecessary complications, repugnant infections. What this world, this breeding race needs is hygiene. We need to clean ourselves until we shine.'

Momma had an answer for this like she tried to have an answer for everythin and she had used it that very mornin on the way to the fair.

'Aperille, I'll give you some advice no-one gave me. I had to learn this some hard and terrible way. Yea, *you* know that. Just keep walkin. If anything doesn't look right, seem right, it probably ain't right. Just keep walkin and don't meet nobody's gaze. If you do anything, just whistle some tune and look as though you have no other care in that world.'

But the slicked back man caught my eye or thereabouts and stopped talkin to the two men standing in front of him and just held on tight, not looking anywhere part from near me. I was flesh and blood to him. I was the middle distance. He could see me cos he needed to. I proved his point. The man took a moment to clear his throat real noisily and spit sharp into the dusty earth. Then he raised his voice like he was givin a speech not just havin a quiet neighbourly conversation. This wasn't polite. Momma said that when people raised their voice to her, she would bring up her own voice, a sweet singin voice and let some tune dance around her head until she couldn't hear nothin but her own pretty song. 'Cuts out a lot of ugliness, Aperille.'

Before when she had spoken like this and then sung at the top of her voice people would gather and watch with their mouths open, their hands raised up to the sky.

There would be shouts and cries and more often than not something hard would be thrown through the air and momma still singin would take some blows and cuts before all she could do was run away, takin the trails of laughter with her, the long distance spits of hate.

'Look what the world coughed up, boy.'

The slick backs could take a voice, snarl it up, mash it up with that ugly stare.

Momma wasn't no moron. She had a tongue that could be as sharp as knife when she wanted it to be and she had words for every moment that she wanted to count. When some Sunday-dressed woman snarled 'slut' at her as she was carryin the bakin into the fair she turned, smiled down and breathed out real loud.

'Aperille, when you get older you'll learn that some people just want to make life harder than it already is. Just walk on as proud as anyone.'

Momma should have walked out of that barn with her head held high. She should have hurt him, wrenched it out of her and left him squealin like a pig and gone to watch the farmers runnin after their stock or the kids settin all the chickens free. Yea, things would have been a whole lot different if she had cut n bled that pasty man. She could have got away and just listened. There was so much laughter to be heard. Just not in that barn.

***

Galt was used to the organisers of local fairs like the one being held in Toleka. Ridiculous little men full of their importance, which was hardly their own, borrowed from some pioneering spirit long since bred out of them. The Toleka mayor was no different. He wanted Galt to see every inch of the fairground as though the calf throwing contest or the pie eating extravaganza as the mayor called it would be of any interest to him. He did however show him the barn where his colleagues would be joining him and while this was important it didn't merit the speech the mayor gave. While the little man prattled on, Galt's eye was caught as it often was by the unusual, the out of place. People told him he had a sixth sense about these things. Some called it intuition. Whatever it was that attracted his stare, the mayor's voice retreated into the background noise of the fair.

Galt knew straight away. Here was the future that shouldn't be allowed to happen. He could tell by her unseemly height, by her wide girth, by the way she moved – a lopsided gait, a weak neck causing her head to loll to one side as she talked. This was another sign. Her tongue was so loose there were saliva trails running down each side of her mouth. As the mayor embellished the basic appeal of the fairground site, Galt watched as this bovine female lifted large boxes on to her stall. Galt was surprised by the tone of her muscles in her arms, the sturdiness of her legs. Even as the mayor, a little put-out by Galt's lack of attention, wandered off, Galt did not flinch from his stare as this large woman, mouthing off to anyone who may or may not have been listening, reached over her stall, the hem of her dress riding up her calves.

***

The fair got busy real quickly. I was goin to do a tour, take a roundabout play through the dust and dirt, the bawlin children, the shoutin dults and work my way back to momma's stall, just in time to see her as people started to get either ugly or hungry. It felt good when she was at her best. She would be so busy that she forgot to talk, forgot to keep her mind on her heart and her tongue rootin out her soul. She was told that made it easier for everybody. And everybody sure wanted it easier. Simpler. This was good. That was bad. Talk about love and people started to get real fidgety. It was only momma that wanted to hear about that and it took a line of people stretchin real far before she lost me. There were too many things to do. I would have to wait. It has to be said even though it feels like a rip across my skin that this was a moment when no-one would bother her, when eyes were carin only about stomachs.

The fair hadn't been open that long but already people were deep around the livestock shows. It was all there. Livin, breathin examples of the best there is. Pigs in their prime and cows that had been shined so much they caught the sun and the judge's eye. Proud farmers were rushin across the field, makin sure everything was ready for judgin and little girls were sweatin in the heat as they brushed down the horses, combin their manes like it was their own fine blonde hair.

While I drifted, watchin them get the horses ready, more slick backs and suited-up types walked by. You could tell em apart. Not just the clothes but the look they had and gave; the way they held on to their prissy little kids, not noticin but you know really noticin anyone that seemed, like, wrong. They had that kind of dee-mean-our that said they were better than most folk and far better than someone like momma. They were a breed apart and they had one of those badges that a few people, local and strange, had been wearing. I hadn't known what it was but one woman in her Sunday best, a sunflowered dress, told a neighbour to go along to the barn, the one with all the lights, and maybe she could get a badge too. 'It's a real honour,' the man said, when he pinned it on me. '"I have a goodly heritage" is something to crow about that's for sure.'

The sunflowered woman raised her voice just a little more when a 'po family from down the Hernish road walked by, ill kept with dust on every part of their skin. They were salt of the earth and the dirt on the ground. Depended who you listen to, if you listen to anyone at all.

'Yes, mam, while the stock judges are testing the Recksteins, Kerseys and Whitefaces in the stock pavilion, they are gonna judge the Holsheys, the Rendamers and Johanns in the barn.'

I saw a sign hangin from an old poplar tree and felt somethin. I was comin near full circle and the fair was jumpin so much it was gettin hard to see on the ground, legs were gettin thicker and the dust could choke you to death in a matter of minutes. The sign was all lit up on a bright sunny day, kind of strange but it worked. The words were comin through the kicked-up clouds.

Fitter Family Competition This Way

Whole families of dressed-up people were getting baked in the heat. It was an or-der-ly line and real quiet like there was dead folk ahead and no words could be said. Yea. I caught sight of Little Bo through the heat and skipped over to join him. He was balancing himself on one of the old fences that ol Mr Flurn kept on sayin he would mend them when some young kid or some old drunk fell against it and wood n nails would go flyin everywhere. Anyhow, sat beside Little Bo and it looked like he'd had the same idea as me. We heard a voice call out, 'Settle down, ladies and gentlemen, and please be patient. The future is going to happen very soon.'

2

'Yes sir, yes mam just sign up here and we'll be glad to give you an appointment. No sir, there is no charge for this service. We, at the Eugenics Record Office, feel we have undertaken a service to the community and, yes, to the nation. It is our duty, God given and state authorised, to administer these tests for the greater good. Yes mam. That's certainly true and we are proud of such integrity even if some might find the results not to their liking. What good would be a test if everyone was right? If everyone was *all* right? We are not seeking to alienate folks but to identify what we see as a very real and pressing problem. The tests that have been devised have an international reputation all the way to Europe, and they are the most sophisticated available. We are proud to be able to bring them to the good people of Toleka. Sorry sir . . . ? Yes certainly. And the not so good people.'

*

Jusrus Holmes had been up since dawn. The night before he had checked into the only hotel in Toleka – which the ERO had block booked for two nights – along with the other officers and admin staff and had said his goodnights quickly knowing that he needed to be fresh for the following day. He left Galt to report on the two days he had spent in the town. He smiled when he saw young Shinton on the edge of his seat, bursting to tell what he had found out about the town and its inhabitants. It was the same wherever they had been.

It was always an exhausting time being on the road but it was truly where he felt he belonged. Some of the other officers preferred the dusty paperwork of research and the meticulous presentation of all their scientific papers and public information announcements. Of course, Jusrus knew this was an essential part of the ERO work but as he himself had pointed out to his colleagues just before they had left for Toleka and the other county fairs due to take place through all of August, all the behind scenes activity counts for nothing if they do not perform and actively seek their objectives. And that was the key, he told them all, in his now customary speech before reaching any fair. 'Let's be careful out there. Let us educate and stimulate; we must find, not blind, with science a way, a route, a method to making people understand that action is needed now. The situation is simple and far from irrevocable and that should be our message. Defective persons are a menace to society.'

The county fairs were always the hardest. It was at these that Jusrus and his team from the ERO had their work cut out for them. Back at head office some people questioned the wisdom of going to the county fairs at all and thought that the finite resources of the ERO should be concentrated on the state fairs and in the principal cities. This was not an argument that Jusrus agreed with and he became suspicious of anyone that put it forward. It was an indication he felt of a moral laziness, a meek methodology. It had the reek of a blanket positivity that was like a cancer riddling the true aims of the organisation. In the dirt and dust of these fairs were the root and causes of present and future problems. By taking the whole roadshow – the lights, the signs, the tests – the ERO could affect on a local level and not simply react at a national level. Using Galt as a kind of advance guard helped them speed up the procedures that were part of the contests and allowed them a level of accuracy that could never have been garnered from afar. Galt was a fearsome foot-soldier.

He knew the other ERO field operatives thought his methods too military, too snarled on regimen and directives but the fieldwork had to be carried out to a prearranged plan – not because he needed everything to be accountable to him at every moment of the day.

Despite what people whispered about him, he was not like that. He believed in meeting people with a smile. He would rather disarm with friendliness, than gear up for war. No, there had to be a plan because of history and because county fairs could be chaotic events. In the early days not that long ago when the ERO was just a few enthusiastic scientists aided by a worthy team of volunteers they had encountered quite a few problems. In Fairlax, the farmers, enraged that city types were taking away audiences from their pig shows, came after them with pitchforks and they had only just managed to escape intact, unholed. And, in Rentool, everything had gone well for most of the day with healthy lines for the Fitter family examinations and good-sized crowds gathering round the Mendel and light-o-meter displays. Gone well, that is, until it came to be that there were a lot of families failing the test. Of course they weren't to know that Rentool was such a place – a lost cause of a town decimated by weak pedigree – and the announcement of results was now more carefully controlled. Individualised and, in the case of the female contestants, recorded in accordance with the Big Aim. Jusrus shivered a little in the heat of a hot Toleka morning when he recalled that day. They lost a lot of equipment when those not of a goodly heritage rampaged through their displays. A number of volunteers never came back after that. They were all sickened by what they saw but, for those with a stronger stomach, it was grist to the mill and fuel to the flame. Jusrus raged his way through the other counties and such a thing was never allowed to happen again.

The other ERO operatives were not surprised to see that Jusrus had already had his breakfast and been up for some time on the Saturday morning, the day of the Toleka Fair. His bulky frame was standing away from the dining-tables and his large, bald head was pressed close to the window. He had seen something and they ate their breakfast in silence. Waiting.

They didn't have to wait long. He broke the early morning silence with a thunderclap of his hands; the palms of his large hands struck once and then they were lifted to the side of his head, pressing against his ears as if it was something he had heard not something he had seen.

'There you have it, ladies and gentlemen. *There* is the living, breathing proof that we are both needed and necessary here. In this beautiful, early morning scene where the good folk of this town are raising themselves to blithely meet another day with spirit and strength, there lurks and then meanders a darker element. The sign of these times, such times that we live in now. An imbecile or should I not say im-bee-ceele. It's not the pronunciation that we should care about but the procreation of such a cyst, of this myth that everyone has a role to play. We are being degenerated and dragged further and further back by such attitudes and it is because of this person that we are here today, and tomorrow in the next county. It is of course too late to stop this man from walking the streets although there is a strong argument for him to be kept in one of the many institutions that are thankfully being constructed for the feeble-minded. He has of course certain constitutional rights. But so do we and we shall have more. We have earned the right to restrict, to predict the future of our families. Ill-fitting individuals shall not progress for they by their restricted intellect, their limited means can only be a burden and our future shall be shaped by lightening the load, our load.'

The operatives knew what to do. They stood and applauded, surprising the few other diners in the restaurant who quickly assumed some kind of evangelism without knowing the cause. Jusrus nodded his acceptance of the applause and in particular the energetic thump on the back he received from young Shinton Galt. Already the firebrand so early in the morning.

Old Man Flurn dragged his weary carcass past the hotel and looked in at the hullabaloo startin up. That hotel had some stories to tell that was certain. From the murder in the bar to the death in the master bedroom, an old lady conking out in the bath, one leg over each side. It made him smile then laugh and he chuckled to himself all the while grimacing through the pain of the hunch on his back. 'C'mon, old fella,' he said talking to himself and the hump in particular. 'We'd better git movin. The fair'll be over by the time we git there.'

***

Little Bo jumped up n out of his scrawny skin.

'They is here. They is here.'

Now, I wasn't sure what he meant or who was arrivin but when someone gets that excited so that they holler so loud that bumps are pushed out on your arm and leg skin, you take notice and take notice quick.

'I guess these are the stars of the carnival.'

Little Bo was lookin down the track and I saw what he meant. Toleka had seen nuthin like it or so I heard later as the crowd grew and gathered around the barn. No doubt some of the other stallholders got a little antsy about the number of people flockin away from their sheep or guns or hams gettin cured in the heat of the sun but there was no denyin it. There was no cure for this, that was for sure. It was a wagon like the kind you didn't see much no more cept this wasn't no ordinary vee-hic-ile like the ol pi-neers tore up the lan with. This was like something no-one had ever seen. The oohs and aahs kinda proved that and where the track wasn't wide enough for the wagon people staggered back a few feet and had to be held by folks behin. I guess everybody was caught off balance by the scene, yea, the spectacle.

The wagon was black. A black jewel that shined in the sun; a dirty great beetle scuttlin along the dusty track. It took people's breath away, took the air into people's bodies and then nobody said a word like the silence was all their own. To keep. Yea. People watched the pro-cess-ion. I chased after Little Bo and got right behind him so that legs he picked and kicked his way through made some room for me too. When folks cursed the blows from Little Bo they had nuthin to say to me. It was like I wasn't there. Yea. I was a shadow they had burned in the sun.

Anyways, I got a real good view of that dark wagon makin its way to the barn. The big wooden wheels had been polished and the black leather straps holdin down all sizes and sorts of trunks were slick with grease. These were city folks that was for sure and the two men sittin like they were watchin for trouble were smartened up as much as their wagon, n black as too. Head to foot in the dark stuff. Must have been bakin in the heat that's for sure. The driver had a whip ready in his hand and was lookin to use it and not just on the horses while the other man, tall and strong with a preacher's hat, sat with his back straight and his eyes straight forward.

Looked like he knew where he was goin, like he knew what he was seein.

But this was new, all of it. No-one had seen this before and even the farmers were standin starin and scratchin their heads. This was excitin. This was more than the fun of the fair. Out the back of the wagon a city boy, real young like maybe ten, was leanin out and throwin leaflets up into the hot air. He was dressed like them, tight-suited and black, from his polished shoes to his neat back and sides. The paper hung in the air, kept hangin there by the heat, and Little Bo grabbed one. 'Say, what does this mean?' he yelled after the wagon. 'Some people are born to be a burden on the rest?' The city boy either didn't hear him or didn't care for his tone and the black wagon rolled on, its wheels turnin silent as anythin could be on the dust and stones.

'In the past but especially in the present there has been a reversion to mediocrity but now the future, ladies and gentlemen, has arrived. Get in line now. Be part of it.'

Little Bo scrunched up the leaflet and kicked it towards the crowd now pressin in on the field with the big barn in it.

'No sense just nonsense. And look at the people go. If this were cattle, the ranchers'd be takin aim.'

***

'Yes mam. The process is very simple. You've made a wise decision. Some people are a little afraid but there is no need to be. There is no magic to what we do just pure science. Yes sir. A Christian science that is about as exact as you can get and there are no better tests around. I understand, yes, I do. We have gone for so long hoping for things to get better that we have lost the ability to make them better. Hope is, if you don't mind me saying so, for fools and gamblers. Yes mam. Fools and gamblers. If I can, before we take you through the tests, direct your gaze to the sign that we have hanging above the consultation area.

How Long
are we to be so grateful for the pedigree
of our livestock and then leave the ancestry
of our children to chance or to blind
sentiment?

'That sure is the sweetest sentiment, don't you agree? Uh huh, exactly. It says it in a way you've been saying it to yourselves all along when some fool gets in the way, when some family moves in close by and messes up your life with their noise and violence. And then the next thing you know their kids are everywhere, cluttering up your school, in every class taking up precious teaching time with their slow understanding, beating up the very walls of the building with their angry blows. And then it gets nasty, the thing which we at the ERO are determined to do something about so that no generation will have to endure what we have seen. The young ones will grow old enough to make their own babies and soon your peaceful town will be swarming with imbeciles – idiots who are violent and morons who could kill perfect children and rape fit women. You think so, ma'am, you think it could never get that bad in Toleka? Take a look around, while you wait for your tests and tell me if you still believe I am exaggerating. Take a look at the evidence we have displayed. The horror in Harkan; the grim reality in Fencer and my very own account of the tragedy in Rentool. These are events that are true and honest witness to the threat of the status quo. The future of our race depends entirely on whether or not we decide to do something about these events.'

Jusrus let the husband and wife drift over to the line forming by Galt. He was pretty sure they were going to be a borderline pass despite their efforts to make themselves smart. If they were, the sharp-eyed Galt would sort them out. He had seen it many times before at countless county and even state fairs of the last few years. Word would get around that they were going to be in town and whole families would turn up dressed as tight and smart as though they were going to church. People hoped that this would be enough. A few easy questions later and then they would pass, get their badge and then their photograph in the paper. It was clear to Jusrus that some families with somethin to hide would do anything to get their badge. In Harkan, two families as beautifully turned out as you could want didn't even make it through the first test. The Hereditary Test. Turned out they were smart only with their clothes. The family of four was really a family of six and the two, youngest boys had been left dribbling in their cots, ridden with some affliction that had been passed down one side for three generations.

Still another family, in Fencer, a large family of two boys and two girls hoping no doubt to win the Larger Fitter Family Accolade which guaranteed them front page of the local newspaper – the newspaper stand put up close to the ERO wagons said as much – got through the first stage only for these children to fall profoundly at the next. The Intelligence Test. The categories of reasoning, judgement, memory and the power of abstraction were failed in such a spectacular way that the family was evicted from the barn with great speed and a certain aggression. They had wasted everybody's time and there isn't much left.

Jusrus moved amongst the throng in the barn who were looking at the exhibits, queuing for the tests, and allowed himself some satisfaction. The air was thick with a sense of expectation; the familiar huddles of hushed awe as country folks' faces were lit up by bright display lights brought a smile to his lips. Even the kids more used to driving their parents ragged with their energy were subdued and kept at heel, the youngest ones scared of the synchronised Mendelian eyes. Of course there was a sense of the circus to it all that the pen pushers back at the head office didn't understand. They couldn't see the need for the painted wagons, paid actors and elaborate displays. To the academics and scientists, truth was enough. It was all simply a case of good versus bad; identify and rectify; educate and eliminate; test and result. Jusrus argued, and got his way each and every time, that the ERO depended on the transformation of statistical truth into pragmatic plans. 'We can't build a perfect society in an office,' he reminded them all.

Pure science would not work.

***

I saw momma from a distance, tho she didn't see me. She was talking to me. I could see her lips movin, her arms reachin out then embracin. There was all the love in the world in that movement. Came from the heart, it did, came from the muscle and soul of a good strong heart. Not that you would know it from the way other people saw it. Even from a distance I could see them jump like they'd stepped on a rattlesnake; like they'd stuck their hand into boiling oil or on a burnin stove. Men laughed, women scowled and children danced around her like she was a fairground ride, an attraction all of her own. And she did. She did have an attraction all of her own. Maybe it was in the way she moved her hips, or pouted her lips, and I may indeed be nothing more than wishful thinkin that's for her and only her, but I think there is always something to hear in men's laughter that isn't funny, always something to see in the way their eyes drop then stare.

Momma was in a good mood. Every last sweet thing had been sold.

'There's barely even a crumb left, Aperille. I'm so happy. Seems like people just couldn't get enough of my bakin this year. That's a good feelin.'

Just like always, momma couldn't keep the good feelin to herself. You always knew it when she was happy. I always knew it. There at the fair she put her arms around me and hugged me until I let out a sigh that was so strong it went from me and back to her leapin out of her mouth, a spine tickler, a hair raiser. People saw her hug the air, her arms missin me and cuddlin only herself, her hands racin up and down her back, her lips air kissin with feelin. Not everybody saw it the way she did. I did and I wasn't even there.

Maybe if she hadn't been kissin n huggin; maybe if

she had taken a moment to look around where her laughter and joy had taken her, far away from the place reserved for the food stalls. Maybe if she had seen the bright lights, the lines of dressed-up folks and the men in black walkin around givin out paper, she would have stopped and considered. Considered somethin. Yea. It's not that she got ahead of herself as some people seem to think she had by sellin her bakin when she couldn't even count. Or maybe actin too high for her own good, makin herself just to fem-i-nine to all those 'po hungry men'. Quite the contrary, I'll be damned (and I was). Some thin and pasty man got ahead of her. Saw her comin and started thinkin things only a man would think.

The bright lights blinkin on then off caught her and she was just kind of pulled in by the swell of the crowd. The man in black beside the flashin-light machine was standin on some ol crates, shoutin at people, lecturin them fast and furious. 'Feeble-minded people are multiplying at twice the rate of the general population and what do we get as a result ladies and gentlemen, what do we get – and this, this, mind you is no off the cuff figure, this shocking number is the result of exhaustive scientific research and may it strike terror into all our hearts. If we allow this to continue then we will be allowing more feeble-minded children with which to clog the wheels of human progress.'

Momma couldn't take her eyes away from the lights. Yea, the city man couldn't take his eyes away from momma.

'Every fifteen seconds a hundred dollars of your money goes for the care of persons with bad heredity.'

The sweat was drippin off everybody and it was a struggle even for the man in black all suited up n hot with words but momma was not carin, she was lovin it all.

'Every forty-eight seconds a mentally deficient person is born in the US and that is something that is going to haunt us all.'

Yea. There she was twirlin, yes, twirlin with happiness. People made room. They had to. This was momma in full flow, all rhythm and light on her feet without a care in the world.

The city man held out his hand and joined her dance by stayin still, pulling her to him, like he had a rope round a kid drowin in the river.

'It is illuminated, yes illuminated, for us all to see. The saddest fact of all and the light which remains dark for too long is the one which tells us, based, I remind you again, on pure scientific fact, that only every seven and half minutes do we enjoy the birth of a high-grade person. Think about that as you walk through this brave new world.'

I stole some time on momma and went on ahead into

the heart of the barn where people were jammed closer than close to each other. Sweat was drippin from the wood of the ol barn and pourin off the stilted man standin about ten feet above everybody else and stridin thorough the crowd, rhymin his words as though his height wasn't enough to git people to hear. 'Crime, insanity, mental defects, alcoholism and indulgence are products of bad heredity; moral strength, industriousness, abstinence and intelligence are signs of a good heredity.'

It was some sight, I can tell you, but people didn't know which way to look. It wasn't just the flashin lights that were dizzyin people left and right but words, rushin, furious words which were flyin bout more than the bitin gnats pourin into the barn from the woods behind the field. Yea. It was the hum and buzz of life, stirrin up the heat in the barn, makin people crazy, makin sure of some strife.

'NO, NO! I don't believe it, I don't believe you. My da was a good man . . .' A young women dressed up with a Sunday-best hat all flowers and bows pulled at two young boys, maybe twins, both dressed the same anyhow. She pushed through the crowds of suited and dressed-up folk queuing way back from a sign hangin from the beams. *Heredity Test for Small Families Here.* The woman stopped at the entrance to the barn just as two men closed in on her, their arms spreadin for some kind embrace. She shouted back into the barn, 'It's not your his-tory, it's my his-tory.' It looked like she wanted to say more but her kids started to wail and the men kinda lifted her off her feet, her arms still grippin her kids, one in each hand, and they all flew out of the barn, not one foot on the ground.

It was easy to lose people in the heat and clamour of the tent and I had lost momma. She wasn't the lining-up type but there was a whole bunch of people starin at the photos of people just like themselves, all dressed up and serious. A black-suited man was telling them what they needed to know. 'These people, ladies and gentlemen, are winners and runners-up of the competitions we have held all across the state, in Harkan, in Fencer and many, many other places. Winners of the both Large and Small Family competitions, they all have a goodly heritage and all have had the privilege of appearing in their local paper. See how proud they look.' When people turn away from the man and his photos, the fathers tighten their ties while the mothers touch their hats and smooth down their children's collars. Everybody wants to look their best.

But I had still lost momma. Little Bo had disappeared into the crowd. The only place I hadn't looked was the far corner of the barn which had been separated some by a black curtain. In front of the curtain was a small wooden table with a man ready with pencil and paper one side and two empty chairs on the other. A sign hung on the black curtain.

Fitter Family Physical Examination

I guess this kind of explained somethin. The photos n talk about how good things could be or how bad they could get was one thing, sure, but not many it seemed wanted to be touched. The man at the desk was a real city type. Thin and pasty-faced and he looked like he was bout to faint on account of the heat. It wasn't hard to get past him. He didn't see me as he stared out into the crowd.

***

Walking slowly through the barn, checking progress at each of the testing stations as he liked to call them, Jusrus was content just to bide his time and act as overseer. He had been trained up in all aspects of the Fitter Family Initiative including the IQ testing, the Wassermann test and the Hereditary tracking questionnaire which all families had to complete and which were then matched to existing county records. Jusrus wanted to keep the paperwork to a minimum but both the trustees back at the ERO HQ and the local administrative agencies wanted meticulous notes kept of each entrant into the competition. Jusrus understood this but nobody knew what it was like to work in the field, in these scorched fields, as much as he did.

'Go beyond appearance but don't ignore it,' he advised the operatives. 'Most families will make an effort when attending the fairs to create a good impression. Expect this but don't rely on it. Dismiss the ragtag, the ill-kempt, those with vagabond airs poorly disguised. On the other hand clothes do not have to be pristine or expensive to purchase but they have to be cared for. A repaired but well-sewn garment for example indicates a level of skill and inherent intelligence. Hair for all genders and ages does not have to be elaborately styled – we are not in the city after all – but should be tidy and in addition look at the skin. We are not seeking an alabaster quality but if there are lesions or sores especially around the mouth then this should immediately raise your suspicions. Be vigilant but at the same time do your best to appear genial rather inquisitorial.'

In the beginning when Jusrus had been keen to man the testing station himself he had come to rely on his intuitive rather than his administrative skills. He ignored the trustees' decree to keep detailed notes to help build the case for the political agenda and of course for the BIG AIM and played things his own way when it came to the entrants to the competition He confided in his protégé, his aide de combat, Shinton Galt.

'You can't determine unfit human traits, as the pen pushers would have us call them by simply ticking checklists or asking banal questions, you have to get on their level, look them in the eyes, get inside their mouths, feel their bones, test their verbal dexterity with quick-fire questions and get them to prove their moral fibre, their sexual stricture with surprising action.'

Galt, tall, strong yet fine boned from an aristocratic heritage and a family with two members on the board of trustees was a zealous adherent to Jusrus's views. In Rentool he had enraged a family and a farmer it must be said by grabbing a borderline imbecile out of the family group and in order to demonstrate a particular part of the physical test proceeded to open a horse's mouth to inspect its gums and teeth before pulling on a pair of gloves and opening the mouth of the human subject. The little girl went screaming back to her family but the point was well made.

In many ways, although Jusrus was in charge of all field operations and led the wagons as they ceremoniously entered each town the day before the local fair, it was Galt's energy, his quick-witted investigations that inspired Jusrus and led him to give instructions to the testers that surprised more than just a few of them. The intelligence tests – the spatial and mental abilities – should be followed by sexual morality tests that required the subject to give an opinion – if they could – on what was acceptable and what was not. This would then be followed by intimate questions during personal history tests. For the squeamish amongst the testers he had no reassurance to give.

'This is the nitty-gritty of why we are here. Science has shown us that feeble-mindedness and sexual deviance are inextricably linked. Remember what has been taught to you, "A borderline family in which illegitimacy runs high is not able to care for itself in organised society and as a result a family where moral rules are not enforced, where moral code has not been inbuilt into the genes and has been diluted by perversion and deviance, will produce offspring which will inevitably lead to sexual and moral disarray. Therefore, any tests that we undertake in the heat of these barns amidst all the turmoil must have the due benefit of being calm, efficient and unrelentingly thorough. Remember, one generation of imbeciles is enough."'

Of course, such comments inflamed some participants and stupefied others but the recognition and status accolade of the Fitter Family contests were taken lightly by no-one. Being placed highly in a Fitter Family competition opened doors and created powerful cliques in communities that would have benefits both socially and financially. As Jusrus told the operatives, 'There is much to lose by evading the uncomfortable. We seek to engineer an evolution and that was never going to be easy.'

Galt exalted in the lurid biographies and pornographic revelations that spilled out usually through spite rather than from a need to unburden conscience. 'Some people put the burden on to others.' This became the catch-all heading for the sessions that Galt took charge of under the watchful eye of Jusrus. Galt's smooth, breezy confidence was ideal for getting contestants to spill the beans on neighbours, on bosses and workers and estranged in-laws. For every man or woman who was as clean as they appeared, as prim and righteous as they said they were, there were another two who had something to hide, something they wanted kept dark.

The excited Galt was quick to praise the manipulative tactics that made the fairs dynamic affairs rather than the dry statistical events the ERO seemingly would be happy with. It helped too that by the time they got to Toleka the winners and runners-up for all categories of the Fitter Family competition were offered handsome cash prizes as well as extensive coverage in the local newspaper. The money as it turned out was put up by trustees with at least half of it coming from Galt's uncle, a fervent supporter of all things eugenic.

'Out of all the trustees, Jusrus, he's the one that seems to have the vision to take all this to the next stage, the political stage – the most important stage of all. You see what I'm getting at?'

Jusrus had given Galt for the first time his own

examination area, cordoned off by a black curtain to enable physical examination to take place with some degree of privacy. The barn in Toleka was the biggest space they had yet occupied with the most displays and information stalls at the ready as well as cordoned-off areas for the hereditary, psychological and physical tests that were now the routine for the competition. It seemed right that Galt's enthusiasm should be rewarded with more responsibility – a point Jusrus believed wouldn't be lost on the trustee uncle who had kept his nephew informed of the next big milestone for the movement. It was the logical outcome for the whole movement.

'The legislative stage, Jusrus, that's where we will be sooner than most people think. It's not enough to identify defective people. We have to stop them coming into being. We are diluting ourselves, our strength, and the effects are already being felt. The true offspring of unregulated pregnancy is shown in the doubling of urban violence, of countrywide criminality and a national reduction in the average IQ. We are in danger of being swamped by incompetence. If we bend over backwards to help lesser souls then all we shall have is a broken back. The support is there, the majority is on our side and compulsory sterilisation of the feeble-minded is within our grasp. How many generations of imbeciles can we endure?'

Galt was in full swing now, his voice rising into a near

howl of excitement. Jusrus watched the eyes of his young colleague widen with every sentence as the ramifications of his grandiose claims radiated through him. The same eyes would narrow when faced with a dubious candidate, a borderline participant. He took any opportunity he could and soon the contestant would be trying to improve his chances by ratting out the competition.

'Yes sir, that's right, cousin with cousin, uncle with niece night after night and they don't care if the children watch because they just beat them to make sure they say nuthin. The babies are born on the back porch and if no-one wants them they are taken out to be left in the street, bawlin until someone finds them.'

There was a lasciviousness to Galt's inquisition, a quick lick of the lips as he listened to the telltales sell their souls for the thrill of being superior. Galt was looking for and exalting in their failure. It made him the perfect investigator. In the end Jusrus felt differently, he pitied them, their aspirational needs, their hopeful notions of acceptance and achievement. This was the feeling he had come to accept as part of the job. He was battle weary, anyone who took the time could see that in his too distant stare sometimes, his irritation at the slightest of things, his quickly surfacing need for cruelty to anyone who happened to be near him. Still, he was a hard-working man and he had been charged with many duties and he was not about to renege on any of them. A certain amount of delegation made perfect sense. The fair would go from strength to strength and in Toleka, the most ambitious so far, he let Galt, wild-eyed and gurning, have free rein. He could do what he saw fit. Fitter, even. With that thought, he drew the black curtain and pushed out into the throng.

***

Lord knows what made me want to go behind the curtain. Just about anybody could have told me that there wasn't goin to be anythin I wanted to see or know about behind a black curtain. There was too much black for a sunny day anyhow. The black covered wagon circling the barn like there was about to be some kind of battle; the men makin like soldiers or rustlers, lookin like they were going to beat up on you at any moment and the black drapes with photos and signs hangin down from the beams of the barn, big announcements for all to see and read.

And hear. And hear. I put my ear to the soft black curtain and heard what I didn't want to hear.

'Bitch. No good blasted bitch.'

Of course it didn't sound good. Didn't sound like no fair test. Out in the field, the pigs were gettin sized up and by the stalls men were gettin muscled up but there sure weren't words like these.

'Fucking, feeble-minded bitch.'
Or sights like I saw.
'You need some of what I've got.'
I squatted down and put my head round the curtain.
'This'll mend ya . . .'
I had found momma right enough.

For Solace Fled to Parts Unknown

Video home system

'HEY, SOLACE, HOW'S it hanging and wait, let's see, yep it is hanging, isn't it? Too cold in these parts, in *those* parts for anything to be stiff.'

 The video shop owner wasn't called Randy but since I have never learnt his real name it will certainly do. People grow into their names as I am sure he would agree. I'm just amazed he's still as energetic and seemingly upbeat as he always has been. The shop is just off the high street with the pretty plain and self explanatory name of *Video Emporium*. If he was on the main drag no doubt he would have been priced out of business by now but he had enough of a regular clientele to somehow survive. I guess there were some genres format-change took a while to catch up on and in some cases could never replace. This was a favourite topic of Randy's which is kind of what you would expect.

'People keep expecting me to go under now that VHS has gone the way of BETA and god knows how many other formats that people, straight men mostly, ooze and booze over, getting their facts mixed up with their nostalgia, ending up with a big pile of memory shit right in front of them. Steaming. Rank and not in the film sense. There is a new world out there that can be copied and presented on to something fine, thin and shiny but so what? Most of the stuff I look for that people are still buying is never going to be seen in any other way. People might get lucky and catch some repeat on the Nostalgia Channel and watch some pretty thing from childhood that brings goose bumps to their everything but then it's the age-old problem of being in the right place at the right time. Of course even if you do see it some conglomerate will have spliced it with too many commercials and so the trip back down memory lane turns out to be a microwave dinner.

No, what I have here and so it follows what you have here is access to the real thing. It's all boxed and ready to go; technology preserved, memories reignited and everybody's happy. Nothing is collated here. Everything stands on its own. It's the good old-fashioned world where you have to buy three things if you want a trilogy.'

Randy liked to talk and his conversation, when it

wasn't one way, was a cut and spliced version of everything he had ever watched. He would swerve from Jamaican patois – he was a fat dumpling of white man – to French porn pro – he was a long way from ever being pretty and the bulge in his tight Farrahs was a sugar lump even to the most kindly of glances. 'Of course you remember . . .' would be his conspiratorial sales pitch; an unsurprisingly effective starter that would implicate the memory of the would-be buyer. 'You're looking for something from XXXX and you don't know this . . . ? Wow!' Randy railroaded people into identifying shows and films they could not even remember. He prided himself on sourcing the most obscure television show – the 1973 pilot of a comedy series that never got made – and then selling it to anyone who had even just a passing interest in the subject matter.

'It's got SR in it who is just incredible when she plays opposite the Divine One. The friction rubs off on the dialogue and you can feel the sparks fly even through those cheap visual effects which just seem so charming now, pioneering even. It's such a good example of how short-lived programmes can have a long-term, inspirational impact.'

That was typical of Randy's approach. He mixed showbiz chat with some casual name-dropping while throwing in a little techy stuff to impress the easily impressed. Of course, he was as camp as a row of tents and some people probably just came in for the show.

'I found something just for you, Solace. A rare gem that is going to break that little bank of yours but then I'm sure we can . . . come to some sort of arrangement.'

You had to be in the mood for these theatrics and I usually wasn't and when I heard a couple of guys snigger a few rows down – they were at the Horror/Roger Corman/John Waters section – I hurried Randy on.

'Tell me what it is and I'll tell you whether I can afford it. There's not too much of my soul left to sell.'

Randy laughed, a pig squeal that got swallowed into something vaguely sultry.

'Who gives a fuck about your soul. They're usually over-priced anyway. The video I know you'll want is a copy of the first series of *The Life and Times of Grizzly Adams*. It'll make you cry and it'll make you want to save every little critter you can on your way home. It tugs all the right things. As, it must be said, do I.'

'I'll pay whatever you want.'

Memory triggers

I wasn't talking or at least nobody was talking to me. That came later too for different reasons. This is a fading memory, hobbling and crippled, already lurching into forgetfulness. It is also a photograph I keep on what laughingly could be called a mantelpiece. The chipboard is badly sawn and stained with old red wine drips and coffee circles. Its surface is cratered with what looks like knife holes and then bumped with chewing gum. In the photograph the blinds are partially drawn and I am at one end of the couch. My father is beside me. On his lap is my sister and then to his right is my elder brother. Everyone's been caught in that photo kind of way, the moment's just a little too early or too late; a smile has turned into a squint; a wave has turned into a rude gesture and the sun delicately strafing through the Venetian slats has created bars, long shadows that have us all imprisoned. There is no escape from this kind of sentimentality. Welcome to my memory.

Nobody is really caring what we are watching. My sister is playing with her hair, trying to push it into my dad's mouth — for the hell of it I guess. She's about nine with me two years younger and my brother two years older. I was in the middle. My brother looks like he would rather be anywhere else than on the couch on what looks like a pretty nice day and my dad seems, well, just busy. Three kids I guess. For him everything was always happening around him. For me it was all on the television.

This is the only photograph. At some point it all stopped. There was nothing to record that anyone wanted to keep, to remember. With no visual evidence it was easier to be out of sight and out of mind. Out of my mind. Out of their sight. There was never any agreement, just the slow tortuous descent into estrangement, that developing state where as many emotions as can possibly be carried are bundled up and trussed to the heart.

That came later, but it's worth noticing that in the only photograph which survived the rip and tear I wasn't even there. Actually but not really. I was in the trees. Truly. I was on the green slopes of the rolling hills, sitting by the campfire listening to words I didn't understand, absorbing pictures of wildlife I had never seen. I was not simply a watcher but a participant. I was interactive before there were buttons to be pushed. Eventually, everybody got up bored and critical from the couch and moved on, one by one scattering listlessly through the house and I was left living alone in the room, left to push myself closer to the screen and turn up the volume.

What?

To turn up the volume so that everybody could hear. He was the first man I fell in love with.

Maybe it wasn't love, but it was an attraction, a strong attraction. It was hardly a unique phenomenon, half the children at school were falling for long-haired singers in American sitcoms or getting wild and native with other long hairs in exotic settings. It was the time, I guess, when TV families found themselves in wild circumstance and tempered it, survived it with charming domesticity. Nature was tamed by ingenuity and conservative values. Sure, all manner of criticism was levelled at the naive utopian, waspish state of it all but I was too young to know what I was being sold.

The busiest section in the Video Emporium was the family section and on a Saturday afternoon there was always a hum of remembrance around the shelves where fathers showed sons glazed with headphoned music what it had meant to them.

All I knew was that a) I wanted to be there on the rolling hills and b) I couldn't take my eyes off the main actor. I can remember the twinge, the subtle contraction of a muscle in my groin. It could have been the beard, the bear or the fact that the guy was just so heroic the whole time – saving kids from fires, and small, cute animals from, well, fires. The dangers got kind of samey after a while. It didn't matter. He was always in the right place at the right time and soothing violins and heart-tugging everything-turns-out-well-in-the-end finales always got one eye tearful while the other kept watch on the living-room door. The programme was a different world but I didn't want to get laughed at in this one.

It was *The Life And Times Of Grizzly Adams* that started it all. Please do laugh if you need to but fuck you and fuck your dishonesty if you do, you know, as if anyone's heart can exist in a vacuum. Believe me, I've heard it all before. *You watched what? You remember that? You care about them?* I know some people like to collect furniture or get hot about property acquisition. Me, I'm aspirational for some wholesome memories. Yeah, just like everybody else, I want something I haven't got. Something needs to keep the blood flowing and for me it was being somewhere I was stimulated, absorbed and trusting. And this was TLATOGA. It's easy to identify because it was the first. It got me hooked. It formed the first of many habits and I would, with religious fervour, quote hippy truisms and invoke natural philosophy on every occasion I could. No wonder my parents went off me, no wonder they started to concentrate on my brother and sister.

'Two out of three ain't bad, Maude.'

No, they didn't say that.

'What are we going to do with him?'

Yes, they did say that, whispered it in fact behind a closed bedroom door but loud enough for my ear pressed to the keyhole to hear the deep sense of worry in their voices.

I wanted to be somewhere else? Crazy fucking kid.

When the programme died an unexplained death, I moved with the indecent haste of a child losing a kitten to the wheels of a car to the next family adventure. *Little House on the Prairie* grabbed me for a while but the kids praying on the prairie began to irritate after a while. It didn't have the space of TLATOGA even though it rolled out of a similar countryside. The kids whined and cried more than was realistic and they were just too damned good. They spent more time in church than they did in trouble. After that, I watched anything and everything, flicking between the two-channelled choice. That in itself became another habit that annoyed everyone else in the family and sent them scurrying from the room.

I quickly, with the fickleness appropriate to my age, moved on from my bearded man and found swashbuckling women with long flowing hair, with tanned and muscled bodies. I couldn't believe it. My sister and the girls at school were snivelling, crying creatures with strange views on just about everything but these Amazonians were like nothing I had ever seen before. My mother tutted when she saw them, averting her eyes to the TV schedule hoping that there would be something else to watch. When I went to sleep at night I could smell the sweat of these women, feel their strength as they hugged me until I could barely breathe. *Thank you* I whispered into the dark. My mother would leave the room without a word.

This back and forth between worlds, of programmes, was no-one's idea of entertainment and I was left to switch from a desert island to Film Foundation kids getting caught by crime and grime in an urban sprawl all the while proving themselves to be both plucky and poor. This was my kind of thing and I sucked it all in until I was dragged kicking and screaming to eat, sleep or, for some stupid reason, breathe fresh air.

Video voyeur

'You know, with good quality erotic entertainment you gotta get a feel of the cassette, don't be shy about getting to know the taut feel and look of a tape, following it up with the slow insertion into the slot ... Solace, you have to look beyond the packaging. Never mind the format feel the quality. Good slogan, eh?'

On a nearly daily basis Randy tried to offload some of the two tons of VHS erotica that were forming some twisted – sure, perverted – pile at the back of the shop. Such was the rate of his acquisition of rarities and exclusive home-mades that the fat little queen was positively oozing celluloid.

'Out with the old, in with the new, out with the old, in with the new ... yep, sex is still possible when you are old and redundant, you just have to make sure you keep yourself oiled and dust free. You could last for just as long.'

Randy was proud of his esoteric collection which would have all been top shelf if he had had enough top shelves to go around. Having said that, he did try to grade them according to some kind of morality, to some degree of accessibility.

'That's correct, no children or animals were harmed in the making of these films. Everybody was taken care of.'

When pressed about the nature of some of the tapes which had no sleeve or artwork of any sort, just a cataloguing number, Randy was pretty evasive it has to be said and it's also worth pointing out that these tapes were always hardest to reach – either beyond anyone's height or buried beneath a mountain of seldom viewed *Electric Blues*.

'These are the equivalent of a well-known director's first film: film school, low budget and black and white of course. Like *The Grandmother* or early Jarman, that kind of thing but with a little less horror or angst. Many of these films are collectors' items and I have built myself a good database of interested clients. I can put your name on the list if you want.'

It sounded to me when Randy talked like this and refused to look me in the eyes, his coiffured head looking the other way as soon as the tapes were mentioned, that I might as well take myself off to the authorities and get listed if I was to sign up for any kind of club that Randy had going. My tastes were pretty simple, low-level and innocuous. I liked my erotica to reassure me that I still had desire to erect myself, to still have some surge and urge. It's not that I didn't try some of the harder stuff – I tried tugging to *Zoo Show* and *Paraplegic*

Playthings but they didn't really mesh the cerebral with the sexual which after a while is what you crave. If I had to see one more window cleaner meets bored housewife with a clothing problem I would go limp. In the end some of the films he foisted on me were completely uninvolving. Bored, I just ended up watching rather than taking part.

Randy liked to think he knew every customer in his shop within five minutes of watching them interact with his stock.

'Whether a guy is going to suck socks or beat himself blue with a chair leg, you get the idea pretty quickly. They don't even have to speak or pick up a tape. It's the way they browse, walk, fondle or not fondle themselves. In this business you learn how to watch without looking. What do I care what they like? If I've got it, I'll sell it. It's as simple as that. Whatever's wrong has already taken place and Lord knows people are fucked up well before they come in here. This here is a dispensary. You take what you will or must have from here and it may or may not cure or pure your ills. Always read the small print. Nothing is permitted, everything is allowed. Yeah, I know, I borrowed that from somewhere.'

Video grizzly

When you watch on your own you don't really watch solo. There are accompaniments and companions. It would be easy to become a victim of my own circumstance, become a stereotype of the cliché, that sort of thing. You've seen it, heard about it and no doubt had a checklist on how to avoid or spot it. Thirty something, neither in nor out, neither up nor down, living alone in a flea-pit flat with limited practical and domestic skills. Broken family life – usually by messy divorce except in my case by statistically premature deaths in close sequence to each other.

I remember . . . No . . .

That's why . . . No. Let's stick to the picture we've already seen, many times over. Lonesome man with no job and poor social skills squanders time and life with peculiarly male activities. He is splayed out in a darkened room with MSG snacks piled on his fat stomach, one hand on the remote, the other down his rank trousers, fingers curling optimistically around the first erection of the day. If he's got money there'll be beer and cigarettes and if he's skint there will still be rolling tobacco. The scene is set.

I can be that. I can set that scene and have done. I have filled the sink high with plates encrusted with mould; held glasses up to the light that have been stuffed with pizza crusts, fag ends and soiled tissues and watched how the light somehow diffuses through the congealed mess. I have not touched the bathroom with domestic fluids for long periods of time so that the dark marks spread out to become bleak foul-smelling patches; so that the seat of the toilet no longer moves, stuck by its own juices to the enamel. I can do that. I can leave the sheets unwashed until it feels like they will snap in half when I pull them over me on a bitter winter night. There is no smell. It is beyond smell. The next layer of fluid and dead skin has grown around me and the bed-crumbs have taken on new partners to create life forms that crawl under me as I sleep. I have wrapped myself in my own semen, spreading it like paste, to glue the sheets to my ruined body . . .

The truth is I have been this and now I am not. I am not fat but have been bloated. I have lived in a foul den and now I live in a characterless flat. I have grown up and become comfortable with my discomfort. What does it matter anyway? How the room was, how the room is? When you are in the video world, when you are a voyeur in the emporium, a VHS aficionado of lost films and recreational memories, then how clean your sink has become matters only as much as you want it to matter.

In the only photograph that is left my calm, quiet mother is hardly there. She is there as a shadow, a miscued and blurred snapshot, a slender streak either entering or leaving the room. It is difficult to know. If you can't remember something imagine it. Such adventure. She served us hot teacakes and orange juice and my father put out a hand to brush her waist. A soft 'thanks' and the music from the television lifted a crescendo just at the right moment.

I live here. After all these years, I live here. The gentle touch of a mother healing some wound; the violent shove of a father as I am disavowed for lewd and perverse behaviour. Such memory is simultaneous. It co-ordinates the rush of the varied past, creating a pincer movement on the present. Grizzly Adams brewed up coffee as mother poured some tea. I stretched out on the couch in the flat and watched them both at home. In our suburban life we were at one with our nature. We grunted our thanks, rushed for the teacakes and slurped our tea while even my father tried to move quickly before everything was eaten and my sister for a moment dangled precariously on one knee and we all howled. In his natural home Grizzly was a refreshingly domestic man laughing as some critter had a go at stealing his beans cooking slowly on the open fire deep in the mountain woods. I want to be there.

When the night has worn on, as neighbours' beats and voices have slowed, I am able to stop the video and lean back on the couch. Around me is not the scattering of debris that might be expected of one such as me. There are no pizza cartons or beer bottles; no tissues or towels. Now after all the rush and fuss, the joyful noise and the wrecked hullabaloo, there is an uneasy peace. An awkward stillness, an eerie hiatus between the storm of youth and the bitter truth of approaching middle age. The mayhem of the crowd has been replaced by the quiet of the loner. From a flat filled to the gunnels with gurning partying strangers taking advantage of my brief financial inheritance to only my own voice repeating words or phrases that make no sense as I withdraw from intoxication into a room that has been stripped bare, a jolt of minimalism.

I colour my own present now with a touch of the past. I don't bother to get undressed to have sex with myself. I can lie where I have been all night and squeeze myself. No-one is going to come in and complain about my state or turn their noses up at the smell of me or the sight of me getting flushed, my eyes glued on the screen. The tingle is not the same. Of course it's not. You can't go back. But back I go. The bearded man seems a trifle unpleasant now, his machismo not nearly as attractive as it had been to such early desire. But he is man enough, outline muscled enough to spur me on to the next thing. A cut-up fantasy like they always are, a quick change – a delicate insertion of the tape as Randy would say – and I am with the Amazonian women that Randy has so skilfully found for me. As always he works miracles with my memory. I remember and he supplies. The toned and natively dressed seem more Hollywood than Amazonian, but it is enough. The present is enough. The past is too much. There is a balance to be had.

Like other solo men I have found ways to keep on keeping on, to grasp encouragement when it is served to me on a plate drizzled with new-male clichés. *Are you in touch with yourself?* Yeah, fuck you. I throb with the best of them, mate. Like other solo sensitive men I have even been tempted by spiritual reassurance when it has been offered in the street or on screen and have dismissed it like all the other panaceas and spiritual cure-alls that are there, wired or hired, for one such as me. Like other solo men I drift off to sleep with the fuzz of static dancing in front of my eyes.

A job to do

'What do I do? If anybody asks, I say I'm an artist. That covers just about everything.'

'Cute, but I was asking you if you needed any spare cash?'

Randy and I had been talking while he carried tape towers from the entrance inside the shop. 'I just got a job lot of family stuff in and I'm having to clear the erotic stuff to make room. Typical, I was expecting it tomorrow but it came early. Story of my life, premature baldness, premature ejaculation and now premature deliveries.'

It was a good question and one which I took a moment

to think about. When I was orphaned some years ago I was left some money, taxed and tearful but still a tidy, shoebox size (six) dollop of money. As a result I don't think I slept for six months and for sure I had a good time, I just can't remember it. I partied and fucked myself into a delirium so chaotic that I didn't know who I was. Ho hum. Yeah, so fucking what I hear the cry go out. Could be there was a breaking point when I was hanging out of my window coked up so much my body was making the window vibrate. I was shouting something to do with loving everybody and how the whole world should come and party with all these wonderful people around me. Of course you know enough without knowing me one iota that I no longer love anybody and those wonderful people are long since gone. Only the glass marks on the mantelpiece remain. That's a tear-jerker, for sure, and I don't buy those.

Could be there was a moment of clarity when I found myself fucking some man's hairy ass while a woman was sitting on my face. There was so much movement – the thrusting of hips, the licking of tongues, the pawing and clawing at skin and bone – that I got dizzy then nauseous and had to break off and throw up on the floor. When I raised myself out of my fugue I was lying in my own vomit watching the two people I had been attached to still going at it.

It all just stopped, there was no miraculous intervention,

nobody came along and saved me from myself. You fall into dark water and wave for help and when no-one comes along you either drown or your wave becomes a stroke and somehow you swim to safety.

Yeah? Well that didn't happen either. I didn't escape anything. People escaped me. Left me when I didn't understand their garbled mess, their emphasis on how we all should dress. I was too dark to see the light. They left me to myself because I was told I operated best alone; that I, Solace, possessed an uncanny ability to survive all that life had thrown at me.

Anyone for treading water?

'What would I have to do for it?'

Randy let the last box of tapes drop on to the floor. His bald head was red with exhaustion and an unpleasant, acrid aroma wafted out from his armpits. It was possible he had been at least cute when he was younger and one time I caught sight of a bunch of photographs of a fat but cute kid in sepia tones laughing as he rocked on some horse. When I mentioned it, he seemed embarrassed, said he had been tidying up some old family things and rushed to squirrel the portraits away. As if that was something to be shy about. I'd worry if people didn't know how they looked when they were younger.

'I see. Don't worry, you won't be paid in kind. You'll

get paid in cash. Minimum wage will be the maximum for you, my boy.'

'Okay, but what would I have to do for it?'

He looked at me with despairing eyes, a sudden surge of stress sharpening his tone, narrowing his stare.

'Do? What the fuck do you think you will do? I would like you to start buying in pet food for when the whole video business goes tits up and I'm left weeping on to metal discs that would be better served as coasters or school art projects. Do, Solace? Tell me, what have your years of self-education in the art of fuck-all learned you exactly? Take a wild guess.'

'Stock the shelves?'

Randy gave me a look that he usually reserved for people asking a) have you got the latest Van Ram movie or b) have you got this on DVD?

'The shelves aren't stocked at the Video Emporium, Solace, they are *adorned*. A subtle perhaps ostentatious difference but not to me. Supermarkets are stocked, warehouses are supplied however this haven from the multinational is adorned. Adorned with what you may ask.'

'I didn't.'

'It doesn't matter. What matters is that I have been bequeathed an incredible gift by an old friend who sadly passed away some months ago. He was rich having got filthy with the pink pound, cashing in on the boom on safe sex paraphernalia in the eighties. A sad but essential market. Anyway, over the years he bought every commercial 'family' based film or TV series that came out. Not only that, he had good contacts in the US, Canada and the New World and managed to find things on or transferred on to video – lost episodes, unwanted episodes, outtakes etc. – that few outside the production company had seen. This was a quirk of his personality. He liked to source the obscure and have the unattainable. The more normal, value-affirming the better. If I remember accurately, a lot of his boyfriends fitted that description – the unattainable I mean. We were good friends for a long time and he knew that I would love to have the collection but would be unable to pay market value for them and so, I am blessed indeed, he left the whole collection to me.

'Hence the boxes.'

'Indeed. Your job, should you choose to accept it, hardly a chore one must say, is to adorn the shelves with the likes of Renny and Flow in the Australian Film Foundation 1956 film *The Retrieving Kids* which sees Renny, Flow and their traveller family making incredible structures out of garbage from the dump they live close to. Or the Robinson Crusoe series, you know the black and white one that everybody tries to remember the music to. So elegiac and poignant. Less elegiac but even more collectable are the outtakes that have the poetic Crusoe scratching himself and chain-smoking reefers. It's all there. And so much more. These shelves are not to be stocked but adorned with possibilities, the hopes and cruelties of humanity, the society of our spectacle.'

Randy shut his eyes at this point and was lost in some series, in some film reverie. With his eyes still shut he whispered, 'I wouldn't ask just anyone, you know. I would rather kill myself with the strain than ask someone who just wanted to watch Van Ram all night.'

That wasn't me and Randy knew it. I wasn't sure about his rapture, his camp overture, but he was right. When dripped dry of the erotica I would always head for the family section in the shop quickly skirting the classic horror section.

'Okay, I'd be honoured. Free rental on all that I adorn?'
'Done.'

His/story of my sex

I tried to ground myself with images that made me fly. It was a foolish attempt, like the creation of a cumbersome machine that was never going to take off. I ricocheted out of my flat bouncing off walls and stood vibrating on the landing.

My last girlfriend noticed it.
'You tremble when we fuck.'
'I get nervous. I'm sensitive.'

'Oh.'

That was some time ago. My last boyfriend had noticed it to.

'You tremble when you suck.'

'I get overwhelmed with emotion sometimes.'

'Oh.'

You can imagine how this went down, especially when the boyfriend/girlfriend scenario kicked home, dragging some pretty past the groans, moans and bass thump of my neighbours before they were enveloped by my flat in its various states, none of which was generally attractive, of chaos. Still, at least most of the men and a few of the women didn't care about that. Maybe they were too out of it to notice, to care about the feng shui of my living space – when I was playing the dating game all that mattered was that I had some alcohol, condoms and emergency porn. But they noticed the shaking, the trembling of limbs that would set off the ashtray on the table and have them reaching to steady themselves with a firm hold on the couch.

'My, you're a passionate one.'

'Steady, mate, you're not gonna come just yet are ye?'

By the time I was out of my partying phase and into seclusion I had heard it all. I was pinned up as a sensitive amouroso or shot down in flames as a weirdo, a pale thin ghost who wasn't alive but rather existed, a plod along some urban deserted street. Thanks. To one and all. Thanks for the memories which come shuddering back as I stand on the landing, trying to root my self in the present, anybody else's present. Thanks for the brief seconds of orgasmic joy, thanks for having a body that I wanted to devour. Thanks for not coming back.

Maybe I had one night stand written all over me. That's just the way it was, the way it had panned out. I made my own bed and now I was the only one lying in it. Of course, there was plenty of time in between tapes to work out how and why things had gone wrong, why I wasn't holed up with lust, nesting with the love of my life. The simple truth was that no-one stuck around long enough to hear it all, hear the history of my sex, the nitty gritty of who I have been. They could probably tell pretty quickly. There was little that was straightforward and little that was sufficiently bent. I was falling between two camps and fighting and batting for both sides. And yes getting shot by them. Time, intent, promises, delusion. I will do this, I will become that.

None of it truly worked. No-one said I was a hard-hearted fuck-up who needed to get in touch with himself; no-one said it was okay to lose it on and off for two decades, with each moment of grief, each personal disaster, each love hereafter. In the end the truth of it was that no-one said much at all. This island's mine? Your island. Fine.

*

Sex exploded inside me. One moment I was cute and innocent with a tingle as a foretaste and the next I was a greased-up monster with a purple swelling that broke through the tightest material. This is textbook of course. Nothing was under my control. Sex and sexuality weren't emerging with the grace of a young deer staggering to his feet with the nurturing licks of his mother to steady and reassure. I found myself drop-kicked into a world of desire that I didn't know I was ready for.

I had my first orgasm on my grandmother's soft bedspread. I remember the bedcover because I could go further back and recall wrapping myself in it when we stayed over, camping out with a torch under the soft material. This was the virginal pop that has never been forgotten. Maybe it's some male equivalent, who knows and no doubt who cares, but the intensity was enough to make me retch with surprise and to reel back, trousers around my ankles on to the bed. 'What is that?' Yes, I had been that well prepared. Maybe I was an early developer but I don't recall any wildlife talk from my parents nor video presentation from nervous teachers. It just happened, there and then while my grandmother was having tea with my parents, while my goody two-shoes siblings were supping home-made lemonade.

I like to think I was the black sheep of the family. I did my best to make sure that happened and the soft bedcover was just the start. *A Boy's Own* story no doubt, a girl's guide to the horror of the nascent male sexuality probably, but within a couple of years I had lost more than my virginity. Inhibition soon went as, teenagers, we rucked and dry fucked on beaches in summer, swung with zeal from one fumble to the next – the boy on girl proudly on display for all to see, the boy on boy kept hidden behind the sheds while we pretended to sharpen our tools.

Of course it all came to a head and GA would have been appalled. He aimed to live in harmony with all creatures, man as well as beast up there in those secluded mountains and he would have hated to see and hear the rancour and heartache that rushed on into our family. But let's keep this short because there was nothing long-winded about it. I pushed and pushed, kicking down doors with my erupting temper, absorbing the drinks cabinet even after a lock had been put on and when I brought back X one night to explore our male on male sexuality it was too far for my father, for everybody I guess. There was turning a blind eye and there was shoving something hot and sticky deep down someone's throat. X and I tried to fuck and I yelped so much at the hot friction that . . . sure, my father came in maybe expecting us to be yelping with pleasure over our train sets – okay, maybe not – and instead sees me splayed out, my beautiful buns in the air.

It's nothing really. You walk with schisms, hand in

hand; shit happens because it has to. All of it. At the time there was drama and more drama; parental meltdown occurred along with the 'get out of this house' kind of thing. Anyway by sixteen the rest of the world seemed like a great place to be. I said nothing to my parents as I left, slurred a goodbye to the drinks cabinet and my shellshocked brother and sister and shed many tears for Grizzly Adams who would no longer have anyone to watch him save all those poor critters.

On the shelf

This is what I do. If people ask – which they don't – then I tell them I adorn shelves. I'm first assistant to a retailer of reassurance. Randy seems to be happy as long as something sells. He grabs the money any which he can and after a few months in the shop I can see why. People browse but don't buy and this always drives him crazy, mad enough in fact to cough unpleasantly behind people who have been staring at a cover a beat too long.

'They'll come in with a friend, laugh at the horror section, look serious in the foreign language section and then fall apart when it comes to family shelves. "Oh . . . my . . . god . . . have you seen this . . . do you remember this . . . Oh . . . my . . . god . . . I must have been about seven when I saw this, every Sunday curled-up on the couch watching and believing everything I saw . . . everybody else hated it . . . but . . . oh . . . my . . . god . . . I loved it." And while people are immersing themselves in their past, bringing it up like a private smell nobody else can get to the shelves and some days, I swear, the shop can be empty everywhere apart from the family section and it'll be like a chorus line from the people-free musical section where a whole line of so called customers will be ooohing and aahing as they rediscover how it felt to be entertained by family values.'

This was the spleen he vented on a daily basis made worse by fewer sales but I had already seen another side to Randy, actually another two sides. Firstly, he railed against the sentimental journeys stopping for too long at multiple copies of *Swiss Family Robinson* or the *Partridge Family* but I caught him looking a few times, a smile pushing out from his fat lips, a thin tear streak making its way down his jowls when he saw some loner freak blanching when they came to a rare copy of the first Lassie film and rushing to Randy just about bowling him into the back shop. There was then an eruption of thank-yous and laughter and the tears of joy Randy shed would inevitably become part of his cash flow. As a bystander to people being reunited with something from their past it was a strange ritual to witness; it was both knowing and innocent; there was both a mawkishness to the reunion and a heartfelt and spontaneous celebration to the smallness of the event.

Sure, some bystander.

'I know.' I heard Randy reassure a fifty-something client

as he packed up three tapes of *The Sun Seekers*, a sixties tale about surf and drug life on Bondi that must have been pretty cutting edge for its time with its hip music and cool blond dudes hanging out with other cool blond dudes, 'This is a homoerotic masterpiece that was way before its time. It got pulled after one short series because ABS couldn't stomach the cult following it had attracted, the critical newspaper reviews that declared it a celluloid cancer on the skin of our nation or the fact the actors seemed to be enjoying themselves as they made it. It's beautifully shot, sweeping pans across the sunset, close-ups on the reefer smokers as they laid back on the sand. This is a purchase to cherish my friend. You must look after those memories or they just go, getting lost in the horror of the present, becoming submerged by everyday detritus that stops us from living usefully in the past. Friend, when the present isn't all it's cracked up to be, these moving images we sell give you the opportunity to make a stand . . .'

The fifty-something shopper might have had to endure a lot more of Randy's philosophy if he hadn't managed to squeeze in the class line 'it's for a friend' and quickly made his way out the shop with Randy left misty-eyed and fired up, declaring that this was the best job in the world. Sure. That's what it was like. Feast and famine. Tirades and triumphs. The reassurance business was full of ups and downs I learnt.

The other side to Randy, the side which he stays

remarkably mute about, lies behind the door to the back shop, the keys to which hang on a hook under the till. When he thinks I am absorbed in adorning his shelves, he lifts the keys off the hook and disappears for half an hour or so and then returns closing and locking the door behind him and then replacing the key. His movements are full of the memory, like his muscles and limbs would go through the whole procedure without his consciousness present. This was something he had been doing for a while and who knows how much time he had spent there when there was no-one to squint over the shelves at him. The door chime, a poor electronic version of the Radio Shack Family theme tune, would warn him of any customers. Of course anything could be happening behind that door. Knowing Randy anything probably was.

His/story of my sex: part two

Nobody told me anything. Nobody told anyone anything. If you hid your injury no-one got hurt. If you kept shtoom you didn't look dumb. Some philosophy. Doesn't even rhyme. My parents must have known they were on to a loser when they caught me listening at my sister's door trying to work out why she was crying, sobbing the kind of tears that were being muffled by an old teddy already worn to its last thread. Still. Something soft. Something reassuring.

'Solace, that's not polite.'

When they caught me watching my brother playing with his soldiers, peering past the slight opening I had made with his bedroom door, they shook their heads as though it confirmed something they felt they knew about me.

'Solace, he's quite happy playing by himself.'

Later at night, much later at night when the house groaned its release of ageing woods and decaying stone; when the fridge shuddered and the radiators bubbled with unbled air, I had my young ear to their door and heard their squabbles pushed into pillows, their tense silences broken by the heavy turning of their bodies back to back on the matrimonial bed.

For sure I swore that would never be me. I exploded out of my inert upbringing and made a movie that had already been made. This was its pitch, queered then cleared. It's now in post-production. You've got sixty seconds. Picture this:

> Solace [cute and highly sexed] runs away from home to the big city.
> Has no place to stay and no money.
> He turns tricks in the park.
> And gets beaten up before finding an older man who takes care of him.
> Solace gets tired of men and makes himself available to women.

- Many turn him down but one stays with him who introduces him to a party crowd.
- He parties for as long as he can and longer than most.
- Eventually exhausted by it all with creeping paranoia and incipient delusion he holes up in an apartment, alone, discarded and damaged.
- [Here's the denouement] With what's left of his mind he reconstructs a sense of self worth, of individual grace from shards of memory [that aren't necessarily all his own].

'You've got yourself a hit, mister, an art-house biopic that everyone will warm to, that every parent will warn to.'

The ending hasn't been reached at least not for me and hence not for you. But in scenes 5, 12 and 19 of my history the ending was uneasily reached first for my mother (cancer), then my father (heart attack). It was scene 19 however that stretched the film's narrative arc, that had viewers at test screenings scratching their heads and turning the notes they had made earlier in the film. This is, what? A true story, a magical-realist fantasy with a timeline twist and darkly comic feel? The producers will be nervous and the writer, incognito of course, will squirm in his seat. This is the writer's first job. This is his big break and he'll think of all those hours he has put in, locked into a stinking apartment that has only creeps and bleeps for neighbours. He has not given into the strain and pain of creating another world, the diuretic flow of his consciousness has found life in characters so close to home, to his heart and mind. It has to work. They should believe.

The brother and sister in a scene that has to be saved for the end are twisted beyond recognition by a car crash so violent the car no longer resembles an estate, so concertina'd is it by the force of the crash, into a brick wall. The impact had crushed the organs of the sister who was driving and the arching arm of a streetlight, uprooted by the force of the crash had spiked into the brother, impaling him deep in the earth. It was some hours before they were cut free and some days before Solace was tracked down and given the news.

Each time he was given bad news he found a new landing place. The only photograph that was left has stayed with him – sometimes propped up against a bedside lamp, sometimes briefly held in a cheap frame from a charity shop until some drunk – often him – has picked it up, laughed and thrown it against a wall. Call that a memory! Now, in what may well be a final landing place, it is held by the sticky glue of old alcohol, its tone fading, its glossy coating scratched by tiny fragments of glass. (In moments revisited time and time again, I could see my brother and sister lying still, their skin glistening with thick slicks of glass flowing in blood.)

The film closes with a brief kiss as Solace's lips touch the fading image and for just a moment the mechanical pulse, the electronic thud and the clattering fingertips of his neighbours pause and everything turns sepia, locked in memory tarnished embrace, but still, somehow, a childhood caught, an adult released. The End. Cut.

Not quite

I've called them Lick and Spit and they have become firm friends. I don't know what it is about this life that I've led, this life you've read which could be better, could have had less sham and more decent truth; could have at least sought some honest emotion rather than a fabricated lotion applied to such obvious wounds; a makeover cream indeed that will cover all blemishes. A Story. No warts at all. Believe it or not. But still, Lick and Spit have been good to me, they treated me like no-one has ever treated me in my life: not distant parents with their hands-off care; not my brother or sister with their who the hell are you stares; not my partying friends who may or may not have moved on and carried on but are now minus one if they have even noticed. Ouch. And even Randy, good old Randy who has kept the flag flying for all things technicoloured and sympathetic: he lives in a world free of irony, a truly dramatic and wholesome place that fights to preserve against the onslaught of forgetfulness and post-modern creativity. God fucking save us from that. But the buck stops with Randy because the fuck didn't start with him. He wanted me to swing as far I could in his direction; he gave me a job and hoped I would give him at the very least a ... Sure, maybe things would have got that far. What the fuck. I've been through all kinds of weather, what's another shower. Bring on the deluge. Bring on the next storm that fate may forecast on my behalf. Not much death left except my own; not much sex left except my own. But then, just what you least expect, just when you least expect it. Randy would be singing that when he found out. No doubt.

I sneaked in while he was on one of his extended Friday lunches with a bunch of rotund retros who liked to gather and talk about the good times of bath houses and chic houses; of Fire Island and that lively cottage on the coast. There could have been anything in there. He was running a hideous trade of bootleg porn that saw innocents slaughtered and buggered into oblivion; he kept a sex slave that he visited several times a day either to feed or to fuck, his podgy prick quivering as it entered some emaciated refugee. How could I think that, how could the purveyor of reassurance possibly have been involved with such illicit habits? Because from what little I've learned and sure what little I know, when it comes to sex anything and everything is possible. Whether it's on display for all to see or kept locked away, it's already there. It's already happened. What the hell were the Dark Ages for anyhow? When it's all over including the shouting, the tears, the self-loathing, people will run for cover and seek some kind of reassurance. These people, all our people, will binge their pain, eat their soul or daydream their aspirations. For me, it takes the combination of the only photograph that is left and a bearded mountain man to quell my terrors. I've tried everything else. And for Randy it was a blow-up world, a blow-up family.

They were all shapes and sizes; ages and ethnic backgrounds. It truly was a diverse collection he had created. The back shop wasn't a large area and I had kind of expected just more of the same, the overspill from the shop, videos waiting to be adorned. There were a few tapes and a few original ad posters and life-size cut-outs of forgotten or never known stars but the small room was otherwise filled with the blank stare of sex dolls. It was kind of eerie. As far as I had known these dolls were the preserve of stag nights and Secret Santa presents, where the object was not the gift but the ritual of humiliation that would follow from smirks to out and out riding and simulation at the end of the night when the drink had kicked in. I guess, however, as is the way with these things, there would be a few men thinking the end of the night wouldn't be a total waste if they ended up alone with some pretty asian-style doll.

Of the two dozen or so dolls, most had their faces turned to the wall, their bloated bodies slightly askew as though drink rather than deflation had taken its toll. One or two lay where Randy had left them or perhaps was expecting them when he next jangled his keys and turned his lock. It was obvious from these pert and well-inflated examples that Randy liked his dolls on the boyish man side, but with some muscle definition which in the case of the most prostrate doll in the middle room had been carefully defined using a thin black marker. It was obvious too from what we all know of Randy so far, that although I am sure these dolls come in many variations, the puckered rubber hole between the two bubble buttocks was going to be the only hole that mattered to him.

When I turned round one dark-skinned doll, it was a shock to find a familiar face. When I turned round a pink-skinned inflation I met another slightly less familiar but still recognisable face. In fact this particular face had lingered at the desk a week or so ago as Randy tried to convince him to buy a studio cut of *Alpine Adventure: A Family gets lost in the Wilderness*. It seems Randy loved his customers, appreciated them more than his short temper and irascible capitalist bent indicated.

The security camera had been used to snap the cute, the vaguely manly and the attractively weird men who had come into the shop and then, with a little digital dexterity, their faces had been printed on to acetate before being carefully fixed on to the dolls. It was clear that Randy liked to get much closer to his clientele than I would ever have guessed. The greased-up feel to some of the latex was testament to that and somewhat endearingly in moments of passion he appeared to exorcise some sexual ghost, some need to get closer, by reversing their head as he pounded his little rocket into the reinforced aperture, the doll's face was in his own, warm lips on warm latex. No wonder he looked more relaxed when he left the back room.

And yes, in case you are wondering, you are perfectly right and have asked the question I would have asked. If you have spent a lot of time with someone and discovered what they did for pleasure, who the hell wouldn't ask?

And finally

So I have house guests. It's been a long time since I have had house guests and the ones I have had in the past have usually been inadvertent crashers, too drunk or drugged to move from the floor; too desperate not to leave without a rub from someone. Sure, with such house guests it's never exactly been ironed dressing-gowns and freshly squeezed orange juice in the morning, but after a while it's not hard to crave something more, something that can kick you out of the torpor of ritual, the humdrum, the diet of memory . . .

Enough is enough. This slice of life has served its purpose. One sorry tale with some pathetic twists and turns of fate is very much like any other. I don't want to blow things up into what they are not. Actually, that's not true, that's exactly what I want to do. The girl, Lick – the only female doll I could find – and the boy, Spit – unused possibly because of slow puncture in his buttock – have been liberated from their secretive incarceration in Randy's back room and they have come to live with me. From the look they give me, they seem pretty happy about it and consistently so. 'You wanna stay with that balding, podgy fruit who gets the squeals when it comes to the female side of things? A hole's a hole for a' that. I'm not fixed. Come with me and I'll love you both more than myself.'

They have no baggage attached, and they don't just travel light, they are light. Lick and Spit are not looking at me wondering what I will do next, they do not swerve away from me when I go near them and they do not tell me that what I feel is wrong and that I will never amount to any good. Lick and Spit are the best thing that has ever happened to me. They laugh at my jokes, comfort me if my memory's knives get too sharp for my blunted defences. If I have finally cracked under the pressure of this life, its burden still present from the past, they will at least stand by me. Their egos haven't been inflated.

Raul and Petra, Uri and Renzo

Scene 1

FOR URI, MARCATA was a town viewed initially through the blurred lens of jet-lag. Uri had got the news late of the final go-ahead for the commission of *The Energy Cult* from his agent and after a day of hectic web surfing and phoning he got on the first flight he could to the US. Touching down in Eureka, California, customs had been edgy about some of the recording equipment he was carrying but he had travelled enough both to the States and Latin America to know to carry the right permissions and credentials. He did however appear nervous going through security with the micro cameras and audio recorders and noticeably blanched when one officer lifted the main camera out of its tiny case and drawled knowingly, 'Yeah, I could use this for my wife. Sure like to know why she's got such a big smile on her face when I come home from work.' Uri laughed this moment off as soon as he passed into the arrivals hall. On the phone to his agent, he made the point he was keen to stress to everybody he talked to. He was here to listen, to observe, to record. Not to judge.

Renzo Capaldi had worked, doing the sound recording and taking B-roll footage, with Uri on two previous projects: *Colombian Nights*, a documentary about the ongoing drug war, and the award-winning *A Spy in the Cab*, the fly-on-the-wall two-parter about life inside a yellow cab that had made Uri's name. Renzo cancelled with little hesitation his proposed work on an undercover abortion film in Ireland. He was keen once filming was finished on this to head south to the coast, and remind Uri of another project they had talked about; a film with the self-explanatory title of *Where Have All The Dudes Gone? The Missing Surfing Generation.*

The pair – renowned documentary maker Uri and Renzo, experienced cameraman and sound recordist – met at Newark and greeted each other with a hug, a continental kiss and a street handshake.

Scene 2

Raul, a 52-year-old second-generation Mexican-American, is sitting at his Yamaha keyboard in the Yoga Studio. He has been awake since just after dawn. The Marcata climate can be variable and unpredictable in early summer but it is warm enough for him to be wearing just his shorts. Most people are surprised to learn of his age when they encounter this lithe, muscular man with his mane of jet-black hair. In his book, *The Energy of Body Music*, he extols the importance of physical condition as benefiting the spiritual self. 'It's not,' he writes, 'just a matter of being what you eat; we must take a holistic view of our condition – diet is just one part. Our breath, our energy, our sexual life all play an important part in creating our true unhindered self.'

Raul likes to run through his music early in the day. Here, we get a rare opportunity to see him at work on his latest composition. 'I prefer to make my own music for each couple's weekend. Too many practitioners use pre-recorded music over and again and this depersonalises the experience.'

A kind of aural wallpaper, you mean?

'Exactly. The music shouldn't be in the background. I'm not interested in creating just another new age soundtrack. There are plenty of those already. I'm much more interested in 'old age' – recreating sacred music with samples from Gamelan rhythms to Tibetan singing bowls and everything in between.'

Do you play any of the instruments yourself?

'I'm not a musician. I prefer to think of myself as a technical facilitator. Taking these ancient and sacred sounds and formulating them in such a way that the music becomes like a companion, sometimes reflective, sometimes energised, for the workshop participants. Our couples are usually very happy with the music. It's a soundtrack to their weekend and I am delighted for them to take away a personalised copy.'

The Yoga Studio itself with its smooth wooden floors, white walls and elaborate, erotically-shaped incense holders is designed with acoustics in mind and when, during workshops, the three sets of French windows are closed, the pulsing rhythms of what sound like Native American drums fill the room.

Scene 3

Uri keeps his eyes shut for most of the journey from Eureka airport to Marcata. In *Colombian Nights*, he had insisted that the minder who picked him up at the airport blindfold him and Renzo so that they could travel impaired to the hinterland. On his arrival in the remote location, a humid conflagration of jungle and hot scrub, one of the cartel's lieutenants had been impressed by his attitude, his preparation and it was considered one of the film's highlights the warm embrace Uri received from the soldier. In *A Spy in the Cab*, his agent had arranged for him to be picked up by a succession of cabs ordered to his hotel in Manhattan at different times of the day and night. Posing as a partially sighted guest who had to rely on an extendable white cane when he was in unfamiliar territory he was led anywhere he wanted to go and when in the cab he maintained the impression.

Why, Uri?

'When I'm starting a new work I don't like to have my vision cluttered with visual detritus. The perceived visual impairment helps me see things a lot more clearly and people always behave differently if they believe you can't see properly.'

At the only hotel in Marcata – a quaint mix of the gothic and folksy – Renzo helps him out of the cab and guides him to the reception desk where he deals with the checking in, lifts the baggage, negotiates the small lift for the two of them and their belongings and even leads him to his room. The receptionist at the hotel, which is to serve as their base while they recce for suitable locations, seems quite taken with the two of them.

'I can't imagine what it must be like for him. Surrounded by people who can see things he can't.'

Scene 4

Petra, a 47-year-old Californian, is walking around the large, mature garden of the *Spiritual Home*, the name she gave the house two decades ago when she moved from Haight-Ashbury, San Francisco to this sleepy town. Before Petra took over, the garden had mostly been neglected, the lawn concreted over and the property a virtual dumping ground for wrecked off-road vehicles and machine parts.

'You wouldn't have believed this place. It looks so different now. I nearly cried when I saw what I had bought with the money. I mean, don't get me wrong, I was ready to leave, nothing was the same anymore, but I had to really stay focused on what the house could become rather than the way it was. And you know, I kinda like that as a metaphor for a lot of things. For myself and Raul being part of our generation's exodus from the city but also for those couples coming from all over the state and country. Our couples come in all shapes and forms, orientations and repressions, but nothing in life has to remain fixed. That's one of the many things we teach as part of Loving and Healing courses. The energy that we found to transform this house into the Spiritual Home is akin to the energy we all have potentially in ourselves. The question for us and for our couples is how much do we want to use that energy to awaken ourselves to.'

Petra walks through the first of several flower arches which have been placed at intervals along the winding path leading to the house.

'This is what I do when Raul's composing music. I like to walk around the garden and make sure everything is just the way it should be, just the way it looks in the brochure, on the website. That's very important.'

You've found that advertising on the web is important?

'It's crucial. The website allows us to reach people who are isolated in terms of geography and deprived in terms of their local amenities. We get people from San Francisco who have been told by a friend of a friend about the work we do here and that's great but I love it, absolutely adore it, when we get a couple from some southern town where there is no sense of anything being alternative, or from some inner city where people are just too scared to explore their neighbourhood never mind themselves. So, I like to make sure that when people arrive, what they saw online is what they are going to get.'

Petra steps up on to the decking, sweeping off some soil from the surface with her bare feet. There is a large, round wooden table with eight directors' chairs and beside this is a sunken hot tub lined with carefully tiled images of various eastern deities.

'You know, this is my favourite place in the whole garden. When we first moved here, there was an old pond that actually had the skeletons of frogs still lying in the water. It was awful and we decided that this would be an ideal spot for the hot tub or *Wishing Water* as we like to call it. On a day like today, the evenings can be so beautiful here and after a long, hard-working day we always invite our couples to share some time in the water, a slow unwinding of any residual stress, a gentle gathering of our energy. It can be very moving. I've known people to break down in tears when they are in the Wishing Water.'

Scene 5

Renzo is taking a bath in the old enamel tub that serves the three other rooms on their floor, although it seems that Uri and Raul are the only guests. Uri appears unhappy that Renzo has got in before him.

'Christ, Renzo, I was really looking forward to a long soak. I've been travelling all day.'

'Yeah, I know, I was with you for most of it. Chill, Uri. I'll be done in say half an hour.'

As Uri kicks the door he shouts something unintelligible before returning to his room, this time slamming the door. It is unlikely that Renzo heard the swearing or the door slam. According to his profile, in his twenties he could stay under water for over four minutes and in the warm tropical water of Phuket and Nha Trang he was known by locals as the Sub-Mariner.

'I love the water. Diving into the swell, waiting for a wave, grabbing the sides of the board, standing up somehow in the offshore breeze and then just taking off. It was a really special thing to do and even when I froze my balls off or half drowned on more than one occasion, I still wanted more. It's my thing, you know.'

What about Uri? He doesn't seem very happy.

'Happy? Uri? He always gets nervous before a gig, you

know, before we start filming. He's just the nervous-energy type and sometimes he needs to kick a few things to make himself feel better, like he's more in control. I wouldn't worry about him. He winds himself up like clockwork.'

Renzo doesn't want to talk any more preferring instead to dive back under, communicating with us through a series of air bubbles.

Uri? Are you okay?

There are quite a few bumps and muffled screams coming from behind Uri's bedroom door. The door opens a few centimetres, allowing his arm to reach out and hang up the Do Not Disturb sign. Putting his mouth to the door like that with the toothpaste dribbling down the paintwork, he knows it will make a good shot and of course our cameraman can't resist a tight close-up on his cracked lips. We are getting to know what makes Uri tick. He is, as many people in the industry have said about him, a documentary maker's documentary maker.

'You know. People think making a documentary film is easy. Stick your ass on the wall somewhere then point and click. It's not as simple as that. It's not as mechanical as that. There are lots of documentary makers out there who just rely on effect, on the immediacy of visual impact, gratuitous shock images – or GSIs. Or they get breathy over some less-than-dangerous situation like some gangster or tiger is gonna jump them, when in reality the threat in question is restrained or chained up to some wall. There should be a sense of wonder to what we do, to what we show. Above all, there should be a sense of truth, unalloyed and if necessary uncovered. In some cases, however, we have a duty to point out where truth begins because it's not always easy to know.'

Scene 6

Raul is in the kitchen which opens out on to the decking and the garden beyond. From the studio the droning tones of the singing bowls mix with the sound of the Italian food processor.

Are you happy with the music, Raul?

'Absolutely. I couldn't cook if I wasn't certain the music was just right. I don't like to leave things half done and for me this is the best way to hear the music once I have composed; hearing it from a distance gives me an idea how first-time listeners will hear it.'

The kitchen has been expensively equipped. Most of the appliances are professional quality and European in origin while the solid maple floor and units have been made from regenerated wood sourced not far from Marcata. The wooden gantry with its half a dozen halogen spotlights casting tight pools of light on key surfaces is another local product Raul informs us, as he holds the blender bowl up to the light. He appears to be checking both its colour and texture.

A lot of thought seems to have gone into the kitchen, Raul?

'Absolutely. Years ago when Petra and I first started doing these workshops back in the city, we would always provide good wholesome food. Of course, back then it was big all-in-one-salads with sprouts and pulses and as many leaves as you could jam into one bowl. We've moved on from that now, our tastes and the expectations of our participants have become more sophisticated but the need for good food in a setting like this, in a workshop like this, is essential. I mean it would be totally contradictory to do a long, complex and energising structure in the morning session and then give people burger and fries. It just wouldn't work. You can't make people feel good about themselves by giving them that shit.

What are you making right now?

'I love this. I think it's my favourite. Its a variation on an Italian dish called rotolo and so instead of pasta we have used a potato roulade with the slices of potato mandolined as fine as they can go. And then the filling is just a wonderful mixture of ricotta, pine nuts and spinach. When we serve it we still have the big leafy salad – the leaves grow so well round here – but we also pick up the tempo by dressing the plate with chilli, basil, pesto and a good quality balsamic reduction.

Raul moves to the large Smeg fridge and pulls out three large bunches of asparagus.

'But first things first. Asparagus soup. A gentle but intense aphrodisiac.'

Is that good for you?

The smile is wide and a little mischievous.

'Sure. And it's good for business too.'

Scene 7

'Are you getting this?

Uri is walking out the hotel as Renzo is trying to explain to the shocked receptionist that Uri's eye condition is brought on by long-haul travel.

'It's a strange thing. One moment he can see and the next he can't. Something to do with the air pressure we think.'

'Renzo!'

Marcata's quaint amalgamation of small-town stores and hippie chic dates back to the protracted implosion of the hippie lifestyle and its association with California in general and San Francisco in particular. A whole generation went on the move and scattered themselves all over California with many finding a home in Marcata. They reoriented both their lifestyle and livelihood. This neo-hippie, shifting population established itself side by side with the old logging community and where old-fashioned hardware stores remained new stores selling hemp clothing and organic soap sprung up. While the relationship hasn't always been an easy one, it is generally agreed that the town is a good example of mixed-culture cohabitation.

'Look where we have arrived, Renzo!'

Renzo is adjusting the mini camera he has hidden behind the buckle of his Rancher-style belt.

'You rolling?'

In the digital world this is of course answered by a couple of clicks and a nod from Renzo as he hitches his trousers into place.

'Let's make film!'

Scene 8

Petra is moving slowly around the *Love Room*.

What's so special about this room, Petra?

'Well, you know when we first started, before we built this extension on to the main house, the participants would all sleep, dorm-style in the Yoga Studio. I kinda liked that – we worked, ate and slept all in the same room. It made it like, intense, you know. There would be a few weekends when everybody would be on such a high, so full of energy and love that they would not mind sharing the space and not mind making love with others sleeping in the same room. But times change and although people could be, as we encouraged them to be, as open as they felt comfortable with in the sessions, they would comment at the end that they felt frustrated that they couldn't put into practice what they had been learning. But, it's not just that. We started to get people who were survivors of sexual abuse, couples who had been through a lot, and it was never going to be easy for them to be so open. So we built separate rooms, each one a different price and decided to have one of the rooms really luxurious. This isn't a hotel, it's a house we share with our guests, but the sleeping mats on the floor and eight to a room of bugged-out strangers like we had back in the city sometimes – all the time really – wasn't going to work. We've all moved on.'

Perhaps you could tell us what makes this room so special?

'We want a feeling of peace and security in the house. In The Love Room we wanted to recreate something a little more than that. We like to think of it as a blank canvas, a space where people can make their own impression.'

It's very white, neutral.

'Sure but not sterile. You know I love the mixture of Egyptian cotton and local wood, the smooth textile complimenting the grain of wood like maple and western walnut. I'm a real fan of the Shaker style; beautiful heirloom craftsmanship, elegant lines. We didn't want to make some kind of pink boudoir or purple harem feel that a lot of people go for. We wanted to get away from such bohemian affectation.'

But Shaker was all about purity, wasn't it?

'Purity is in the soul of the beholder. Being pure isn't

necessarily a bad state. Purity of thought, purity of love and purity of action are all part of our energy. I don't accept that purity has repressive overtones – that's a common misconception and something that we have our ancestors to thank for, something that we have organised Western religion at its least tolerant, most restrictive to thank for. If we can recover the innocence of the child in our adult states then I believe we can begin to awaken our energy.'

You've put a lot of thought into this room?

'I understand the notion of feng shui but it's always struck me as a little too fussy. We just wanted to make a beautiful room and I think we have. That's a king-size bed with a good quality meta-orthopaedic mattress; all the wooden furniture – the candy wood bedside cabinets, the Baltic birch table by the window there and the large chest of drawers – are all made for us by an old friend who lived a few a doors down from our house in Haight. Another old friend designed the en suite for us and found that wonderful old bath tub at an auction down in Marcata. The taps and many of the other little touches were sourced by Raul at a house sale near Eureka. So much of the house might look new and modern but most of it is recycled from something old.'

Is there a metaphor there?

'There is, I'm glad you mention that. Raul and myself have transformed ourselves. We were on a journey in

San Francisco, a journey towards a sense of personal truth that got derailed and then delayed for a long time by the oppression of the state, the repression of ourselves, the entertainment of strangers. I'm not looking just to blame a society that has imploded with greed, sexual mortification and a head-on rush to nowhere but we've moved on. We have taken ownership not just of this house but this life and by opening up our home to others we have put ourselves after all this time back on track. The purpose we serve is to serve ourselves and help kindred spirits on their own journey.'

Scene 9

Uri and Renzo are walking around Marcata. There has been some argument as to what they should shoot as background and atmosphere but Uri likes the light and they agree to stop outside *Hemp World: All You Need. Naturally.*

'Marcata. Friday 10.00 a.m. Here in a place which has probably more new age travellers, spiritual tourists and sawn-off war vets than any other part of the world, we are looking for what has become a multi-million-dollar industry and a haven for healing. If you have problems with sex or perhaps even have a problem getting sex then Marcata may be the answer.'

'Stop.'

Renzo seems agitated.

'What do you mean, stop? I'm just getting the flow. You don't stop the flow when . . .'

'The flow of what, Uri? Flow of shit. 'Sawn-off war vets.' What the fuck is that?

'It's a nice visual metaphor.'

'Nice? You don't know shit. Firstly, these guys fought a war that no-one believed in. A lot of them were drafted and a whole lot more were either poor, black or both. I've no idea what kind of pain they're in but I do know the life they knew wasn't the same when they came back. And secondly, Uri, I assume you've noticed that there's quite a few about. They might not be able to run after us if they hear you but I'm pretty sure they'll have good aim, you know what I mean?'

'Listen, Renzo, you're doing camera and sound. Now that's a pretty important job and I don't think you're going to be able to concentrate on getting that done if you are worrying about whether I am offending a few stoned war vets. Have you ever thought that they might have got tired of people being just nice? Satire isn't about healing wounds.'

'That's what we are here for, satire? I thought we were here to investigate the sexual healing industry or whatever you call it. Observe and record, you know.'

'That's what we should be doing if you would, as the saying goes, get the lead out. C'mon.'

With Uri marching off to film the window of the

record shop with its fading Altman Brothers record cover and Frank Zappa T-shirt sale, Renzo seems to be hanging back. He reaches to the small of his back, and flicks the recorder to off.

Something wrong, Renzo?

'Sure. No. Not really. I'm used to this. It's just nerves. He's getting on mine. He's not really such an asshole. He likes to work himself up into some kind of froth. He thinks it helps him cut through the shit, you know, cleanses the visual palate; reconfigures the ways of seeing. It was like this in New York. After we had gone through his blind man thing through the lobby with lift attendants and baggage boys falling over themselves to stop him falling over himself – which is kind of embarrassing when you knew he was just "in the zone" – after all the shenanigans, he let rip in the hotel room. Not at me but at Federa, his agent, who's a pretty nice woman and good at her job. Uri needed to wind himself up over something and so he stood in this plush Upper East Side hotel room swearing blue down the phone.'

You are here again, working together in California.

'Yeah? Go figure. I have my reasons and whatever I think of his methods, this is a good idea and obviously other people think so too. These kind of commissions with a good amount of development money don't grow on trees.'

Scene 10

Raul is taking some time in the middle of the day before his pre-lunch meditation to complete *The Love Story* in the corridor that joins the kitchen with the large Yoga Studio.

Raul, you seem to be enjoying yourself?

'You know, I've been meaning to get this done for ages.'

What is it you are doing here?

'Well, we like to record the weekend workshops that have taken place here over the past two decades nearly. We wanted this wall to be a photo history of the love that we have been privileged to share with our guests. And you know, we always ask if it's okay to take some discreet photos and you would think that a lot of the couples who come from very mainstream lives with pretty ordinary jobs and day-to-day concerns would be pretty wary about being photographed, taking part in what many see as wacko sex ritual porn parties. You can imagine how it could be painted by the jealous, the repressed and the ignorant. But hardly anyone has refused. There is a sense of trust and we are not interested in taking exploitative, pornographic photos of our guests – I've seen firsthand what that kind of thing means back in the city and that's the last thing we want to do here. Don't film this yet, wait till I've got the last few up.'

No problem. But you mention pornography. Would you say that your exploration of sex and sexual technique is different from your life and work back in San Francisco?

'Man, the two don't compare. I mean, in the seventies it wasn't about the technique of love and ecstasy – it was about the freedom and the political right to explore sex and sexuality; to swing, to take drugs and fuck in the park; to raise awareness by taking our clothes off; to make people aware that love wasn't about marriage and kids; about conformity and patriarchy. I mean it's true. The ultimate act of revolution is to change yourself and that is what we were about. Still are. Sure, sometimes we got it wrong, a lot of the time we were all over the place but we were stoking up a fire to burn under what was expected. We were the heat.'

Is all that now forgotten, then?

'Far from it. You read a lot these days about where have all the hippies gone, where are the flower children now, and you get this shit doled out left, right and centre as though people want to know that we have fallen, like they take pleasure knowing those hippie freaks have become cogs in the wheel, that we have of course sold out because we are just like everybody else. They need to be reassured by our failure. But we were never some corporate venture, we were a collective, a stretched-out meeting of minds. And that's a pretty elastic thing, you know. I know people right here in Marcata who are the same as they ever were, getting high, making a buck here and there and that's about it. Some music, maybe a little poetry and that's it. I know others who are worth millions but who aren't selling guns to babies, just taking one of many good ideas that were about – soy, hemp, renewable energies – and doing something. Yeah, sure and make ice cream.'

And you've made something of sex.

'Not just sex. Energy. Spiritual health. Human relationships. And we have achieved this because of our past experiences not in spite of them. And despite the fact there were some difficult times back in the city with friends freaking out and dying, with people being imprisoned for being different or disagreeing, with developers ruining a community already made fragile by municipal shit, I wouldn't take back one day. This is evolution. We are here now. We have self-awareness. We have woken up to the power of our own energy.'

Scene 11

Uri is some way ahead of Renzo as they reach the outskirts of the seemingly still sleeping town. Renzo has been hanging back taking sideways footage and has already stopped at several stores. Some of the time he has just stood on the sidewalk with his eyes shut.

What are you thinking about right this moment, Renzo?

'Well, I was just thinking about how much I love it

here. It's like got so much peace to it. I mean I know it's early and the whole place could change – I've been in plenty of places that can thrill you by day and kill you by night – but you get a real sense that there is some established serenity here. I've lived in some of the busiest cities in the world – New York, LA, London – and you get so whacked out trying to keep pace that you forget what it's like to breathe. And man, that air is so good.'

Uri seems keen to soak up some air in the woods.

'Yeah, this is Uri doing atmosphere. He'll wander around for ages doing his commentary and filming what he thinks will work. When we were filming *A Spy in the Cab* he was doing his blind thing and he worked it a lot more than he did here. I was filming, recording and acting as his PA all rolled into one. I was pretty squeamish about it actually. I mean everyone bends the rules, some a little, others a lot. That's documentary for you. Show an audience a bunch of lemmings and a cliff and make sure they do the rest. Make believe.'

You are referring of course to the infamous Disney film White Wilderness *in which the filmmakers create the impression that lemmings culled their own population by throwing themselves off a cliff as one suicidal herd . . .*

'Sure. I mean that's a classic example of a documentary maker wanting to take a subject and make it into something much more dramatic and I can understand that, sure I can. I guess I just didn't like Uri pretending to be blind . . . my grandfather went blind and it sucked the life out of him so much he only felt alive at night. But Uri and the visual thing . . . I mean it wasn't in the pitch, we were just gonna do a fly-on-the-wall, a spy-in-the-cab thing, getting some good stories from the drivers about their – usually immigrant – lives. But Uri played up the blind part so he could get a reaction be it hostile or compassionate or whatever. He was manipulative, when I thought we should just be sitting back recording the ride.'

Uri and Renzo enter the woods which lie to the north of the town. After just a mile from their hotel, the town disappears from view and there appears to be an uneasy silence between them.

'This is a nice walk, these old redwoods are amazing Uri, but why are we here? I thought we were going to try and find a sexual healing group to film.'

'That's exactly what we are doing. One of the websites I had a look at said that there were a number of secretive Tantra sects holed up in the woods.'

'Okay, but it doesn't sound very likely. Isn't a lot of that sort of thing gonna be, you know, indoors? It isn't that warm for . . . well.'

'I'm sure these people warm up fast . . . it's in their blood.'

The sound of the chain-saw stops both of them in their tracks.

'This could be it, Renzo, split up so we can get two different angles.'

'They're chain-saws, Uri . . . what do you expect to . . .?'

The woods to the north of Marcata are made up of redwoods which have federal laws to protect them since the time they were nearly wiped out however it is widely known that illegal felling does go on.

What do you think is happening here, Uri?

'Shut the fuck up. We need to get this on tape.'

'A forest, Friday, 12.00 p.m. Just a mile or so from Marcata we have come across deep in the redwoods, one of *The Energy Cult's* secret locations. After extensive research we have managed to locate perhaps the most outlandish of them all. Participants in the Earth Shakers are known to indulge in days of extreme meditation, intense psychosexual activities and biorhythmic dancing that can send people into prolonged ecstatic states.'

'Uri, you need to take a look at this.'

'These woods although close to the town are notorious amongst the locals who have seen wave after wave of hippie incomers invade and then evade into the redwoods. Here, beyond easy reach of law enforcement, cannabis plants can be grown and ritual nudity is encouraged even among the many long-haired children.'

'Uri, you really need to take a look at this . . .'

'What the hell is it, Renzo? That's the second time

you've interrupted me. You're not the fucking producer, you can't just decide when we stop filming.'

'Whatever, but those "chain-saws" don't belong to tantric folk and the people they do belong to have kind of noticed us, and you know it's worth pointing out that they are coming this way and do not look too happy.'

Away from Uri and Renzo, the five men in checked shirts and baseball caps fanning out from their two pickup trucks which have managed to push into the forest up a steep track away from the main path have begun to shout and although the words are not clear their aggressive tone is confirmed later in post-production. Renzo however has seen enough to start running, tugging at Uri's arm.

Uri, have you seen Deliverance?

Scene 12

After a long Iyengar yoga session followed by meditation, Raul and Petra are both sitting cross-legged in the Yoga Studio. Petra is assembling the *Love Kits* for the three guest bedrooms while Raul is working out the plan for the weekend workshops.

Petra, what do you put in the Love Kits?

'Well, there are a few secret ingredients which I'm not going to tell you about and I will leave your viewers to take a guess at what they might be. Let their imagination be their guide as we hope our guests will be guided by theirs. In addition there is a nice selection of condoms because we don't assume anything about our participants' status or their procreative intention. Also we include some locally made massage lotions, fruit-scented body drops, beautiful hand-crafted candles and even a feather – freshly fallen of course – just to add to the local and erotic touch.'

Raul, are you able to tell us about what you plan for the weekend?

'Sure, I can give you a broad outline but we don't like to set out an exact itinerary or a schedule of activity. These workshops run best if there is a strong element of the moment, of reacting to the needs of the couples themselves. Obviously the encounter session is important in building up confidence and a feeling of personal security. When people are coming from, say, a competitive environment or even one where personal security is under threat on a daily basis, it is important for our participants to know that the Spiritual Home is a haven from a physically aggressive and emotionally transgressive world.

'We take our time with the encounter session allowing the couples to speak, to share their fears and their hopes for the weekend. This comes easily for some and not for others. We understand this and want to help people not to feel isolated within a relationship, not to feel that they have to repress themselves in order to be a part of a successful bond. This introductory course is just that and we encourage everyone that comes to sign up for intermediate courses which take place over long weekends once a month. We take things further.'

What do you mean by 'further?'

'Further, deeper if you like. Having looked at the fundamentals of a relationship, of the sexual and spiritual energy within the context of the relationship, we then aim to make our participants more highly skilled lovers and in particular we look at male sexuality and explore the man being a master not a slave to ejaculation. At how both people in the couple can become multi-orgasmic. It's fun stuff.'

What methodology do you use?

'I'm not sure I like the word "methodology". It conjures up restriction or an academic syllabus where in actual fact we are aiming for a pedagogy of the soul, for liberation – from ourselves, from a society that reinforces repression of the self. Both Petra and I have trained in the varied and wonderful techniques of Tantra, which is an ancient form of sexual practice and which seeks to evolve our spirit and awaken the life energy often trapped in our bodies. We want to encourage pleasure and pleasurable feelings.'

Scene 13

Raul and Uri have temporarily separated. It is now late afternoon on Friday and they are still without any significant footage for *The Energy Cult*. Uri has gone to a

'Tantric Time Out' lunchtime session a few streets away from the main square. Renzo has taken a moment to himself on one of the benches donated by the Vietnam War Vets Association. He is smoking a joint.

You seem pretty relaxed, Renzo, considering what just happened?

'Man, I've been chased by a lot worse. Nearly gunned down by drugged-up Colombians or run over by a New York taxi-driver. It's Uri, you know, it's what happens with him. If you hang around with a bad kid you get into trouble.'

Is this because he is, as his agent described to us, a cutting-edge documentary maker who consistently puts the story before his safety?

'Yeah, I know the puff but he is stream-of-consciousness, you know. He doesn't set out to take risks but he puts himself – and me – in situations without a script or outline except for what's in his head and I'm pretty sure even he doesn't know what's going on in there half the time.'

Doesn't that bother you?

'Sure, sometimes maybe even a lot of the time he annoys the fuck out of me and doesn't listen to me even when the advice he is getting is something he should prick up some ear for. But I'd rather be here than having to lie in mud for a day making some wildlife thing, or worse, having to follow some fool around a suburban home waiting for something melodramatic to happen. This is work. You have to sweat and shit yourself to get something out of it. And besides, the stream-of-consciousness thing is exactly what I want for my next project, *Where Have All The Dudes Gone?* He's the best guy for it. I can film the beach, the waves and soak the tape with atmosphere and he can search out the surfers who don't want to be found, the spirits of the waves who didn't sign up for corporate sponsorship and who got wiped out by fickle fans. Yeah, we'll make history with that one.'

And in the meantime?

'In the meantime, Uri's gonna check out this meeting and he could get some good footage if he can talk his way into it. Then tonight we are gonna get drunk in that bar right there because tomorrow I've signed us both up for some Tantric workshop thing.'

Does Uri know you've done that?

'No, but I'll sell it to him and he'll buy it as long as he feels it's his idea.'

Does that sound like an ego out of control to you?

'You've got a camera, a microphone, you tell me.'

Scene 14

The building Uri is standing outside is the Marcata Community Hall. Built in 1980 by locally raised money it has been a multi-purpose venue hosting a wide variety of events; from fundraisers for the local school to Astanga yoga classes and transcendental meditation sessions.

A number of people are gathering outside the hall and Uri appears to be hanging back from the entrance.

What are you going to do, Uri?

'The usual shit, you know. I'm passing through town and I've heard this is a great workshop to take . . . The thing is with these Tantra people, nothing is what it may seem. Even in a new age haven like this place they have to careful; certain by-laws prohibit male sexual organs to be displayed before 6.00 p.m. or prevent nudity in a publicly maintained building, that kind of thing. So, they get round this by billing it as some yoga or Tai Chi class and once everybody's in the doors are locked and the Tantric sex machine goes into action.'

What do you think happens in a Tantric workshop?

'I've got an idea, from what I've read and from some of the QuickTime promos I've seen, but you know I'm going to be as much part of it as I can. I would never go in there with all cameras blazing. That's not what the documentary maker does. We let truth show itself.'

Scene 15

It's Saturday morning. At Raul and Petra's house the first couple have arrived and Petra is showing them the garden.

Raul is in the Yoga Studio, arranging his CDs by the PA system.

When is everyone arriving, Raul?

'Well, there's been a cancellation but, as you see, the first couple, Susa and Jono, have arrived. They've come all the way from Toronto.'

What about the cancellation? Does this happen a lot?

'It does but not usually at such short notice: we only just found out last night. We ask for a deposit, we have to, and people do lose that but on the other hand we understand that people cancel. For some couples this is the biggest thing they have ever done either as individuals or as a couple. Don't forget, people come to us sometimes to make a good thing even better but a lot of the time people come to us to save them from themselves, save themselves from the fate of an otherwise rich relationship floundering on the rocks of inhibition, the reefs of repression. We never get to hear the conversation that leads to the cancellation but I'm pretty sure how it goes. Within many relationships there is a fear of intimacy. You can fuck each other, you can breathe in the scent of each other's sex, you can urinate in full view and yet there is still that fear of intimacy. We believe this is because the intimacy stretches or lasts only as long as the sex and when this is over, when there has been orgasm, each person retreats back into their own body, their own smell, their own sexuality. The shields that we have in place on a day to day basis slam back into place. The loving gaze is replaced by the middle-distance stare; the erotic touch is changed to a peck on the cheek. You understand what I am getting at. We are offering something here this weekend that will enable people to move on from this freezing/thawing model. This is not just about how to have great sex. We aim to get our couples to identify and manage their priorities in all aspects of their life.'

Is there anything you can do about the cancellation? How many people will be here?

'We only ever have three couples here both because of the accommodation and because we believe that is the maximum number of people we can give quality attention to. But we were lucky this time. A couple phoned up and were looking to see if we had space at short notice. It was just great. I love it when things work out like that. It's always for a good reason. We wish the cancellers well and hope that they rebook but we are especially looking forward to our last-minute guests. Two guys too. It's been a while.

Two guys? Does that not change the dynamic of the group.

'Not at all. This is not a weekend for groups. This is about the love that exists between two people. Love does not discriminate.'

Scene 16

Uri is in the Marcata Community Hall. There are around fourteen other people in the hall and we join them part way through a Sun Salutation or Surya Namaskar, a series of twelve postures which are intended to be fluid in terms of their motion and co-ordinated with the breath. Uri appears to be struggling. Around him there is a great deal of expertise, at least none of the other participants seem below an intermediate level, while the teacher quickly goes through each posture before instigating further repeats. It would seem also that Uri is having a problem filming the session since there is both a lot of movement between postures and a degree of inversion of the body. The bandana concealing the camera has slipped a number of times and the elastic of the loose-fitting trousers he wore in order to blend in better seem unable to support the weight of the micro recorder discreetly. Struggling to conceal and maintain posture has caused him to lose his balance several times.

We are unable to speak to him while he is in the hall but two hours later he emerges.

Uri, can we talk to you about the session you've just taken part in?

'Fuck you. Fuck them. Were they shitting me? I feel as though I have just been indoctrinated into a world of unnecessary pain. I mean if I was wearing the right incense or smoking the right hemp vest then I might have been okay but otherwise I feel as though I have been steam-rollered by a third-rate kindergarten gym teacher.'

What did you learn about the use or possible abuse of Tantra and sexual healing?

'Shit all, mate, that wasn't Tantra, that was paying twenty dollars to get nauseous as some fucker encourages you to bend backwards and hold yourself there for as long as you can. Yeah, getting there was the problem. I mean what the fuck is all this about? I didn't know that in order to get sexual healing you have to be like some kind of gymnastic Ghandi, all Zen about getting into a pose that would cripple most people. This is sexual healing? This is some kind of beat 'em up where you pay your money and forget about whatever sexual shit is going on because you're too damn sore. Ommmm, my ass. More like Ouch.'

Was there nothing to direct you towards members of the Energy Cult?

'You ain't listening. I've had more sex between two pillows than this shit. There was nothing here, it was time wasted. This was like a crochet circle for acidheads who got scared and turned organic; this was for the casualties from the war on our bodies. Carrot juice was dripping from their skin instead of sweat and I swear, I swear, I have got some kind of lung thing, from being cooped up in there, some kind of shit you get from passive incense smoking.'

So, what next, Uri?

'I'm gonna get some last-gasp footage of these losers leaving and then I'm going to join Renzo for a vast quantity of beer. I only hope that the Wheatgrass Inn serves something that isn't green. Jesus!'

Uri crosses the road and sits on a vet bench. He is leaning forward so that he can zoom in as close as he can to the yoga class participants as they leave the hall. He speaks quietly into his mic.

'The session threw up a number of leads and possibilities. These men and women you see leaving now are well known in the area for this kind of activity and many of them have taken part in similar group sessions in San Francisco. They have brought it all with them to this small, sleepy town. The footage shot inside the hall, the grainy, jerky movement of limbs in motion accompanied by the grunts and howls of those being led in the direction of spiritual ecstasy, is not the tip of the iceberg but the hot fundament of erotica that is embedded in the counter-culturalists of this town. While the gun shop down the road has opened for business, there is a strong sense of something far more dangerous being sold here.'

Scene 17

Petra has kicked off her sandals and led Susa and Jono into the Yoga Studio. A few moments before you joined us, she held their hands and told them, 'This is your weekend. This is a wonderful opportunity not just to get to know each other better, to learn how love and intimacy are the bedrock for your relationship, how the exchange and explosion of each other's positive energy can enhance your relationship and how we can all learn to trust one another in an increasingly sceptical world. Not just this. More. We will have fun and you will meet other people with the same trepidations and uncertainties, people who too have just taken a step towards fulfilment and awareness.'

With a nod from Petra, Raul presses the button on the hi-fi remote and the first of the tracks he has composed begins its long, ambient build-up.

'Don't dance, just shake your body whichever way you want.'

Susa and Jono close their eyes and begin to sway. As we join them in the studio, Petra has rushed across the solid oak floor and welcomed the couple from Wisconsin who have just arrived.

'Put your bags down, you do not need them right now. If you can, join us. We have just started. You've had a long journey, I know, and you may want to just relax in your room and I can certainly show it to you but if you don't want to do that then, please, come into our Spiritual Home.'

There is no hesitation. As can be seen, the two newcomers are ready and able to join Jono, Susa and

Raul gliding across the floor, hips swaying, feet lifting up and gently kicking, their eyes raised to the sloping glass ceiling of the studio.

Petra, this is straight in at the deep end, is it not?

'Perhaps, but that's why we always give people the opportunity to ease themselves in at their own pace. But you know, most people just kick off their shoes and join us for this energy releasing structure. I love this part, you can just shake off all the accumulated worries and concerns of the day, the stresses and strains can be pushed out not held in.'

And the last couple, when do you expect them?

'Hopefully, any moment now.'

Petra joins the two couples who have all closed their eyes.

Scene 18

Renzo and Uri are in JD's, not the only bar in Marcata but the only one that stays open late. Its clientele over the years has been mainly college students from the nearby Standard University. Renzo and Uri have been at the bar for more than two hours. There seems to be some disagreement.

'Why the hell would you want to stay here? I mean firstly what the hell would you do? I don't imagine there's any great call for documentary film-making here. I mean you could maybe make some series about how the best way to save the environment is to landfill this hole, but that's about it.'

'I could use this place as a base, go off and do that dude docu I've been wanting to do and, you know, just settle for a while. I've been moving about so much this past decade that I don't know where home is anymore.'

'This place is making you sentimental, Renzo. Home is wherever you mic up, wherever your eyes take you. But maybe you're getting sucked into the Great Sexual Con. The best thing you could do is to set yourself up in porno. You'd make good money, work in some luxurious locations and the view would be pretty good. Close-ups wouldn't be such hard work and I'm sure there would be a lot of extras.'

'Sex doesn't have to be pornographic.'

'Give me a break. The proprietors of the Great Sexual Con are making millions out of people's desires. They set up shop and offer people tutelage and reassurance; they say that fulfilment of their sexual desire, eradication of their sexual trauma is just within their reach if only they could commit themselves to x number of sessions at x dollars a pop. You think criminality is always with a gun and a snarl. Renzo, sometimes it's done with a kiss and a deep-breathing exercise. This is about money. This is about indoctrination. This is about commerce. Sex is the great equaliser after all. You don't have to be rich to do it, you don't have to be spiritual about it to know what you want. It's all there. You can mail-order any kind of sex shit from anywhere in the world. Have your Jungle Sex Juice deluxe pack couried to you and everything will be all right. You can get some miraculous penis pump airlifted to you cross-continents from a dodgy address with a Californian seal of approval and everything will be all right. You can go to some weekend course and learn the basics of getting back to basics; you can learn to do what you can already do and you will find that wisdom comes at a price. A very high one.'

'Whatever, Uri, nice script – the mic's on I take it? Anyway we're still going to go tomorrow, yeah?'

'Oh yeah, I wouldn't miss it for the world. I love my work, Renzo, you've seen how much it means to me in Colombia, in New York and I haven't run away from anything, even when it seems like I'm a blip away from being face down. But, you know, what I'm not doing is running *to* anything. Patience and objectivity. These are skills, Renzo, and you know, well, it's always the same with you, isn't it? You recall starting to empathise with the drug soldiers in the mountains . . . ?'

'They were conscripted kids, Uri, and you know that . . .'

'And you got friendly with one of the taxi-drivers and let slip that everything is not what it seems. Fuck, Renzo, wake up. Of course not everything is what it seems.

Some things are hidden. Some things are to be found. That's what we are here for.'

'To make things up?'

'To tell a story in whatever way it takes. The truth is essence.'

'What?'

'Anyway, Renzo, if we are going to do this thing tomorrow we need to get some sleep. This Spiritual Home place is a few miles out, so we need to order a cab and then we just turn up and join in with the happy clappy group. I tell you, though, I ain't doing any more fucking back bends. I feel as though I need a good massage from something Thai and tight on a white sand beach somewhere just to get rid of the shit I had to endure today.'

'You are remembering what I said, Uri. This is a weekend workshop for couples.'

'I know. We should get all the footage we need since by the sound of it sex is high up on the menu. I'm looking forward to being multi-orgasmic in one easy session. Oh, but wait a minute, I already am. In my heyday I could splurt six times in a night and still have enough left to share. Hope these couples ain't going to be too shy.'

'We are one of the couples, Uri.'

'What?!'

Scene 19

Here, outside the headquarters of what has become known as the Energy Cult, we are just about to enter and see for ourselves what goes on. The setting is idyllic, pastoral even, and is certainly a long way from a city red-light district or even the idea of a tolerance zone as established in some places. The activities here are much more covert and pseudo-serious. The activities of the leaders of such groups as *Tantra Travellers*, *Holistic*, *Happy* and *Healing Inc.* have been well documented and support groups for those who have experienced something less than wholesome have become widespread. We will certainly aim to include as many contact details as we can for these groups at the end of the film.

In the meantime, we are here to expose the fraud that is being perpetrated on perhaps some of the most vulnerable people in our society via something so personal and intimate. Sex. The Tantric groups we have come across consider sex and its actions to be proprietary information; only they can unlock the key to happiness and satisfaction. That unlocking as far as we have been able to discover – and it is a secretive and coded business – involves the appropriation of people's hard-earned money and 'must-have' products which can double the price of the holistic healing.

Uri and Renzo have been skirting the picket fence

surrounding the Spiritual Home for nearly half an hour. They have both been filming. There seems to be more to it than setting scene.

'You're making us late, Uri. How much atmosphere do you need?'

'Fuck me, Renzo, I don't know. No, wait, don't fuck me. Just yet. I'm sure that's gonna come later.'

'Christ, Uri . . .'

'Now I know why you are so keen for me to work with you on your pet surf idea, which by the way has been done a zillion times – *Dogtown, Riding with Giants*, etc – I understand now. We were gonna get real close as we worked.'

'Yeah, I was gonna retitle it *Where Have All The Prudes Gone?*'

'Cute.'

'What I don't get, Uri, is what the problem is. You're the cutting-edge documentary maker. This is cutting edge.'

'You're making us late now, Renzo. But let me get this last bit, right here, by the entrance to this paradise.'

'As we enter the workshop, neither of us know what will happen. In a place that should be about what people can achieve, what they can dream, we are mainly concerned that in somewhere as remote as this, no-one is going to hear a scream. But we will leave you with this quotation from a devotee of the Hindu goddess

Kali: 'Those most fit for Tantra almost never take it up, and those least fit pursue it with zeal.'

Scene 20

Raul and Petra break off from the moving couples for a moment. The air is thick with incense and warming up with the heat of bodies. On previous occasions, Raul informed us, the studio has become like a sweat lodge without the need for heating even in winter.

'Pheromones are the body's natural scent and they are produced in order to communicate with others nearby. We don't rush to open windows as we think that this build-up of scent and smell is both healthy and invigorating for the others. This kind of communication isn't direct like a conversation, it's general and the osmotic nature of pheromones means that their impact is without prejudice. It's such a good icebreaker.'

It seems though, Raul, that there is more than just a pheromone scent in the air.

Raul's glance at the couples in mostly rhythmic movement is followed by Petra's. And they both move to corner to confer in private. Accompanying the pheromone scent building in the studio air is the equally pungent smell of alcohol. Not fresh exactly but rather stale, the kind of alcohol stench that leaks out of flooded pores, the toxins rushing and pushing their way out of the body.

Raul and Petra come back from their huddle.

'This happens, we can accept that. People gather up courage in whatever way they can and a few of the first timers do get a little drunk either before they come or during the stay. It's unusual for the men to get drunk however as there is always the fear that this will impair their sexual prowess. With first-timers there's always a certain amount of education, health training and hand holding involved. What we actively discourage is any kind of drug taking. I don't know, but maybe people read our bios on the website and see where we have come from, our age and assume that we smoke pot 24/7. Man, if we did do you think we would have ever got this far? No way. And people from out of state look at where we live and think this is Cannabis County where everybody gets high just by being here. So, there is no smoking and if somebody produces weed after the meal and everybody is relaxing maybe just about to get in the tub, we ask them politely to refrain. The focus isn't on hedonism. It is on spiritual fulfilment. It's taken me most of my life to realise there is a difference.'

Are you going to say anything?

'No, he doesn't appear to be drunk now which would be a concern, so we will just continue the encounter session and take it from there. I'm sure it will be fine. But, one thing's for sure, his partner likes to move. He's got a natural fluidity to him. Lovely.'

Scene 21

Petra is explaining to the couples what the next structure will be.

'This is more than just simply a massage and we have timed it to be the last structure before we break for dinner. This is a really good way to finish the first session and it allows you, after the movement, encounter and group work, to be solely with your partner.'

Raul sets up the music then joins Petra and lies down on the bundle of blankets and cushions Petra has assembled. A gentle pulse emanates from the four speakers angled down from the studio's ceiling. Outside dusk is falling and Petra has lit the erotically shaped candles.

'I'm going to demonstrate on Raul. This is not a remedial massage, you are not trying to heal something, erotic massage is about the sexual energy so often trapped in our bodies by inhibition, by ignorance. The first step is to cleanse the aura, don't touch just glide your fingers around the body, just a centimetre or so away from the skin. With practice you will be able to feel the energy from the body you are close to. You are touching, it's just not the skin you can feel. The next stage is to press firmly into the contours of the body and not forgetting to include the fingers and toes. As the receiver, if your arms get sore from being above your head, relax them by your sides. Giver, go round like this twice. There is no hurry about this or anything that we do here. There are so many times in our lives when it seems we have to be quick, we need speed, our life and limb depends on rush. But this is not one. Sex should never be like that and yet for so many people that is exactly what it has been reduced to. A quick orgasm, a hasty climax and a fleeting intimacy. If you take nothing else away from this weekend, take away this. Make time for love. And we will come back to this again and again.

'Once you have gone round twice with the firm touch, go round again but this time pulling at the skin, dragging out the body's resistance, the emotional toxins, squeezing out of it all the accumulated negativity. I love this next bit. Surprise your partner, awaken his or her energy and pluck or tweak at the skin around the contours like before, do it randomly, teasing your partner with this sensation. It's great fun and it is a wonderful preparation for the last but most significant part of the massage. The erotic touch.'

Raul and Petra swap places. Raul takes over the instructions.

'The key to this part of the massage is the lightness of touch and the wonderfully slow movement of your fingertips as they travel across the skin of your partner. The touch should begin with the body's contours but soon you will progress to any part of the body you feel drawn to. Feel the heat coming from the energy you have awakened.

Do not be afraid or embarrassed by arousal or by your breath – this is a beautiful thing and you are completely safe to explore this, be like a child without any of the fear you have learned or been told to have; simply let the touch make you fizz with energy, come alive to the most neglected of our senses. Touch. And with your voice bring out all that has been kept silent; breathe out all the air that has gone stale, been held for too long. Listen to the sounds around our Spiritual Home, listen to the music which will help bring you to a state of spiritual, erotic ecstasy. For this moment and many moments to come, you will know what it is like to be free.'

'Shut the fuck up!'

There is a sense of a spell broken as Raul jerks back in shock from Petra's body and Susa screams.

'What's with the camera? You think I can't see it? You think I don't know when I'm being filmed? What you gonna do with it, eh? Make some home movies?'

Uri has suddenly jumped up, his face red, his skin streaked with sweat. He breaks the circle formed by the other couples, tearing his hand away from Renzo's strong grip.

'Where's the trust, you freaks, where's the fucking trust?'

Uri kicks the tripod of the camera set up for recording the session for would-be trainers and rushes out of the Yoga Studio.

Renzo is shaking his head and appears to be close to tears. He walks after Uri, wrapping the purple sarong he bought in Marcata. He ties the ends tight around his waist and then stops, speaking quietly to the group.

'Listen, I'm sorry, there's something we need to tell you about, that I want to tell you about that. We weren't here for the right reasons and that's a terrible thing. But right now I need to go after Uri.'

What do you think has happened, Renzo?

'You tell me. I mean I could tell right from the beginning that he was pretty unhappy with the dancing stuff, especially when Raul started to move in sync with him, matching him move for move. It was pretty funny really, Uri had the flexibility of a board. I told him to think of it as a workout but he kinda pushed me away, still freaked out I guess by the fact that we were being seen as a gay couple. He knows that's not true so I really don't understand the problem. In the encounter session he looked like he would rather be eating his own leg.'

Were you surprised by this lack of joining in, for the sake of the film at the very least?

'Yeah, I was. I mean in Colombia he sniffed coke until he talked himself hoarse, so he seemed to be pretty okay about role-playing there and he loves doing the blind thing.'

So what was it? Why the sudden exit?

'You know, I could feel the freak-out building in him

and I just tried to hold on to him as firmly as I could. I knew he would be thinking about how he was going to tough out the massage but if I'd had the chance I would have said, what's the problem? There are worse things that you could do. There's no malice here and, from his point of view, the close-ups and commentary are like docu gold. He just couldn't do it, I guess. It's sex, isn't it? It's sex that people get fucked up by.'

The two couples look pretty shaken but Raul and Petra nod silently towards Renzo as he walks out the studio.

Has this happened before, Raul?

'Well, it has but I guess not for a while. It makes me sad but it is the way of things. What we are awakening here and what we are releasing from within ourselves is a powerful thing. It's not just the guests that get something from these weekends, Petra and I both do, still do. We are not gurus. We do not sit on spiritual thrones and hand down advice. We are learning about ourselves all the time and there have been many times when we have both been in tears or energised to such a high that it feels like we are kids again. These weekends are about rejuvenation and continuation.'

Even for someone like Uri?

'No. We've only just met him. But no.'

Would you care to expand on that?

'Renzo, I think, has a feeling for what we are doing here.'

But you've only just met him.

'We have a sense of these things.'

Of him belonging and Uri not?

'Yes. It seems to us that Renzo looks at the world with a wide-angle lens. In the encounter session he seemed to be open to questions and the answers of others while Uri seemed to be uncomfortable, the stress of control showing through his constant need to touch and rearrange his bandana. Uri appears to be tightly focused on what he is doing. Such a state can lead to a kind of sensory impairment, an inability to see anything that matters.'

You can tell that already?

'The self-deception is there for all to see. From his outburst it seems he is afraid of a camera which is not even focused on him. He is afraid of what it might reveal and show but most of all he is afraid of himself. Perhaps he believes the camera never lies.'

Miss Globe X

Translated from the Romanian

'THOUGH I CEASE to be Miss Globe, I have not ceased to be Sera Lanic and from time to time you will hear of me and you will see me. I know that I give up this crown with all of your support for my personal future.'

***

I unzipped the smile and paused for photos. Three days in total, I have estimated, three days in total for pausing moments which turn out to be lengthy trials of being stuck to a spot by some photo-hack dribbling on to my silk sleeve with enthusiasm, constantly being called 'hot' by some schmuck telling me to brighten up their readers' lives. Imagining lies. In the three lost days, I have paused in Pennsylvania and waited in Wai Kung; in that still life I was foreground to beautiful settings, added colour to tint product. I adopted a posture to sell the brand. In the three lost days, my legs would bulge with tiredness, my arms could barely be straightened after a day of hugs and hand tugs and my lips would be cracked and dried from air con air. Oh God, in those three days what I could have done that has now been lost . . .

'Congratulations.' Miss Estonia mirrored my smile, she reflected previous dreams. I could have whispered something into her ear as I lifted the crown on to her head. There was every opportunity. By the time the organisation's heavies would have realised what was going on, I could have easily sullied some innocence, wrecked with pain and jade the hope of someone so young and giving. Just as I placed the crown at a prearranged angle on her hair and head, I could have rushed into her ears, invaded her head and said, 'Get out while you can. If you run right now they might let you go, might find a way to spin a different win. You could be a loose cannon, an untied thread that came unravelled under the extraordinary pressure and responsibility. They would still be able to find a way out to save face and you could get out of the race just in the nick of time. Go now and live something imperfect.'

So, I didn't. Obviously. Another year, another dollar, another beauty. I'm not a revolutionary. I'm a gender capitalist. I'm not femininista, I'm anachronista. Ex-friends couldn't believe that I was about to go public in a thong, while they rushed to Business MAs and to drink lattes in the city's new style bars. My business was children. For Miss Globes it's always the children. Always the future generalised by the hope for worldwide waifs surviving somehow against all odds.

Sometimes I'm so sickened by everybody else's suffering. Missed Globe, too damn right.

2

They've told me I can stay as long as I like. They told me that they are honoured to have an ex-Miss Globe staying with them, especially one who was born in Brasov; a bumpy, dusty journey from this suite luxury. Here was I, a local heroine come home to roost. Yeah, a real plus for some new economic boost. Everything is incidental I am told, there is no charge for what I need. I am the rider. I know. I have already been paid, in full, tipped over the edge, a most generous provider. It's there not just in black and white but in my head, drip-fed into my soul.

'We must learn to give more and take less.' They applauded politely at my crowning glory, they rubbed their hands when they told my story. I was expected to say something gently unexpected, like the faintest of hiccups in a breathless world. I was asked to think of something that would reflect who I was, where I came from and who I wanted to be. I told them, of course I did, I told them in some brash naïveté exactly what I thought the answers to the questions were. I wrote it down. It came from the heart.

'I am from Brasov. My father is a painter whose work was confiscated by the dictator two decades ago and now hangs in the national art gallery. He made a living commercially, illustrating brochures, but his paintings until a few years ago were either ignored or destroyed. He has lived and continues to live in the social housing the government built. Even when they were new, he found it, we all found it, difficult to live in. In winter we could see our breath when the heating failed or never even ignited and our coughs would get worse as the months wore on. Everyone's health suffered but my father could have endured that apartment – the cold, the lack of fresh or even reasonable food – he could have put up with all of that if it hadn't got so damp. When his paintings began to curl off their mounts and mildew grew across his landscapes he would weep and we would join him. United. Pitiful.'

It was moving stuff, even MJ, the head of the organisation, said so but perhaps, she smiled, it needs a more uplifting ending. 'We want our stories to inspire not expire.' MJ was the founder, the brains behind the beauty and a woman in touch with everyone apart from herself. She had been a beauty herself, I was told, in her day, in her prime. You could see it in the fading light. Tall, elegant in a furred kind of way with high cheekbones, expensive hair design, expensive layer design – everything arranged as neatly and as perfectly as it could be. Nothing was to be out of place, everything was to be on message.

'Perhaps if you just added this . . .'

I didn't write this. It didn't come from the heart.

'He was so proud of me when I decided to enter the competition for Miss Romania and when I won against really tough competition he was over the moon. The whole family, my father, my sister, my grandparents were so delighted for me and it seemed the whole of Brasov was cheering me that night. I swear I could hear the cheers from thousands of miles away in Honduras when I won. It was of course a dream come true and my father wept down the phone and despite the hardships he had endured under communism he said he would take up his brush again, so inspired was he by both my win and the Miss Globe competition.'

MJ had a way with words and her tight grip could wring every drop of truth out of them.

There was nobody in the crowd I knew. Just new friends.

Anyway, the circus is no longer in town and I've run away. There are still the post-reign contractual obligations, the calls, the messages, letters and flowers that arrive on a daily basis to my junior suite at the top of the hotel. The same, sweet bellboy delivers them and he knows enough now just to pile them up on the long, smoked-glass coffee table while putting the flowers on whatever surface is left.

There's not much room now. The bouquets from admirers, sponsors, corporate flunkies have piled high. But I won't have them removed. 'Drain the water, but leave the flowers.' And so the dianthus, asters and chrysanthemums slowly rot in their vases. Their decay has been sequenced over the four years I have been in the hotel. The maids know better than to comment although I can feel their sideways glances, their smirks at my state, their shaking heads as they struggle through stalks and stems that have intertwined creating a natural barrier after so many artificial ones. They whisper their gossip as they sweep up fallen, rotten petals but their twisting, ugly mouths shouldn't bother to hide their words. I already know what they are saying. I have been left to my fate. Soon they will be dusting me down.

Cut flowers can never be beautiful.

3

Sweet Valentine. I knew him once. Him and every other man that got close but not close enough. He brushed past the security cordon in Honduras and said he would always love me. His Latin skin was awash with sweat and his eyes were huge and wild. He wasn't unattractive. When the heavies caught up with him, he was still blowing me kisses as they dragged him away on his heels shouting over and over again. 'This is what it's like to feel.'

He had a point but I began to miss what it was from that point on. There were many such admirers during my reign. MJ made the rules pretty clear to me on the night of my coronation. She pulled me aside just as the celebration party was getting going, just as the runners-up were being placated into oblivion, their sorrows not so much being drowned but siphoned into subordinated roles with promises of exclusively limited opportunities. It was always made to sound better than it was.

MJ let me know the house rules for the newly crowned queen of the world:

1. Miss Globe is celibate.

2. Miss Globe shall take a sabbatical from any relationship she might be involved with.

3. Miss Globe shall refrain from initiating any new relationship during her term.

4. Miss Globe shall be chaperoned at all times during her term.

She wasn't kidding. The guy that I had started to see was given the cold shoulder not by me but by the heavies and administrative arrangements tailor-made for the newly crowned. What chance did he have anyway? He was a student like me from Brasov, intense and full of intent, learning his literature, immersing himself in the arts. R was a man like any other but we certainly had something. He had me. I was a virgin when we met and I thought he was smart and good-looking. Yes, the usual but the usual, the simple, the downright fucking boring is nothing to be sneezed at, I would say, now, not to be sneezed after all that I have seen and done. R thought it was strange that I wanted to display myself, be a slave to the flesh when we were supposed to be nurturing our minds but he could see the possibilities, weigh some good and bad and imagine that there would be some kind of balance. How naïve we both were. When I won Miss Romania, I was taken from Brasov to be schooled in London, trained up for my appearance. It was a good story made into a bad film and we never saw each other again

How was R supposed to follow me to London or to anywhere? He had no money and the cordon sanitaire around all nation winners would never have allowed some scruffy student within a hundred metres of a beauty queen. He wrote to me and I tried to write back but there was no time. Photo shoots, travel, formal meet-and-greets, informal cultural and educational exchange. We were quickly lost to each other and when I tried to contact him after my year was up, he was no longer at the university and no-one knew or was willing to tell me where he had gone.

So, here's to you, R. You've probably got some shit awful bar job in Brasov as you wait for someone to discover your genius, where you can pedal the same shit to your customers that you tell yourself. 'Miss Romania/Miss Globe. Yeah, I knew her. I fucked her. I blooded her. She got glittered and sold.' Yeah, I can hear that and it doesn't matter because I heard it a lot. My past life would have caught up with me if I hadn't been running so fast. The bitterness, the jealousy, the intellectual disdain. As MJ said, 'Say goodbye to that life. You won't be going back.'

But it did catch up with me just once. It spat at me before the heavies could do their work. On some godforsaken Czech street, some poor and dwindled protester didn't see the beauty or the charity and got angry, plain and simply angry. 'Such *small* people,' MJ would say dismissively. Of course there would always be ingrates and crazies but mostly there was adulation, cheering crowds and bonered men around every corner. Each day brought more delights of smiling children and fawning officials; of welcome parties and ostentatious celebrations of, as it was called, 'the osmosis of goodness'. But

I remember the past catching up with me that day. I remember the saliva, its heat and stench, as it struck my cheek, as the woman was bundled away by security in Prague. I felt the vehemence, the lash of the spit. Not the force but the source. I shouted to the heavies, 'I know her,' and they pulled her around to face me.

'Hi.'

The smile and the souped-up teeth that had wowed the judges seemed to galvanise the woman's hopeless struggle against the heavies' firm grips. They covered her mouth so she could not spit again, and her arms were nelsoned up her back. But they could not stop her hate-filled stare. It drilled into me so hard, I can still feel the vibrations.

'Hi, Mum.'

4

The bar was busy last night and Ushka, chief whatever behind the bar, surveyed it all with her usual ease. She had seen it all and was everyone's friend. It was in the contract. You could walk in for your first night in the hotel and she would greet you with warmth and fresh nuts, a quick wipe of the already spotless counter and she was ready to sell anything but herself. The guests liked to think they knew her. She was a friend in a stranger-infested world. They liked to think she was always there for them which of course she was except when she was back home in her squashed, damp house with her husband and two children.

I always take the same corner seat and the whisky sour that Ushka brings over to me. Occasionally at the end of a long, long night, Ushka would sit down with me, pour herself a glass of flat champagne and sigh long and hard. We knew what we were doing. We just didn't want to do it anymore.

In the bar, I can fade into the dark wood and sink into deep red velvet, cushioned from the constant stares, the nudge to nudge recognition of whispering fools too drunk to be polite, too shy to be rude. No-one ever gets near me. There have been instructions. There is always security when I am in the bar.

I sink not just into velvet but, when I have had enough whisky, into my mother's cold embrace. When I am in the suite on the top floor, I can see nothing but the last glimpse, the last twisted glare and shout: 'You have betrayed me. You have betrayed yourself.' When she let loose with her saliva it must have been a well-planned operation. Travelling to Prague, tracking my world itinerary and acting quickly when she saw that this would be as near to home as I would get during my reign. She was Party but not the hedonistic sort. A fully paid-up, neighbour-spying communist who had gone underground when the world had caught up. But not my world. She could not, would not accept that. Glasnost.

Not exactly. Proud mom and pop at the spelling bee, screaming for their one and only to beat the opposition into a greased-up pulp? Far from it. She came to none of the low-level pageants that took place in falling-down concrete halls and she denounced their decadent remit, the obscene parade, and by the time I had got to the finals of Miss Romania she would not even let me near the house. She let it be known that any daughter who could so easily be swayed by capitalist infiltration, moral disintegration, was no daughter of hers. My father and other members of my family came early on but they were always uneasy and by the time I won Miss Romania there was not a blood relative in the crowd. Cousins suddenly had work to do, uncles were kept at work by aunts and my father retreated behind canvas. 'I will paint the world for you,' he whispered and quickly shut the door when I called round out of the blue. I had already won. I was Miss Persona non Grata. And my prize?

5

In Honduras, eight white horses took me in a gold and silver carriage to where a hundred soldiers stood with ceremonial swords crossed. They made a formidable arch of sharp steel above my head as I walked on a red carpet unfurled for me by the frantic action of the half dozen young children running ahead, struggling to control the heavy roll. Their glances were acute. Lasting. I see them out of the window of my suite day in day out. They are hanging there for me to see, to remember. I can see them when the bathroom floor-to-ceiling mirrors steam up, my fingers tracing their small bodies on the glass.

If only I couldn't remember. In Peru. Not the bloated ones, not the dying ones with tubes running out of skeletal arms, not the blinded ones with flies buzzing around their useless eyes. I caught the lost stares of well-dressed kids pretending to be something they were not. Comfortable. They had been shoehorned into footwear that was not their own, trussed into jackets that came off trucks from well-meaning charities. Even their bobbled hats were more left behind than après ski. They have always depended on the kindness of strangers.

I had had shelter above my head, I had been fed a basic diet and I had been loved and wanted. Then. And when it most counted I was not forced to sell my slender child body nor was I asked to carry arms for a cause I couldn't even begin to understand. I was asked to shake hands with priests who claimed there were holes in the condoms that were being dropped like propaganda leaflets from planes and I was asked to hold a baby riddled with ignorance, an auto-chaotic disease. I saw power brokers step into armour-plated Humvees and make for their hotels and I was in their parade, ticker-taped, while those we were there to help were left in our wake. If I could only forget that it came down to me.

Impossibly, ridiculously, I carried hope and tokens of luxury. I gave out bite-sized sweets to children that hadn't had a square meal in their lives; I gave toys to boys who had already killed their first man and dolls to girls who witnessed the line-up in front of their prostrate mother. These big-eyed children thought I was Miss Globe, they thought I had grace. After I had left the village, the camp, the hospital, everything would change. Of course it would. I was Miss Globe and I could change the world. It was in my speech. It was in everyone's speech.

I'm sorry but I don't know who I can apologise to. What could I have done? I was believed in, invested in and contracted to charity and product placement. I was the face of decent desire, of wholesome potential, of life-saving possibility. I could save the world with my looks. Any young girl could become me. Any young girl could get to be where I was as long as they ignored the slurps of men and tried hard not to tread on waifs rolling out red carpet.

The exotic destinations began to blur, the journeys choreographed to make the world, my world, Miss Globe seamless. I felt like a dancer, moving swiftly through the air, coming to velvet ground to be spun from person to person, a kiss of air and lip, a handshake of sweat and softness, of gentle touches as though I had the power to heal. If only to be left in opulence late at night with the desire to feel.

It wasn't possible. MJ reminded me from time to time.

'It's only a year of your life, for God's sake. Use your imagination, failing that use your fingers.'

That was typically forthright of her. She had a genuine callousness that passed for efficiency. When one young man threatened to get close to being personal in Vienna, she whispered forcefully in my ear. 'You could shit better than that.' She was adept at being there or employing somebody to be there just at the most vulnerable moments – at daytime press conferences, at parties that threatened to go too far into the night. Yes, I was curfewed, I was as virginal as Cinderella and believe me I have heard all the quips. From the heavies to the hotel bellboys who fondled as they bundled me into my heavenly cage sometimes minutes but usually hours before midnight.

I was anything but untouchable. I was both off limits and fair game at the same time.

MJ said she understood, at least in the early days. She knew that her freshly crowned Miss Globes would need a period of adjustment and not all of them adjusted at all or at all well. Miss Ecuador couldn't stand the restrictions even though she had signed all the relevant paperwork. Showing some spark she decided to make her own arrangements to see an ex and he flew in undercover and under the radar of the organisation. MJ liked to tell this little story, using it as a warning for wanton independent-minded girls. Miss Ecuador's secret suitor didn't even make it to her hotel door, dressed as he was as one of the many bellhops. The security MJ employed had a list with photographic ID of all hotel employees likely to come into contact with Miss Ec and this guy wasn't on it. Miss Ec told me she was left waiting for hours wondering with fading hope then fearing the worst. In the middle of the night, after she had fallen asleep still fully clothed on her bed, MJ woke her up with a room-to-room call. She kept it simple, Miss Ec said, kept the tone pleasantly menacing. 'Your boyfriend has been encouraged to take a return flight to XXX. He seemed to agree it was the right thing to do.'

Miss Ec told me this story when we managed to spend a few minutes alone on the night of my triumph, the last night of her never to be repeated reign. 'But it pours now, for you.' She was high on coke and her minders, cut loose and mellow with some herbal, had got lax and allowed her to go into the ladies' unaccompanied. Even on social occasions as I was soon to discover, the female restrooms were no kind of sanctuary. You'd think you would be cubicled against intrusion and the next thing you would hear whispers about your sloppy bowels. People would have you believe that the concept of Miss Globe is degrading. There was nothing conceptual about it.

'There's no time to tell you what you need to know,' she stage-whispered to me as she laid out two thick lines on top of the white cistern. It was some sight, I can tell you, and I was only just getting to grips with the whole beauty drug thing. On the local circuit it had been non-existent with the beauty queens pretty much happy to avoid any thing more intoxicating than a small glass of red wine. Maybe they were pure. Maybe not but by the time it got to the regional level, diet pills, up and down powders and smoking were part of the menu for just about every girl. Those that shunned the stimulants were never going to make it. Judges even at this level were looking at the ability to play the game; to look like someone every parent could be proud of. How you achieved that status and the way you represented it, was the crucial question. Forget 'how would you make the world a better place?'; try 'how low can you go?'

Ec chopped and delivered like the seasoned pro she was and, anticipating the moment, she closed her big brown eyes and smacked her full, luscious lips. She truly was beautiful but there was no point telling her that. We were all beautiful.

'Expect to lose yourself. No-one will find you. You will touch the poverty of the world through a powdered glove; you will see the horror of humanity through designer frames and you will feel, at times, that there is nothing you cannot do. You will be told that you will change lives and you will but significantly the only life you will truly be aware of changing will be your own. When someone kisses you with gratitude their face is obscured. When someone thanks you for your help you will be left wondering what it was you did apart from being in a certain place at a certain time. Think of yourself as the person you are now and fight your hardest to keep that. Lives have been lost in a split second, and souls have been dulled in the blink of an eye. You have a year in which to reach whatever depths you are capable of. Most people are surprised how low they can go.'

Ec took one long, ecstatic sweep of the coke and held out the rolled-up note, keeping it at arm's length as though it had nothing to do with her. I took the note and cleared the rest of the powder from the white porcelain. I tried to see her kissing babies and kneeling down in orphanages and just couldn't picture it. But it had already been done for me. According to MJ and the Miss Globe publicity office, Miss Ecuador had travelled and seen more of the world than any previous winner. She was the notion of a global beauty personified. She seemed confident enough, on stage she had been a supreme performer, her body glowing, her words flowing from one statement of love to another. I heard it all. I bought it all that night. Who wouldn't? It was real easy to get into that kind of debt of gratitude.

When Ec opened her eyes, it was only to take in the full extent of the toilet wall. It seemed to hold her attention more than it fully deserved but I just thought, 'what do I know?' This was the ex-Miss Globe and I was just a new pretender. I was led to believe that experience counted for something. My dad survived his experiences, my mother proscribed hers. Experience was the future, a tried and tested route out of innocence. Of ignorance. And I knew nothing. I could hear Ec's words as they landed and watched them bounce off me, their meaning elasticated, exaggerated. I was so excited, thrilled and daunted by the worldwide crowning that I needed to get out of the cubicle. The powder had reminded me of the important world that partied beyond the restroom walls.

'Sure, I know, yeah, I really do know. We should go. You should go. Reap the rewards for the sacrifices you have made and I will say nothing more to dim or cloud or darken the experience. It's yours for the taking. Make of it what you will and the best of luck to you. But have this.'

Ec lifted up her gold clutch bag and undid the clasp. I wasn't sure what to expect. I had been told that the beauty queens liked to pass on good-luck charms when it got to the Miss Globe level but no-one had either known or said what it was. An inscribed brooch that could be worn proudly on evening wear or perhaps an exclusive pen with which to sign autographs . . .

Ec lifted it out and gave it a quick dust with her fingers, a quick blow from her breath.

'You'll need this,' she said, her voice crackling with phlegm.

The flesh-coloured vibrator had been embedded with topaz, such tiny freckles spattered along the impressive shaft and in addition the head had been initialled with indelible ink by each of the Miss Globes who had possessed it since its introduction in the eighties.

'This is our heirloom. You might,' Ec said, lighting a cigarette and pushing her way out of the cubicle, 'need some company now and then.'

She gathered a deep laugh from her perfect frame and pushed the restroom door with both hands. There was an audible gasp as she made her way into the crowded ballroom.

6

In the early days my father showed his paintings at the café in the Bucaresti Hotel which gave the hookers and the rich, fat men something to look at as they danced with each other, making jazz out of crackly vinyl. No gallery would show something as modern as his paintings. His world was of the streets, the alleys, the bars and moments that just seemed to catch everything, a visual definition that swelled with meaning.

His low-key beginnings had continued into marriage, children and the communist era. He painted the same. It was the world that changed. And his wife. When he didn't tow the party line, when he didn't even consider joining that party, their marriage dissolved into silence and avoidance. She was too busy anyway to care about what he was doing or how he was faring as the café gradually began to refuse to show or sell his work, as his boho visions and versions of the world suddenly became old, problematic and dangerous.

'The man,' he said to me looking at one of his heavily oiled nudes, a couple in passionate embrace, 'is just a man; the woman is just a woman. Nothing can change that. Believing they should be someone or something else still doesn't change it. Am I the only one that can see that?'

He sends me his paintings. He can't or won't visit. He is old now, I understand that, but each time he sends a painting to the hotel with the same brief, cryptic message – *Something else to look at* – I reply to him, pleading with him to come to the hotel. I could arrange a car, help for his ageing bones, a fleet of ambulances or limousines if needed but he does not reply. Maybe my mother intercepts the messages or maybe there is something else to his notes. Perhaps he disapproves that I have made such a spectacle of myself, that in his world of aesthetic survival, of the imagination and intellect being assaulted by the forces of control, I am now squandering and wasting my time. Not so much Eastern Bloc but new kid. I am after all simply being superficial, throwing out marbles to scatter the serious on their journey. He may be right but my mother remains wrong.

Like the machine she was part of, her words feel manufactured, churned out. Their vehemence is repetitious, her protestations once vocal, once interventionist have become mere observations now that the machine has broken; its operators, its shadowy informers have grown old and weary. 'Since you have chosen to live in luxury you can suffocate in it.'

What the hell did I do that was so wrong? That should have been in my inaugural speech, never mind the sugar-coated crap I agreed to say. If I sat on one lap I was told one thing and if I sat on the other I was told not only that it was wrong but that I was wrong to sit on the other lap in the first place. What chance did I have if it wasn't the one I made for myself? Yes, thank you, I would like to be considered living breathing proof of a New Europe and neither a superficial tart nor a capitalist whore.

Sometimes, I think they are both outside the hotel. At different ends of the street certainly but there nonetheless. My mother is planning a coup against the hotel, an insurgency against the number-one symbol of western greed in the city. 'Start at the suites. The worst of them are there.' Then there is my father, armed with his paintbrush painting from memory the good he sees in me.

Okay, thanks. No wonder I ended up in a G-string and high heels, an ambassador's sweaty hand on my thigh.

I was told. I was promised in fact. Reach out and I'll be there. I asked her. I begged her. 'Sing something to me that comes from you.' Once I got both. A holding mother, rubbing away pain from childish accidents, kissing away tears from bullying incidents, singing me old folk songs that her mother had sung to her – *'a mother's love, a daughter's love, shall be blossom for our winter'd eyes'.*

What lies can be said as reassurance, what cries and whispers can go unheard.

People wonder why I don't just move. I have the wherewithal to be anywhere in the world. I could hole up with a lot of the ex-Miss Globes in South America or Austria and Switzerland. The cold and warm bloods spend their money and take their choice and location but either way, most of the exes are somewhere better than this. Quite a few have grouped together in Geneva secreted in the Grand Hotel X – you can't expect me to divulge the name. But then nothing is secret. Everything is on display. Even your vital statistics become like the GDP of an emergent country – to know the figures is to know the people. Fuck that. MJ says they don't do that anymore. Swimsuits and bust-size are to be ousted in favour of classic prim fashion and home improvement tips. Give me a break. It doesn't have to be flashed up on screen in multi-national configurations for the punter/client/viewer to be chalking up fuckability. When he uses his eyes to strip the girl down to her pussy it doesn't matter if she's got a good tip on how to make your living space chic. If Miss Globe was a business before, that dealt with beauty, MJ has made beauty know how to work in business. Yeah, I believe it, I understand it. Beauty with a purpose; a lurking, foul agenda that giftwraps body and soul, and makes it available for franchise and merchandise. She can be up on that podium, her mouth, her heart just about to say the bravest, most sincere things she has worked on for weeks and the presenter ogles, trivialises and then cuts her short with a thick arm round her shoulder. Apparently she gets what she deserves. To be holed like some pigeon before she even gets a chance to breathe.

The girls in the Grand Hotel X know exactly what they are missing. It's something they lost themselves.

7

In San Paolo, I had my heart wrenched, my soul torn out and my desire teased. It was just another day and night in the life of a Miss Globe. The children's parties seemed to merge into one old nursery rhyme, one big conga line. But, shit, the clowns got me. There was a whole group of them wearing the usual clown outfits of oversized everything and multi-coloured, luminous wigs. You knew they were kids because of their size and I reckon not one of the half dozen or so was over ten. It was difficult to tell much else, even whether it was a boy or girl that I was meeting and greeting, because the clown make-up – complete with the widest and happiest of smiles – was layered on real thick. Of course I know now that it was all a useful smokescreen for less palatable and more adult mutations and deprivations in the ghettos. But then it was another day, another clown.

But halfway through my tour of duty, this one kid got to me. San Paolo was a dust bowl in search of a city, a pragmatic detour between trips to London and Tokyo and it was probably the jet lag that made me hug one of the kids way longer than I was meant to. MJ, smile blazing, had to move in to break it up, worried no doubt that yet another queen was going to flake. Miss Finland a decade or so back had tried to bundle some poor and starving kid into her limo and had had to be restrained by security when the kid's parents objected.

In the heat of the Sao Paolo street, I had my eyes opened wider than MJ would have liked. I thought this was a cute clown dressing-up thing for some orphans which were like the staple for a Miss Globe visit but, no, some careworker came up to me and said that the kids were all terminally ill with cancer and in particular the one I was hanging on to was the weakest and the most likely to depart soonest.

So, as was typical of a routine itinerary, I found myself hours later at a splendid ball held in my honour, the usual glitz of evening gowns, champagne, white truffle canapés etc. and, as my minders sneaked some cocktails, slugging them like there was no tomorrow and getting quietly trashed, I found myself in close-up with some breathy Brazilian, who seemed to enjoy having me pressed to every conceivable part of his muscular body. I just wanted to close my eyes. It wasn't unpleasant but it was unusual and normally MJ or the bouncers would intervene before any cameras would flash, before any headlines like *Miss Globe Gets a Brazilian* had a chance to be written. For a few moments though, the Miss Globe baton, the vibrator passed to me by Miss Ec which had been keeping me vaguely amused – its significance I gather was more ceremonial than practical – was a distant memory and it was good to sink into a man's arms holding me with simple, wholesome desire.

The tight embrace wasn't tight enough. Memory started to drip into the present and it soon became a steady stream of images seen through one-way windows; dusty streets with dogs lying dead, their guts cooking in the heat; bare-knuckle fights erupting from roadside huts, liquor bottles being raised then smashed on bone, tearing skin and there was I, kissing the children goodbye, shaking hands with spruced-up workers before getting into the black Range Rover. 'The windows are bullet-proof,' one of the minders said to me, tapping the glass with his fat knuckles.

*

It wasn't enough to keep out bullets. I felt the memories rip into my flesh, rupturing my veins so that I was exposed, leaking my lifeblood on to the thick, sumptuous upholstery. The diaries of the Miss Globes I have read state that they had all been moved to tears by the sights they had seen, by the people they had met, but it struck me less as an emotional reaction and more as a physical attack, a sudden and catastrophic loss of control. I urinated on to the leather and, as the minder went 'What the fuck' and jerked himself out of the way of the puddle quickly forming on the seat, I managed to close my eyes and feel something. I had been caught up in desire, its expression, its subordination, its annihilation. I had been fighting, even just a few months into my reign, against the prescription and curtailment of me and who I thought I was. I got so angry sometimes I forgot to feel something other than indignation. There I was after another wonderful day, another extravagant party and I was wet with the tears of a clown.

They tell me I should join them, the girls in Grand Hotel X. Like war criminals on the run, they have taken on new identities and are leading alternate, separate lives. Except they are not. The only vital statistics they are interested in are their bank account numbers and their room codes. There is nothing else to remember in the twilight world of the ex. I know it can be different, MJ rammed that home hard enough when I came to the end of my reign and she came to the end of her tether. 'You know, Sera, it is possible to give a few things up for a year and recoup more than you could ever possibly have imagined. Many Miss Globes have gone on to meet important men, raise families and lead fulfilled lives because of not in spite of them being Miss Globe. Jesus! I'm not sure why you think there has to be a conspiracy around every corner, behind every action that we take on your behalf. I suppose it's the Eastern Bloc mentality.'

You want to rip it up and start again when you hear that kind of shit.

8

Angelo, the Italian masseur, has been and gone. I let him use the Miss Globe vibrator. I know it gives him a kick to think where it's been and over the time he has been coming to see me he has become pretty good at using it. When he first started coming he thought one thing might lead to another but of course it didn't. The massage was good, his touch just right and the vibrator fun, of course it was, but the buck stopped there and fuck didn't even begin. It's not what I want. Not now.

And that surprises the hell out of me, and no doubt MJ would pitch on her heels if she thought that I wasn't making seven kinds of love with seven kinds of men in a globetrotting, round-the-world first-class conga of orgiastic sex. She'd never known a Miss Globe to be so horny. 'There are many types of leashes, visible and invisible, and you should know that we use them all.' She wasn't wrong. I was locked in and locked out. I was watched 24/7 and my chaperones were trained in martial arts. It may seem extreme but Miss Globe was a business and titillating headlines were bad for its interests.

Even though I was climbing the walls I didn't really want to escape. I wish I could say otherwise but I didn't stop, mid reign, and go back to my quiet life in Brasov. I might not have known where I was going or who I was becoming but I knew I couldn't go back. What the hell to, anyway? Some Miss Globes lamented the fact that they were too far away from friends and family for most of their reign. I could understand that if you had something good going. Homesteads draped in warmth; little mountain villages with nothing but open arms to greet you. Lovely. The best thing going for me was getting on the 'Beauty Boeing' chartered for the Miss Globe entourage and counting the riches I had dreamed of, the luxury I would never have otherwise been able to afford. I should paint it otherwise? I was being slowly intoxicated and people do strange things in such a state. Fame and celebrity was rohypnol for my soul.

It was okay at the beginning, I think, although it has to be said that much of it now is quite a blur, the handshakes merging with kisses, the exotic getting joined with the erotic, the waif-like children grafted on to the bony elderly men who shook as they grabbed my hand, their whole bodies vibrating with something other than lust. There were just too many people. I was being populated not copulated. By the end of my reign, being the object of lust, the witness to the eradication of even basic humanity, I found myself inoculated against desire.

One old man in Singapore said to me, 'I am blind and I can't see you so I would like to ask you for a kiss.' Only a couple of months into my reign it was kind of a defining moment. Already, MJ and the management were getting nervous about my ability to shake off my chaperones and head either for some gorgeous hunk on the dance floor or for the free bar where the barman would fall over himself to pour me whatever I wanted – 'and yeah, like wow, Miss Globe asked for . . .'. I was a walking headline. A celeb exclusive just waiting to be flashed and column inched. For MJ, I was a time bomb and after having to deal with a pretty headstrong Miss Ec, they took no chances with me and upped the children, the elderly and the terminally ill on my itinerary and kept the ambassadorial receptions to a minimum. These were always fraught with security issues as there were too many people with too much power losing it, on drink, on drugs, and the last thing they wanted was for the world's most beautiful woman to be around such speculative inebriation.

The cameras were poised, lips were parted with anticipation and MJ looked on with amusement. This was the kind of spontaneous moment she loved, this was the spirit of Miss Globe reaching out but without tongues. There was nothing lewd or sexual about this. This was sweet and cute and everything they needed to pump up the image of innocence and purity. No doubt too she thought it would serve me right to kiss some wrinkly and it would serve as a little warning not to get frisky. Maybe that's paranoid and God knows the beauty industry builds that feeling easily but as the old man leant over I just thought fuck her, fuck me for that matter.

He was so grateful for the kiss that he started to cry. Yeah, I know that it sounds both boozed up and sentimental at the same time and that it means nothing except that I've been imbibing a little too much from the free bar, getting a little too high on my own good vibrations. But my job was awash with sentimentality. Day after day the insipid clichés of care and love were the currency I was expected to trade in. This was different. On a simple person to person level it was different. As he was led away beside himself with emotion, I thought he was the only one that could see and that it was everyone else that was blind. Trite enough for you? True enough for you?

In the hotel room that night, I had been planning to try and phone one of the hotel security staff, someone who wasn't in the pay of the organisation but who had the power and ability to get me out of the hotel and into some life, a night that would bring adventure and excitement and above all allow me to feel absolutely nothing beyond the moment. Stepping off the plane it had been the only thing keeping me going through the arduous business of meet and greet until, that is, I met the blind old man.

I guess it took the wind from my sails for a moment and the desire to be seen on some scene, with the beautiful people, drained from me and instead I worked my way through the champagne I had brought to my suite – the security men liked this as it meant they knew where I was and I always doubled the order so they wouldn't get bored walking the corridor outside. By the end I was toasting everybody with a slurred sense of pity and gratitude. 'For my father, my mother, for the city I have left behind . . .' and I remember bumping into the window so hard that the security men shouted through the door, 'Sera, are you all right?' I was fine but I wasn't. I was drunk but I wasn't. I was waking up to many things many people would no doubt think were pretty obvious. The cynics, the intellectuals, the taste elite would dismiss such airhead drama. I had reaped what I had showed and there would be few people that would cry for a Miss Globe. So, we cry for ourselves.

The Geneva girls keep saying that I should join them – six escapees including Miss Ec from the MJ regime. By that I mean they are neither incorporated nor attached to contracts that will keep them in diamonds until their skin is too slack to hold them. That doesn't mean they are destitute or depressed at the sudden lurch back into normality. The suites are large at the Grand and most of them are adjoining so that it feels like a large home, certainly larger than any they were used to before Miss Globe. And there is a sense of family in their post-reign bond, their love of all things hedonistic and the fact that two of them are pregnant with both fathers not encouraged to be part of the picture . . . Yeah, a home at the edge of the world.

I am not sure I am ready.

9

Everybody asks me what am I doing holed up in a Bucharest hotel, just a few miles from family and old friends and yet alone? What am I doing in such a city when I could be swimming with dolphins in warm water; what am I doing smoking and drinking so much that my skin is changing colour, dark circles shadowing my eyes when I could be landing contracts for perfection? What am I doing playing with myself when there is a world of men who would take me? And on. Expectation. Such a fuel for a pointless fire.

I read what I am sent, as it is carried in each day on a silver platter. Some are first-time correspondents who have got in contact via the In Touch Miss Globe programme which allows the many thousands of people all over the world to directly communicate with the Miss Globe they have met. MJ knows the value of follow-up activity both for revenue and advertising purposes and it's written into all the contracts that all Miss Globes must continue to reply to all such communications for at least five years after their reign. The Geneva girls are for ever complaining about this duty but it is well paid and it all helps keep them leading the life they suddenly became accustomed to. They have made an art form out of templating the personal reply; of using a ready reckoner of sincere responses to fulfil their role and quite possibly their correspondents. No doubt, there are quite a few letters processed on individually printed Miss Globe X notepaper adorning the walls of the adoring.

Mostly, however, I keep in touch with the letter writers who write a second or a third time, who become regular correspondents and who mail directly to a PO Box address I can collect from myself. This way the flow is not obstructed and the words are not altered. And it does happen, as the naughty Geneva girls have tried.

Let's have some fun with MJ they always say, like she has become a blood sport all of her own. They make it up, ham it up. A fuck-you reply to some poor man throbbing with desire for something he can never have is no doubt altered to a 'thank you for your kind words' type thing. Dear John, we are all prostitutes, yeah.

    They are amusing themselves in their extravagant suites watching the trembling suitors deposit their worth for all to see. They are a catch. Both desirable and intolerable. Maybe. 'Who the fuck would have me?' Miss Ec screamed down the phone at me late one Saturday not that long ago. I had spent the night in the bar writing this diary and Ec after a night on the town was full of something maybe everything. 'C'mon, who the fuck would have me? Sure I know, you know, we all know. Every fucking man would. Ain't that a hoot. I'm laughing myself to sleep with that one.'

I want to stay here. 'When I touched your face, it made me feel so happy.' Kenyana aged 12. Nairobi. 'A light went out when you left us. Please come back.' Lucia aged 15. Sicily. 'If I could I would travel to the other side of the world to see you.' Santana, Venezuela. 'I know everyone else will say this but you are the most beautiful person I have ever met.' Consuela, Mexico City.

*

Nobody knew what to expect of me. MJ's staff who got to know me pretty well mainly when I was being carpeted in front of them on the plane or in a plush office for not having kept to contract, for not being more demurely Miss Globe in my contract. They probably thought I would blow out the aftercare and refuse to do any of the letter writing and photo signings. I was the naughty schoolgirl being chastised for bad behaviour; I was the bad student who showed two fingers to anyone even those trying to help. Nobody knew me. Why should they? How could they? Humanity was a formula, tried and tested, and fed to all who wanted to believe in it. Not for the first time, I was reminded that Miss Globe was global.

I wanted to stay here. It didn't matter that these kids had been fed formula and were writing to me for more. My anger, the self-loathing that, as MJ would often point out, I seemed to suffer from, had no place in my suite when it came to opening the letters from the kids. This wasn't a set-up, a graceless meet and greet; there were no kids being beaten within an inch of their life to make sure they behaved when the Miss Globe rodeo came to town; there wasn't the scrubbed and antiseptic feel to the square of a town that had been prepared for my arrival; a square that bore no resemblance to the shanty lean-tos that we passed at breakneck speed. The letters were simple in their adulation, their need, their warmth.

The Geneva girls couldn't believe all this when I made the mistake of telling them, after many cocktails, after my hand was limp with exhaustion. Miss Sweden was happy to correct me. 'Baby, if writing is your therapy then fair enough, go with it if that rocks your cradle but we don't believe any of that shit anymore. Love your own, love yourself, forget the manipulative, pitiful words that come to you from across the world. Out of the mouths of babes? You think? From the hand of MJ more like. Just like her to set you up in this kind of emotional purgatory.'

'Come and join us,' she kept on saying. 'Why be by yourself in that godforsaken country that time should've forgot. We are sitting pretty and soon most of us will be free of the last legal tentacles of the organisation and we can really let our hair down, settle down or just mutate into something fat and ugly. Whatever. It will be our choice.'

'It's my choice to stay here,' is what I keep telling them. They laugh and forget to hang up the phone. In the confusion of sound I can hear their laughter, their night just beginning.

I want to stay here.

'It touched me that you came to our poor town. No-one else does.' Safia, Ratanwa. 'I would love to see you again. Do the Miss Globes from previous years come back?' Elsa aged 16. Malmo. 'I pray to the picture you signed for me every night. I think of you when I am awake, I dream of you when I am asleep. Where have you gone?' Juilana, Peru.

The phone goes rarely now. When it does it's usually just Miss Ec or one of the other Geneva girls high and happy. The paperwork and commitments grow less and less each day and soon I will have most of the day to myself. There will still be letters to open, like the one on the desk in front of me as I write this. It's from a charity organisation in Chechnya. A small note reads 'Memories are precious; they should be allowed to live. We thought you would want this.' Enclosed is a photograph taken on a typically bitterly cold day in Grozny. I am wrapped up in furs, head to toe in animal skin, and I am leaning over a young boy, patting his head. He is not looking at anyone else in the group around me. In his small, ungloved hands is a photograph of me, a newspaper shot of me a few days before in Moscow. I have the same full smile, the same sparkling eyes in both photographs. The boy is putting his lips to the newspaper image, his eyes closed.

It's still early in the morning, the breakfast tray has still to arrive and I have not bothered to get dressed yet. There is a glass of champagne left from the night before that I hadn't managed to finish, too worried that it might send me into nausea and the inability to make it to the bedroom. That had happened a few too many times recently. I guess the Geneva girls had someone to look after them when they got into this state. Downing it quickly, the champagne doesn't even feel like a liquid it is so dry. It makes my whole body shake a little and for a few moments my head spins. In the momentary dizziness, it's possible both to forget where I am and remember who I was. In the brief confusion, I am kissing my mother who has shrunk to a street urchin and I am running away from a small child who is sending arcs of spit at my fleeing back; I am being feted by royalty while my father has comically put his head through one of his own paintings with the Geneva girls applauding him wildly and then I am back in my suite, both hands on the desk to steady my roll, to root me back on to the thick pile carpet.

I sit down slowly at the desk, look at the letter again, reading the words carefully while keeping the photograph propped up against the lamp and begin to write. *Dear Zaur, thank you for your letter. Your words mean the world to me.*

Acknowledgements

'Like a Pendulum in Glue' was first published in *Damage Land* (Polygon 2001).

Thanks to Francis Bickmore, my editor; Margaret Blythe and Graeme Hart at Dogtooth Media; Jane Akhurst for the Brinkburn Era; Colin McClear for *Silem Renk*; Frances McKee for the collaboration and more at Crossing Border; Craig Mercer for the limited editions; Mark Waddell and Graham Bell for their performance and editorial skills and to Jim Dodge for crucial inspiration.

I would like to acknowledge the music of Max Richter, David Darling, Ketjil Bjornstad and a big chunk of the ECM back catalogue for the comfort in sound and inspiration they have provided.

I would also like to acknowledge the support of my friends and family without whom, I am pretty sure, these stories would never have been written.